A Hot & Copper Sky

J.M. Ozanne

Published in 2023 by Hollingwood Design & Print Ltd

The book title is taken from 'The Rime of the Ancient Mariner'
by Samuel Taylor Coleridge, 1722-1824.

ISBN 978-1-3999-5723-6

Also by J.M. Ozanne
The Boat Shed
Rule of Twelfths - sequel to The Boat Shed

If you wish to contact the author Julia Ozanne, please email:
juliaozanne@rocketmail.com

Cover and design by Hollingwood Design & Print Ltd
01422 646720
07771 965063
hello@hwdap.co.uk
www.hollingwooddesignandprint.co.uk

For Mac

My thanks to the following:

To my son James for the photography and thoughtful advice, my son Michael for his wise words and company, my brother Michael and his wife Ruth for technical help in moments of panic, my sister Jane for her constant support and Jim Humphreys and his wife Anne for sailing detail.

To Cathy Woodhead, Delfryn Publications for her generous time and sharp eyes.

To Kathy Hopewell, The Freewriter's Companion for her kindness and suggestions.

To The Rock Engineering Company in Porthmadog.

To the staff of the Ffestiniog and Welsh Highland Railways.

And to all my retailers, a special thank you.

**"On such a full sea are we now afloat;
And we must take the current when it serves,
Or lose our ventures."**

Act IV, Scene 3 Julius Caesar

William Shakespeare, 1564-1616

CHAPTER 1

SEPTEMBER 2020

Madoc Yacht Club was packed that night for the first social event since the lockdown restrictions ended. The subject of the talk was 'Further Afield' and the speaker, a long-time member and globe-trotting delivery skipper in his working life, had sailed and raced from the club whenever he could. Known fondly as Zeb, he had acquired his nick-name courtesy of *The Magic Roundabout* and the character of Zebedee, who bounced everywhere with limitless energy.

In his younger days, his racing crew boasted of how their skipper pushed them to extremes and his name had been engraved on many a trophy. Now in his sixties, fit, strong and still full of bounce, he had sailed further afield than most, and after a whisky or two, could be relied upon for the telling of sea-faring horror stories.

Many members raced regularly in the bay; round the cans, out to the Causeway Buoy and even to Ireland. Some cruised to Scotland, the Channel Islands and even France, when time and jobs permitted; some had never raced or cruised at all. They were here to learn.

He stood up in front of the seated members to loud applause and friendly cat-calls. The late scraping of chairs and whispers died away. Then he started to speak, his voice deep, his words carefully enunciated and the subject riveting;

"I cut my teeth on a lobster boat out in the bay. Some of you may remember John Jones who owned the Boat Shed. I believe we have the pleasure tonight of the new owner, his great-niece. Welcome, Cassie."

Heads turned; a hand lifted in acknowledgement.

"John Jones taught me about the waters around here; Tremadog Bay and the approaches, and the sea around Bardsey Island; which areas were good, bad and those to be avoided at all costs."

For an hour, accompanied by images of his own voyages, he held the room in thrall; footage of the Southern Ocean with a following sea as high as a house, photographs from the Pacific, where a typhoon had decimated an island's only marina, and yachts decorated trees a mile inland from the sea. There were pictures from the Bering Strait, where he'd worked with the crab fishermen on decks slick with ice, and in the Roaring Forties dodging icebergs in thick fog.

Then he switched off the projector, perched on a stool, and gazed around at his audience.

"But of all the places I've sailed in," he said, "and there are many I haven't, so I can only speak from personal experience, there are few that match the horror of miscalculating tide and weather around Bardsey Island."

Heads nodded.

"Rip tides, overfalls, whirlpools, standing waves in the Sound, peaked waves in the Tripods if sailing from the north, Bastram Shoal, Devil's Tail and Muddy Hollow if sailing from the south, and Sarn Badrig, that sticks its rocks above the water on low springs, and can smash a boat to pieces. Do I need to mention the Glaslyn Estuary, with its sand-bar, tortuous channel, and shifting sandbanks?"

Heads shook.

"I thought not. It's amazing that anyone comes in and goes out of Porthmadog at all. So, finally, folks, despite those oceans out there, you should congratulate yourselves on sailing from here on a regular basis with such a shit piece of sea on your doorstep. Thank you."

Gales of laughter.

CHAPTER 2

The first week in September and the days were still warm. For a whole hour, I'd sat on the Boat Shed's slipway and watched the ebb-tide run below my feet, slow and lazy, almost at a standstill, then slide quietly past the green buoy that marked the entrance to the harbour.

It was well past slack-water now, and out beyond the bar, the incoming tide had begun to flood in. It would change the face of the estuary for the next few hours as it met the flow from the Glaslyn and Dwyryd rivers, nibbled at the banks, over-topped the edges to cover the warm sand and spread out in a silver sheet towards Harlech. As the water in the channel deepened and the current set the buoys bobbing, oystercatchers on the banks would lift orange beaks from the sand and rise into the air, a black and white frenzy of feathers against the blue sky.

There was a subtle change in the air at the turn of the tide that was not easy to explain or identify; the stream of slack low-water slowed, stopped, as though doubting its purpose, then quivered and stirred in anticipation. From the rustle of leaves on the cliff-face to the swoop of gulls, there was a promise of activity. Out in the deep channel opposite me, a tell-tale swirl and a flash of silver broke the surface and a shoal of mullet cruised up to the harbour wall.

Lost in a reverie, oblivious to anything but the tide, I barely registered the sound of a car and the tyre-crunch on the gravel.

"Hi."

Not a voice I'd expected to hear, after the last awkward meeting. A tentative smile from David Hughes, so untypical of my confident solicitor, then a wary greeting from me, and he joined me a few feet away on the concrete slipway with his knees up and shoes just above the water-line.

"The tide's turned," I said. He looked at his feet and took off his shoes and socks, rolled his trousers up, stretched tanned legs and dabbled his toes in the water.

"Still warm," he said, conversationally. "I thought I'd call to congratulate you."

"Thank you," I said, surprised, and as graciously as my disturbed peace would allow.

At the edge of the slipway to my side, where the water was just deep enough, the mullet slid over one another and intertwined like eels, grey shadows against the sandy bottom but iridescent blue and green where the sunlight pierced the surface of the water.

"Buggers to catch on a line," I said, a dead child's words remembered. "Easier to hit them over the head with a boathook." Tomas had been nine, and no innocent, but the language that had issued so effortlessly from the freckled-faced child with the bright hair, had seemed crude and beyond his years.

David agreed. "That's if you want to eat them in the first place. Grossly over-rated, in my opinion."

"Like garfish. Those disgusting blue bones when you cook them."

"Quite."

We studied the water as the tide lapped, inch by inch, towards us. Is that it, I asked myself? Not easy after the last uncomfortable conversation a week ago, sat on the bench by the pill-box with the estuary stretched out below us and away over to Harlech.

His contribution; an out-of-the-blue suggestion about my business, about the yard, a partnership and funding. I hadn't stayed long enough to unscramble his last comment. I'd asked him exactly what he meant by a partnership; 'it's whatever you want it to be,' he'd said. I think I was polite. I think I said my usual thing, that I needed to do this by myself. Thanks, anyway. I hadn't seen him since. Now here he was.

"Cassie, can we have a talk? Now? Sometime?"

"I thought that's what we were doing."

Safe ground; fish. He sighed, audibly, ran his hand through his hair, the black curls as unruly as ever, the green eyes as attractive as ever. That wasn't the problem. It was his attitude that irritated me and brought out the worst in my responses. He was still my solicitor, but advised me as he would advise a wayward school-girl. I was never sure if I cared what he thought of me or not. Was I trying to impress him with my bloody-minded independence? That was too uncomfortable to explore, so I didn't.

"This is different. Please just listen," he said.

"I'm listening."

The water nibbled at our toes, and we shuffled a couple of feet up the slip.

"I'm sorry about the last time we spoke. I hadn't made myself clear. I went out in *Sylvie* that evening by myself, just drifted in the bay, and asked myself why I always end our conversations by upsetting you, unless it's something practical where you've asked for help or advice, that is. Then we seem to get on okay. I don't mean to be, well, bossy, you know, it's just my way, to try and point people in the right direction."

"The direction according to David Hughes, you mean."

"You said you'd listen."

"Sorry."

"Then I heard about you taking over Madoc Marine. As manager? That's an amazing opportunity. Arnie Blackwell must have great faith in you."

"Considering I know nothing about powerboats and I'm young and female, I agree. I can almost hear the gossip."

"Yes, but you'll have Denise for the admin and I hear Arnie's nabbed Pwllheli's best mechanic for three days a week. Also, I bet your boss will be handling the major sales. You won't be left on your own."

"You seem to know more about it than I do," I said, slightly miffed. "So, I'm just a glorified caretaker. Is that how you see it? Not to mention the fact that I own this shed and the yard with its ever-so-useful slipway, which is something Madoc Marine hasn't got and never will have. Doug Peterson tried and Cadw said no chance. I remember. Historic monuments and all that. Arnie's not stupid. He's a hard-headed business-man with 'opportunity' stamped all over him." Shut up, Cassie. You promised.

Where's he going with this? The sun had disappeared behind the cliff above us, and there was a sudden chill in the shadows. Another hot day was promised tomorrow, and I knew that if I'd been out at sea looking west, I would see the sky painted in reds and oranges and the sun going down in a blaze of copper. I shivered.

"Pannad? I've got biscuits."

He sat on the step to the Boat Shed and I pulled a sweatshirt over my head, threw him a towel for his feet and glanced over his shoulder. He dried between his toes, and put his socks and shoes back on; he had long feet, long toes, and manicured nails; a fastidious man, but I knew that. It ran in his family.

I brought mugs and the biscuit tin outside. He'd fetched two plastic chairs from outside the snack-bar, and I put the biscuit tin on the old oil-drum that served as a table. He carried on where he left off.

"Please don't interrupt me, Cassie. Let me finish. Okay?" He raised his eyebrows, his face serious, intent.

"Okay," I said, curious, and sipped the hot tea.

"You've been given an amazing opportunity to manage Madoc Marine and to show what you can do. One thing you can't do, though, is manufacture the maritime experience you need to give you the status and the credentials to work with customers. You're going to have to talk to them about being out there in local wave and weather conditions. 'They'll want to know what to expect from cruising in the bay, if they're going to spend money here. You can't talk about that with confidence, unless you've seen it and done it; at least a lot more than you've done already, and I'm talking sailboat as well as powerboat handling, riding a jet-ski, safety on the water, marine radio… I could go on. You need more experience." He drew breath. "And I want to help you."

A herring gull perched on the rubbish bin by the side of us, cocked its head to one side with a black, beady eye on the biscuits. I chucked my tea-bag at it and it flew off with a squawk. A thread of interest wove itself into my head; the reality of my new job and then being classed as just a 'caretaker'? People's perceptions and acceptance of me in my new post would be exactly that and I suspected Arnie had hidden agendas. Didn't everybody? But I wasn't going to say 'no' to the job.

But this conversation with David was different to many of the others we'd had, where I'd bridled like a restive horse at his caution, even under the umbrella of care for my welfare, as Denise reminded me. His responses to any new ideas that involved risk-taking, as though I couldn't think things out for myself, had irritated me; the 'I'm telling you what you should and shouldn't do,' conversations. What did he mean this time? I put my mug down.

"How?" I asked. "How could I possibly do any of that in six weeks? Arnie's given me until the end of October to settle in and learn as much as I can before the first proper business meeting. And that's all to do with running Madoc Marine as a business. And it's coming to the end of the season. The weather will change and I'll be busy with the lift-outs for the winter. And don't my trips out on *Annie* count?"

"Not nearly enough. No."

He fished out a notebook from the inside pocket of his jacket; not a suit jacket with a perfectly-ironed handkerchief in the top pocket like his father's, but a soft, brown, leather jacket with slightly worn cuffs. He was a strange man, made up of conflicting parts; one minute, a formal and cautious solicitor, the next a serious sailor with a love of rough seas. What would he be like as a teacher and skipper? Could I tolerate being his pupil?

"This is what I think, if you're willing to listen to the plan."

I nodded. Might as well.

"Each weekend, spend some time sailing with me in the bay, gales being the only obstacle, and a night passage to Ireland for the last race of the year in early October. You'll be a fully trained-up, reasonably competent crew, by then."

"You're joking. I was very sick, the last time, if you remember. I said I would never sail to Ireland again, or anywhere else in nasty seas, come to that." I felt the colour drain out of my face at the thought of it.

"You won't be sick. You've got used to the motion being on *Annie*. You'll have your sea-legs already and with hours of sea-time under your belt, you won't even notice. You'll love it. You'll also know enough to pass your Competent Crew tests and put the training towards a Day Skipper Certificate."

I thought about it. He was so positive.

"Okay. But the powerboats?" I asked. "I don't know any owners. I can't see anyone letting me loose on a fly-bridge."

"I can," he said. "I've a friend. You'll like her. Are you up for this?"

"As a sort of protégé, you mean?"

"If you like." The smile crinkled his eyes. "With the best possible motive, of course."

He stood up and took his car-key out of his pocket. A clean, ironed, and folded handkerchief fell out onto the gravel. Mother's efforts? No change there, then. He picked it up, held it in his hand, tilted his head to one side.

"Well?"

"What motive?" I asked. "Why?" I was bemused, and quietly suspicious.

He opened the car door and slid into the driver's seat. "Because, Cassie, in the unforgettable words of Brutus, 'There is a tide in the affairs of men…'"

"'… which, taken at the flood, leads on to fortune…' Yeah, yeah, I know my *Julius Caesar*."

It wasn't an easy one to forget. How many more surprises in one day?

"My fortune, you mean? And you never told me you knew your Shakespeare."

"You never asked," he said, and drove off.

Denise raised a pencilled eyebrow when I asked her to work Saturdays for me, just for a few weekends, but the tone of my voice precluded any questions. It was my first lesson in being in charge and I felt the first stirrings of power, albeit small ones, but curiously satisfying.

"By the way," she said, "there's been a woman, a customer, in the yard. She said she was just looking around, but she and her partner might buy a boat in the spring. He said for her to start now, to see what she fancied."

"Lucky lady. Arnie'll be pleased. Which boat was she looking at?"

"That Sea Ray with the fly-bridge; the one by the bottom gate."

"Good God," I said. "Hope they've got plenty of money. Is she still here? What does she look like?"

"Jet-black hair, short-cut, big sunglasses, bit over-the-top, if you ask me and a white leather jacket and tight jeans. Complained she had to leave her car on the road outside 'cos of the deliveries in the way. Brummy accent. Have you seen her around before?"

I shook my head.

"Common," she said, and sniffed. "She chewed gum when she was speaking to me; more at me, rather. Right up herself. One of those pursed, thin mouths, like a duck's arse."

"As long as she's got money," I said. "But that's good, and it's only my first week."

"And her hair's out of a bottle, but too black."

"Miaow," I said.

Saturday, and my first weekend on *Sylvie*, the Sigma 38 that David owned and raced. My stomach was in knots. Supposing I got it wrong? What if he shouted at me? What if I shouted back, or cried, or dropped something overboard, or threw up, despite his reassurances?

I arrived early and waited. It was too early in the day this time of year for the reception area below the Pwllheli Marina Office to be anything more than empty. The digital weather- chart with its wind-speeds and wave-heights, helped me while away the time until the door opened to David, a rucksack over his shoulder. His black curls peeped out from under a woolly hat. At the top of the flight of stairs to the Marina Office, he introduced me to the guy behind the desk.

"We'll be training every weekend until the lift-out," he said to the manager.

"Won't there be gossip?" I asked, back down the stairs.

He rooted through the table of pamphlets under the display screen, handed me one with the title, 'Learn to Sail: High Quality Tuition - Certified Yacht Master,' with his name on the front.

"You never said." I nearly exploded. "I can't afford this."

He scratched the back of his neck.

"I've not made myself clear again, have I? Look, there is no charge to you. The training business is only when I can fit it in during the summer. I have a job as well, just to remind you. This is just a weekend side-line. It also helps me to find crew when I want to race. Got it? The next few weeks is purely for your training and my pleasure in having your company for a bit of weekend sailing. All my regular crew have gone back to college, or work, or whatever. This is for friendship, Cassie. Okay?"

"Okay," I said. Ignore the doubt. We stepped onto the entrance to the ramp and the security gate that led onto the pontoons. I'd been in the marina once before, but it seemed a long time ago when I'd crouched down out of sight on a pontoon and watched the life-boat as it towed in the fire-damaged hull of *Pegasus*, and the police removed Gareth's bloodied remains from the cockpit.

The gate was closed. He punched the buttons on the pad at his side.

"This is the code," he said. "Same for the shower block. *Sylvie's* over there."

Three weekends into the month, and I'd learned about self-tailing winches and riding-turns, the difference between the clew and tack of a sail, how to start and stop the engine, how to tie clove-hitches and bow-lines, how to manoeuvre the boat in and out of fenders he'd thrown into the water and how to pick up mooring buoys off Abersoch. The weather was kind and I wasn't sick.

"Can you stay overnight next weekend?" he said, one Sunday night after two days at sea, tacking and gybing until I was happily exhausted. "I'm going to spend the night at Porth Ceiriad, if this weather holds. I'd like you to have the experience of a night at sea; a clear, dark sky and shooting stars, if we're lucky. There's no light pollution out there. You'll do the calculations for the anchoring, as well as all the navigation for the weekend."

He caught my expression.

"Just the two of us?"

"Part of the training. You can't wax lyrical to your powerboat clients if you've never done it yourself. You can have the fore-cabin; bring a sleeping-bag and warm clothes. It gets cold at night this time of year."

It was cold already, the sun well down, and a chill wind fluttered the tell-tales on the mast. I climbed out of the cockpit, ready to go.

"Friend of yours?" David asked, and nodded towards a woman outside the marina office. "She's been staring at us for the last few minutes."

She was slim, dressed in a white, quilted coat with her hood up. She blew a puff of cigarette smoke into the cold air, dropped the butt on the ground and turned to leave.

"Not me. Ex-girlfriend?" I asked.

"Not my type," he said, and wrinkled his nose.

Denise raised both eyebrows at my planned absence for the whole weekend; again.

"Just this once more, I promise. I'll still pay you double-time for Sunday."

"It must be worth it," she said. "Just this once, okay? My man's complaining that he never sees me. What will the big boss say if he turns up and finds you've been gallivanting for the last few weekends?"

"He won't. He said he'd leave us alone until the meeting at the end of October. Anyway, I'm the everyday boss," I said, "and it's all in the company's interests. I'll tell you what I've been up to when I've finished."

A quiet Saturday morning and the marina seemed deserted. We loaded up carrier bags of food for the weekend and I stowed my gear in the fore-cabin, found pillows and unsurprisingly, if his handkerchiefs were anything to go by, clean pillow-cases, ironed and neatly folded, in the overhead lockers. I stood on the pontoon and waited for the now-familiar instructions to cast off. He shook his head, climbed out of the cockpit, and stood on the pontoon by my side.

"She's all yours," he said, and pointed to the wheel. He unhitched the mooring lines on the pontoon, climbed on-board, stood on the deck, and coiled up the mooring ropes, seemingly at ease, while I reversed his precious yacht out of its berth and into the channel. Hands clamped tight on the wheel as far as the Fairway Buoy, I turned the yacht into the wind while he winched up the main and the genoa and studied the snap and flutter of the tell-tails in the wind.

"Excellent," he said. "Watch her fly. Causeway Buoy and then back to Porth Ceiriad for the night."

She flew. The port side-deck awash, the sails trimmed to perfection, the wheel easy, the occasional wave over the bows and spray in my face; David sat on the cockpit seat and adjusted the sheets and grinned at me, then stood up, looked over the pram-hood and up at the sails.

"Doing good. Keep an eye on your speed. If you press her on the wind too much, the speed will drop off and she'll luff up. Good. Better. Perfect," and he laughed as spray splashed over the hood and hit him in the face.

The sun had set behind the cliffs at Porth Ceiriad by the time the anchor slid into the dark water, buried its flukes in the sand and the chain tightened to good holding ground with enough depth to keep us afloat as the tide dropped. He checked my calculations and nodded. I would not make the mistake I'd made with *Annie*, that first time on the reef. It was a safe anchorage until tomorrow at least, with a north-westerly wind forecast later in the morning.

"Not a good place to anchor in strong winds," he told me. "Nasty down draughts off the cliffs but we'll be long gone by then. Oh yes," and he smiled to himself, a small, secret smile as he turned away from me. What didn't I know?

Tired but exhilarated by a day's hard sailing and now bundled into warm clothes, I cradled the mug of hot tea he'd handed me, stuffed biscuits in my pocket and sat on the foredeck with my back against the mast.

"Dinner at six," he said. "Don't get cold."

Mother Hen. The wind had dropped, and the water was now completely smooth, with not even a cat's paw to ruffle the surface. The last tinges of daylight faded away above the cliffs with their incredible strata, the folds of rock now flattened out in the absence of light, into a dull, grey oppressive curve ending in headlands; to the east, Trwyn-yr-Wylfa and to the west, Trwyn Cilan.

With David, I'd sailed just once through the disturbed water around Trwyn Cilan; rough, but mild compared to the 'Tripods', just before Braich-y-Pwll at the end of the Lleyn Peninsula. I'd been told that they were dangerous enough to deter any sane person from bashing through them in the wrong conditions. David described how once, in his early days as a rookie racing skipper and in a hurry to get back after a trip round Anglesey, he had ignored the warnings about wind against tide.

"Tell you what," he'd said, and pointed to the area on the chart. "I've never been so scared in all my life. The waves piled up on each other both sides of the boat, then they towered higher than the boom and threatened to crash into the cockpit. We had to keep going until we could see straight down Bardsey Sound, turned sharp to port and we were out of it. It was all plain-sailing after that. The crew nearly lynched me."

I'd pored over the charts and pilot in the evenings back in the apartment, tucked up warm and safe above the showroom. The pilot's lovely glossy pages of maritime detail and pretty pictures of the bays and harbours around the Lleyn Peninsula, described Bardsey Sound as evil.

I remembered my first fantasies when I first inherited *Annie*, and had nothing in my head but a vivid, rose-tinted idea of perfect, sea-going conditions; sunshine and blue skies, a gentle breeze and tiny wavelets; but ironically, the more I read of fearsome, wild seas and dangerous places, the more my curiosity was piqued; that was until I started to venture out; then I understood. There was always YouTube for a fear-fix, I decided.

During his informal lectures last year, and to steer me away from any foolhardy, complacent ideas about being at sea in these waters, the Harbour Master, Will Roberts had told me that the overfalls around Bardsey Island were to be avoided at all costs in the wrong conditions. Even the names sent a shiver down my spine; Bastram, or 'Bastard' Shoal as I'd heard it called and the Devil's Ridge, showed the differences in depths on the chart. The extreme differences in depths in a small area caused nasty, confused seas. I didn't want to fall into Muddy Hollow, either, tossed around like child's toy; all I needed was enough gentle experience to talk to clients convincingly.

With that comforting thought in mind and being in the hands of an experienced sailor, I relished the gin and tonic placed in my hand before being called below for supper. A bottle of Rioja and proper glasses graced the table, set with mats and napkins, the chilli and rice served on proper plates with a bowl of salad on the side and a dessert of apple pie and cream.

"Do you always treat your clients so well?" I asked, taken aback with the presentation.

"Always," he said. "At least, at anchor or in port. It's about having that contrast between wild and inhospitable outside and civilised comfort inside. Different if we're racing, mind. Plastic bowl and a spoon, if you're lucky."

We discussed the day, the sea and the wind and the sailing tactics and the local knowledge for overnight anchoring. It was safe talk; like fish.

"Did you make the apple pie yourself?"

"Of course," he lied, and cleared the dishes into the sink. "Put your coat on and bring your glass." He picked up the wine bottle, turned the cabin lights off and I followed him into the cockpit. We sat with our backs to the cabin bulkhead, with feet up on the cushioned seats. The boat had swung around with the falling tide and we faced towards the stern looking south, a floating ornament on the black-glass sea. An owl's hoot from inland carried over the water, and then there was silence.

Ink-black, the sea merged with the sky. The stars hung, as though from threads, seemingly near enough to reach up and touch. They glimmered and glittered, nameless, colourless, then a flash and an essence of light streaked through the dark, twice, there and gone in the wink of an eye. I hadn't seen a shooting star since my dad took me star-gazing as a child. I held my breath and could almost feel his rough wool coat next to my face as he adjusted the telescope.

"Meteors," I said, to break the moment. "Just dust. Possibly the Aurigids. That's me up there, above The Square of Pegasus, Cassiopeia, and that's Capella, the name of Hugh's little boat."

"I'd forgotten you knew your stars." He topped up the glasses, tilted his head back and looked up at the sky. "Bright Star…"

"Keats," I interrupted. "Sorry." Embarrassed, it had felt like showing off. "How come you know your English Literature so well?"

"It was my first degree. Then I did law. How come you know your poets?"

"'A' level," I said. "And I like poetry."

"You never told me."

"You never asked," I said.

We clinked glasses. Safe ground.

Late the following morning, after a leisurely breakfast and a practice tutorial on the ship's radio, the first hint of a change in the wind direction slapped wavelets against the hull and clanked the spare chain in the anchor locker. *Sylvie* began to rock in the swell.

"Time to go," he said. "Hold onto your hat. This is where she really flies."

We headed out to sea past Trwyn-yr-Wylfa and the end of the Tudwals, leaving the Bell Rock Buoy behind, then turned and screamed towards Pwllheli on the port tack with a cold, blue sea and cloudless sky, the wind, a brisk, north-westerly. The sea, protected from the worst of the wind by the Peninsula and with little fetch, did nothing to slow us down and we sliced through the water at eight knots on a close reach, heeled well over with the starboard deck awash, the sails taut and the wires singing.

Then I understood the secret smile. "I get it," I laughed, gripped the wheel, and felt the power as he played the sails, adjusted the sheets inch by inch and the speed crept to nine knots. We approached the Pwllheli Fairway Buoy, I turned *Sylvie* into the wind, and he furled the genoa and lowered the mainsail. He took the helm, and we motored sedately into the marina berth and moored up. I was exhausted, elated and lost for words.

"Next weekend, powerboat training," he said, as he closed the hatch. "That woman's there again," and nodded to the terrace in front of the

Marina Office. "Not exactly dressed for boats, is she? And wearing heels? Her feet must be frozen in those sandals."

We walked up the ramp to the security gate and he pressed the button. The gate slowly swung open, and I looked up to see the woman wearing the white, quilted coat disappear around the corner of the shower block. A wisp of smoke hung in the air, and cigarette butts had been dropped on the terrace.

"Lazy cow," I said, picking them up with a tissue and throwing them in a bin. "Hate to think what her boat's like."

CHAPTER 3

Monday morning, Denise arrived for work and called me downstairs to the smell of toast.

"Don's sick. He's got Covid."

"Oh." What could I say? My only mechanic. My first thought focused selfishly on how many viruses he'd left behind on Friday and resolved to clean the toilets and anything else he might have touched. My second hoped he wasn't too poorly. The third how long he'd be off-work. My first major hitch of the week. "Have we got anything urgent?" I picked up the clipboard with the week's work.

"I don't know these people," I said to Denise. "Is there anyone here who could be upset, or awkward?"

She took it from me and scanned down the list.

"What was one of the last things Arnie said to us before he drove off?"

It was a month ago, but I hadn't forgotten. The driver's window was down and he'd rested his arm on the door, the muscles solid and the skin on his forearm thick with tattoos. He looked me straight in the eye; not a look to be avoided or forgotten.

"Make sure you look after my clients, Cassie," he said, and drove off.

I'd managed okay so far. There had been no immediate demands and all the schedule work had been completed, but then no-one had needed their boat in a hurry, what with children back in school and the weather decidedly autumnal.

"Arnie said to look after his clients. Well, we have, haven't we?"

"Apart from this one," she said. "The work was down for this week, to be ready for Friday. I know this one. Mr Robinson. He rang last week to check his engine had been serviced and the work done. He's taking a business client out for an end-of-season jolly. He said he was taking the boat over to Pwllheli on Friday to pick up his guests." She looked up. "He's not a nice man, I seem to remember. What are you going to do?"

"Me?"

"Well, you're the boss."

"Why doesn't he keep his boat in Pwllheli, if that's where he wants to pick up his guests?" I said, cross with a problem I didn't know how to solve.

"It's cheaper here," she said. "You'll have to phone him to explain."

"I expect he'll be okay about it," I said. "I can't help Covid, can I?"

"With people like him, you're expected to be God. Good luck with that. Here's the number."

I ran back upstairs and shut the door to the apartment. Difficult conversations are better handled without an audience, but I read the worksheet Don had prepared and could at least explain about the impellers that needed replacing on the massive engines and the new batteries to be installed. Mr Robinson wouldn't be going to feed lunch to his visitors without his microwave, I imagined, never mind all the instruments. A man who liked to show off his apparent wealth with glitzy acquisitions, Denise said, just to cheer me up.

It started well. I reiterated the work to be done.

"Yes, yes," he said, "I know all that." Testy.

“Unfortunately…” and I explained.

“That’s total crap,” he said. “When Doug Peterson was there, I never had any problems with the mechanics to do the work. Don can still work, can’t he?”

“I’m really sorry,” I said, “but he’ll have to self-isolate until he’s tested negative. Then, of course, he might be quite poorly. I wouldn’t expect him to work if he was ill.”

“Well, get someone else. You can’t expect me to cancel plans just for an impeller. It’s not critical; advisory, he said. He said he’d do it before the main winter service.”

“Yes, I do understand that, Mr Robinson, but as it’s so late in the year, he probably assumed the boat wouldn’t be used again much this season. I couldn’t guarantee it would be safe to use without the recommended work, sir. There is no-one else available. I’m very sorry.”

“Well, you’re a bloody useless manager,” he said, and I held the phone away from my ear. “I’ll tell you now, I’ll be looking to berth elsewhere next season.”

“Good,” I said to the dead phone.

I put it down carefully on the coffee table. If it had been the evening, I would have poured myself a large drink. As it was, I crept downstairs to the office and lowered myself gently into the chair opposite Denise. She looked up and wrinkled her nose in sympathy.

“The joys of business,” she said.

“What will Arnie say? That man’s threatened to take his boat somewhere else.”

“He won’t,” she said and shook her head. “I’ve heard it all before. Bet you anything he turns up and takes it over to Pwllheli anyway, then he’ll come back as soon as he can, after he gets the marina bill. He’s one of those men, Cassie, with less ready cash than he pretends to have. All piss and wind. He’ll be back as though nothing had happened.”

"But if he did take the boat out, would we be responsible if anything happened?"

She rummaged in a drawer and pushed a sheaf of papers over the desk.

"Read the conditions in the contract section. Also, the work-sheet he signed to request the service, not yet counter-signed by us to say it's done."

I felt better after that. He could please himself, I thought, and looked at the weather-forecast for the week and decided no-one would turn up that weekend; nothing severe was predicted, just rain, a light wind and a lumpy sea, due to the swell of something big brewing out in the Atlantic. My training weekend on the powerboat would be restricted to tea and biscuits in the cabin, I thought, but we wouldn't be seeing much bad weather this week, apart from the relentless rain. I didn't think we'd see Mr Robinson, or anyone else, and sent Don a 'get well soon' text.

"I forgot to tell you," Denise said. "That woman came back on Saturday. Brought her partner this time. Bit of a bashed-up face. Looked like a bouncer. He was pleasant enough, though. They made me take the cover off the Sea Ray, the same one she looked at last time. They had a good look round."

"Time-wasters?"

"Dunno. She had skinny jeans again and that cream leather jacket; expensive, but she'd put trainers on this time, not those silly heels. I wouldn't have let her go clunking around any boat in those, I can tell you."

"Did they want to see the boss? Arnie, I mean."

"Didn't say so. They seemed dead interested, though. Looked at everything and took their time. Then they spent ages just wandering round the yard. Did you have a good weekend, by the way?"

"Instructional," I said, and got on with the business of appearing to be running the yard.

The one date in my diary for the following week, the Tuesday, and Helen's Nain's memorial service, was not to be missed and I'd planned my diary to leave it completely free. It hung like a shadow over my head, and blanketed the enthusiasm I tried to feed into my work, no matter how busy I was. The absence of Don, who was quite poorly, his wife said, and without his cheery face and practical hands in the yard, brought back the reality of the deaths that had hit so hard, and the possibility of another lockdown over Christmas. The virus hadn't gone away, and Wales had continued with restrictions.

September had passed without an equinoctial gale but then the weather had turned; abruptly. One minute, it seemed, it was warm enough to paddle in the shallows, the next minute it rained, with a persistent, cold drizzle off the sea, in between storms and provisionally the wettest day on record.

I donned work-boots and a waterproof jacket each day and stuffed my hair under a hat. David texted me. With predictions for rain and gales the following weeks, the race to Ireland was called off. Relieved, I looked forward to a couple of sessions of powerboat instruction at the weekends and expected simply a chat with the owner. The handling of a posh powerboat would have to wait.

On Friday, I walked down to the Harbour Master's office. The dates for the lift-outs for the main boatyards were fixed for later in the month, weather permitting, and I needed to make sure any of my bigger boats didn't overlap for space on the pontoon. Will Roberts looked tired and old, the home-care and then the reinstated visits to his dying wife had taken their toll. She was very sick.

He and Mark were working with charts which showed the updated positions of the channel buoys before they became unreliable during the winter storms. Nobody with a keel boat, in their right mind, would tackle the estuary without an updated chart before next spring. They both seemed distant, as though Covid had sapped their energy, though neither had caught it. For Will Roberts, waiting for his wife to die would be exhausting. It was good to hear him as formal and dry, as usual.

"All well, Miss Jones? I presume you'll be lifting out at your leisure with Don to help, as usual. He knows how to use your crane to the best of its capacity. He's a good man to have around. An excellent mechanic, too. You're lucky to have him."

"He's caught Covid," I said, and hesitated. I wasn't sure. Then I was. "Can I ask you a question?"

They must have noted something in my voice, turned their heads and gave me full attention.

"If a boat-owner chooses to go to sea with a predicted poor weather-forecast, in a boat that requires some maintenance work not yet carried out, is there anything I can do about it? Hypothetically, of course." There was a brief pause. "No," they said in unison.

"You could, of course, advise the owner otherwise," Will Roberts said. "Apart from that, I'm afraid there is little you can do. There are no laws, as such."

"Thank you," I said, and left as quickly as I could. It wasn't my place to discuss the clients.

I walked back to the yard, but as soon as I arrived, I knew that my fears were realised. A four-wheel drive Subaru took up most of the parking space inside the gate and the deep-throated roar of engines broke through the drizzle.

"Told you he'd turn up," said Denise. "He arrived about an hour ago. Said the engine-cooling was perfectly alright and there was enough charge in the batteries. I won't tell you what else he said. Horrible man."

I looked at my watch. "High-tide in two hours. He'll be going out in a bit. Has he mentioned the sea-state? Did you tell him?"

"Not on your life," she said. "If he wants to drown himself, the world will be a better place. You tell him, if you're brave enough. Don't blame me if you get mashed up in the process. He's got a mouth like a sewer and he doesn't like you at all."

I jotted the predicted wave-heights and the sea-state in the bay on a piece of paper. The breeze would pick up in the next couple of hours, and with twin 150 engines, he could be in Pwllheli in twenty minutes, but only under normal conditions.

I'd been out at the Fairway Buoy a couple of times in a big swell. It felt as though the whole of Tremadog Bay had been diverted to the Glaslyn Estuary with the waves piled up, pushing and shoving to get in like an unruly crowd at a nightclub. I wondered if Mr Robinson had ever been caught out in his treasured, plastic possession with its high freeboard and shallow keel and been rolled around mercilessly as the flood-tide gathered pace. I thought probably not.

From the pontoon, I could see him at the engine-controls inside; a big man in an expensive, bright-red, foul-weather jacket, his head bald like a golf-ball with just a few strands of thinning grey hair on top. I called and he turned round. I held out the piece of paper.

He bowled out of the cabin and glared at me, his face like an angry bull-dog with piggy eyes.

"You that woman on the phone? What the fuck's this?"

He snatched the paper, cast his eyes over it, scrunched it up and threw it in the water.

"Have a nice trip," I said, and fuck you too.

I shrugged, made my way back up the ramp, watched him cast off the lines and motor out into the channel. Then I ran back to the showroom to make sure the radio was tuned to dual watch; the coastguard and Pwllheli Marina. His car was gone and Denise said someone must have driven it away but she'd been busy on the phone and never heard it go.

I put my feet up on the desk and Denise brewed tea, buttered some scones and opened a pot of the best raspberry conserve. We deserved all of it. It wasn't long until the radio shrieked for help; not a May Day, but a call for assistance, and the life-boat was launched from Pwllheli. We weren't surprised.

"He'll be stuck in Pwllheli Marina now until the engine's fixed. Cost him a fortune. Anyway, what did you say to him?" she asked, mouth full of scone.

"Oh, just pleasantries," I said. "In case he decides to come back to us. He won't be able to entertain his guests with a trip round the bay, so serve him right. Hope he's left the marina and gone home by tomorrow, though."

She looked at me curiously and, I thought, with a little more respect.

The weather continued grey and drizzly all week and the weather promised the same for the powerboat training that weekend. The Fair Line, gleaming white fibreglass, toughened glass windows and stainless-steel fittings polished to a shine, was a floating gin-palace, as they were often called, and far removed from my shabby wooden yachts in the yard. The fly-bridge was a long way from the pontoon below, and its occupant, as we emerged from the steps up from the cockpit, was not at all what I expected.

"David, darling," a cry and a bone-crunching hug, and David was enveloped in large arms and crushed to a bosom enclosed in a sailing jacket that could have paid a mortgage for a year. I knew about those, being in the business.

"This is Veronica," David said, extricating himself.

As instinctive as a mother greeting a long-lost child, she opened her arms and hugged me, then stood back and looked hard into my eyes; hers were slightly blood-shot with crinkled, faint lines when she smiled.

Tanned and weather-beaten skin on her cheeks was framed by wisps of blonde hair that had escaped from the hood.

"Welcome to *Pegasus*."

The shock evident on my face, I muttered my indistinct thanks. How could I not have recognised the boat? I hadn't seen the name on the stern.

"I know, bit of a surprise," David said. "It had belonged to Veronica and her husband when Doug Peterson 'borrowed' it for the drugs haul. It was fixed up after the fire and then…"

"…and then," Veronica said, "I got what I wanted, didn't I, David?"

"You got what you deserved," David said.

I looked from one to the other, perplexed.

"My divorce settlement," Veronica said, beaming. "David was my lawyer and a jolly good one, too. Ready to go?"

He threw off the mooring ropes for us and Veronica negotiated the berth and pontoon like a pro, turned into the channel and out into the bay. The sea was grey, lumpy, and uninviting. Four hours later, my head full of information and my wits taxed with snappy instructions, she inched the boat back into its berth, barely nudged the pontoon and I heard her say, "Thank God for bow-thrusters," as she switched the engine off.

We drank coffee and ate smoked salmon sandwiches in the warmth of the saloon.

"This afternoon, she's all yours," she said. "You can obviously do as you're told. Just don't crunch it, dear."

"Thank you, but why?" I asked her, at the end of the day. I hadn't disgraced myself, but was still shaky from the responsibility, as she talked me through every manoeuvre.

"Because I owe David a favour," she said. "He rescued me from misery and did me proud. He'll tell you if he likes; I don't want to talk about it and spoil the day, which I thoroughly enjoyed. Also, you'll have been my first, official pupil. How did I do?" and she handed me a brochure with 'Powerboat Instruction' on the cover.

"Early days yet," she said. "I'm fully qualified but it's the end of the season, so I'm not expecting any clients. What do you think? Will you join me in a drink to celebrate?"

I shook my head. "I'm driving, but thanks anyway," and we toasted the day in coffee.

She called over as I stood on the pontoon, and stared up at the boat, hardly daring to believe I'd negotiated that enormous piece of plastic back into its berth in one piece.

"Do ask David for my phone number and address. I have a feeling we should meet again. We girls have plenty to discuss, I think. Lovely to meet you… and well done. You've crammed a lot into eight hours, but then you knew quite a lot before. Your handling of *Pegasus* was excellent and instinctive. Big boat, fly-bridge. Well done," and she scrambled back inside out of the rain.

Late that afternoon, back in the cabin on *Sylvie*, with the heater and the lights on, David handed me a shot-glass of 'Single Malt for special occasions,' he said. This one I couldn't refuse.

"I know you'll do your usual thing and accuse me of being patronising, but it's worth the risk. A toast to you and well done." He handed me two pieces of paper; one for basic powerboat handling, and an RYA Competent Crew Certificate.

"Get them framed and put them up in the office or showroom, at least where they can be seen by your doubting clients. Nothing to say?"

I lowered my eyes to the certificates, shook my head and sipped the whisky so he couldn't see the gratitude and the emotion I knew was betrayed in my face.

"Still friends, then? And crew? You can crew for me any time. I only take crew I can trust to get it right. Your helming is instinctive and you're quick to see what needs doing. Also," he hesitated. "You do as you're told without argument, which I didn't think you could do. There's only one skipper on a boat."

I flew home on gossamer wings, but there was nobody there to share my happiness. Denise was long-gone and Madoc Marine had a desolate, lonely feel; a dead yard, grey in the last of the light, with the powerboats silent, inanimate objects in winter shrouds, like an exhibition of installations in an art gallery. I walked between them, zig-zagging in and out, avoiding bashing myself on the props of outboard engines, until I reached the bottom gates.

I remembered how I'd hidden in the bushes that separated the two yards, and watched *Pegasus* as she motored down the estuary like a white swan, and moor up on the pontoon below me. I'd watched as Doug Peterson talked into his radio. Even then, even without being able to hear the words, I'd known something was up as he and Gareth prepared the boat to go back out on the tide; then the fire at sea, the drugs-bust, and the quiet world I'd learned to live in was filled with NCA guys, police in stab jackets with radios and questions. It seemed like a lifetime ago.

I walked back to the showroom. Exciting though it had been, the day out on *Pegasus* had dragged up the pictures still clear in my head; the stench of the burnt and blackened cockpit, the removal of the body, the weird violence of the gale that hit the pontoon soon after and then the search and rescue for Doug Peterson called off. Then the awful wait; was he dead or had he survived, only to come back and take revenge? He'd hated me from the start; a silly schoolgirl threatening his underworld. It still haunted me.

I couldn't bear the silence inside the apartment, so I put a ready-dinner in the oven and, with drink in hand, wandered back through the yard and over to the Boat Shed, where I fed the gold fish and seriously considered spending the night in there, tucked up in one of the chairs by the fire. Then I remembered the threat of rock-falls from the cliff-face above.

Monday morning, and I handed Denise the certificates.

"You sneak," she said. "Brilliant. I wondered what you were up to. That'll shut people up. Just the training, was it? You and David? Was that all you got up to?"

"Absolutely," I said, and winked, just to annoy her.

"Remind me to talk to you about him some time," she said, as the door shut behind me.

I walked down the yard with Don's work-sheets to see if I could make any inroads into reorganising his work. Why didn't I just say yes, no, nothing, to Denise? Well, I answered myself, 'cos it's none of her business and I'm beginning to get the idea that she knows better than to cross a certain line between friendship and employment. I'm her boss and don't need to justify my actions to her, or anyone, come to that. Food for gossip, that would be.

The day passed without event. I had expected an unwelcome visit from Mr Robinson and prepared myself for polite discussion, which did nothing to help me sleep that night. With the memorial service to face in the morning, I tossed and turned until the first glimmers of light appeared through the window.

Tuesday. It could hardly be called a dawn; at least, not like the summer dawns of glorious peach and copper hues that signified the promise of a fine day in summer, with the sun rising up over the Rhinogs like a great, yellow ball. This Tuesday morning, the day emerged reluctantly out of night, accompanied by a fine drizzle and a grey mist that shrouded the trees on Ballast Island and obscured the estuary and mountains beyond.

It was a fitting day for a memorial service, a ceremony for reflection, sadness, loss, and grief. For me, I needed to put aside the mundane practicalities of managing a boatyard and face the conflicting emotions that accompanied Helen's Nain's death; the death of someone whose life had already been seriously compromised by one of the afflictions that often accompany old age. The inevitable, physical deterioration that would have affected her mobility in the years to come, would have been unbearable for her.

She'd told me so, while sitting at the table in her warm, comfortable kitchen over tea, toast, and a plate of bacon, not long before the pandemic extended its tentacles to our quiet corner of Wales. It was not her fault, or mine, that she caught Covid; my care and protection for her was as assiduous as my affection; the fault lay with one of her friends. The need for silly chat and gossip and to 'cheer Mrs Parry up' her friend assured me, negated any genuine consideration she may have had for her, when she laughed Covid germs in her face.

Her thoughtlessness and ignorance did not excuse her, and I couldn't forgive or forget. I was born under the sign of Scorpio, after all, even though my dad had sniffed at all that 'astrological rubbish.' That woman would be at the service, along with most of the village, but I promised myself to attend to the real reason I was there and not to indulge in judgement and bitterness.

Denise called up from the showroom below, with promises of coffee and early-morning croissants, fresh from the Big Rock Café in town. I had time to change for the service later, and pulled on old jeans and a jumper, opened the bedroom window and scanned the yard below. Most of the powerboats had been craned out and now rested in their black winter covers with the lashings pulled tight to withstand the winter storms. They were lined up in rows with their bows facing into the yard, dressed appropriately for the day as if out of respect.

The scene from the window felt different somehow, to the discomfort I'd felt on Sunday evening; maybe it was because there were humans around to mitigate the stillness; a few owners were down in the yard and Denise was in the showroom. People, I decided, were the key, and their reason for being there at work on their boats and looking forward to the next season.

In the spring, the scene would blossom into the bright-white and silver of polished hulls and stainless-steel, and the yard would reverberate with cheerful voices amid the roar of engine checks and the powerful purr of the crane as it lowered boats into the water. Now it was quiet, despite human presence, and even the usual hunting cry of the heron seemed to have been subdued under the blanket of mist. I shut the window.

"I hate Tuesdays," Denise said, irrelevantly, as I poked my head into the office. "We need to go through these invoices when you come back. What are you going to wear?"

"I'll think about it," I said.

It was so typical of Denise, her front-of-shop observations of attention to detail and appearance, filtered this morning through the croissant crumbs that clung to the lipstick; pink today, but the blue eye-shadow never varied and her blonde hair was scraped up as usual and confined with a band on top of her head. Wisps escaped regularly from this fountain but she just pushed them back into place artlessly, even when talking avidly to customers who were charmed by her concentrated interest in their requirements.

To sell powerboats to wealthy customers required total commitment and expertise; one needed to listen carefully and file snippets of personal information, particularly from those who wished to impress their financial worth on the sales staff before they returned to the yard with decisions. Denise remembered everything, from bereavements to divorce proceedings, illnesses and property developments, car up-grades and how many rosettes their daughters had won at the last gymkhana.

'… and how is your wife? And the dog? So glad. That must have been…'

In the summer, in the odd moments when I escaped from my own yard and wandered over to Madoc Marine to ask for advice, or coffee, or just company, I'd catch her in full-flow and had to turn away and hide my smile. She was very good; too good for me to aspire to and she knew far more about the specs of powerboats than I did.

I was learning as fast as I could, but until today, I'd felt like just a token manager. Now after the last weekend, I could feel my shoulders broader, my head held higher and knew I could answer basic questions; I had experienced what it felt like to be way up above the water on a fly-bridge and tear through the water at thirty knots with a wake like a broad, white ribbon behind, and was now able to return safely from impending bad weather.

With an hour to kill, I walked over to the Boat Shed. The lock for the boatyard slid out smoothly, and I opened one gate and re-bolted it open. The old chandlery lay abandoned, awaiting appeal to the planning department for the re-build. There had been no more clients, the only revenue the small fee I'd charged for the two yachts, safely tucked up for the season in their cradles; they were the only evidence it was a classic boatyard at all; it was only the presence of people that had made it a special place; for warmth and food and chat and the familiar sounds of power-tools and the screeching of gulls as they raided the rubbish bins.

The caravan had begun to look shabby with green mould gathering in the surrounds of the window frames. When I'd moved out of it into Madoc Marine, uneasy with the loss of my old role as day and nightwatchman, the only living creatures left were the goldfish in the shed. I fed them every day but they were useless watch-dogs. Drug trafficking didn't go away and the gangs had long memories where large sums of money were concerned. I still found it difficult to throw off the feeling that somehow someone still stalked me, and retribution had yet to come.

"No way, bab. That's all finished with now," Arnie Blackwell had said, when Denise announced him as the surprise new owner of Madoc Marine. I told him about my anxieties and doubts when he offered me the new job and the apartment over the showroom to live in. "Sort out the CCTV and I'll pay. Can't see who the hell would want to come nosing round here, though," and he gestured around the yard. "There's nothing worth stealing. It's not as though someone's going to run off with two old yachts, are they? Can't see it myself."

"It's not the yard or stuff in the shed," I'd said. "It's me."

"You get settled in and you'll feel okay," and he'd rested a strong hand on my shoulder. "Clear your stuff out of that old caravan. You can keep an eye on both yards from the comfort of the flat. It's yours for as long as you want it. At least, until I do," he added with a grin. "We'll discuss that in the first proper meeting in October. Learn as much as you can from Denise, read up about the different powerboat models for sale. We'll knock out the details then."

He didn't hang around after that, just downed one glass of Cava, smoothed his moustache, tugged gently on his gold earring, and fairly bubbled with enthusiasm over his new purchase, then drove off back to his scrap emporium in Dudley. It was only after he'd gone, that the reality of his wealth hit me. Hugh had done some research and guess-work. The only thing I'd known about Arnie Blackwell, for sure, was his generous, big heart, his gentle hands, and the propensity for an incandescent, violent temper when he was crossed. And he was huge.

"Are we expecting a customer?" I asked, back in the showroom.

Denise had cleared the mugs and plates away and replenished her lipstick.

"You never know," she said. "Now, what are you going to wear?"

The apartment spanned the whole of the top floor above Madoc Marine, with its huge glass-fronted showroom filled with a specimen boat-of-the-moment. A retail section for clothing, chandlery, and cleaning materials, was tucked in a smaller showroom at the back and behind the big office, a small kitchen and stock rooms.

The living accommodation upstairs was modern, luxurious, with stunning views from the balcony over both yards and over to Ballast Island. I could hardly say it harboured the ghost of Doug Peterson, as he had hardly ever been there, and the furnishings seemed as new as the day they were installed, courtesy of 'Tradewind Inc.'

I ran my hand along the back of the white leather sofa, and thought of Daniel as he soaked up the sun, worked and sailed his boat in his native Trinidad and wondered how the sales of his firm's UK marinas were progressing. I also wondered if he'd ever regret his company's decision to sell Madoc Marine. Just because of Covid? I found it hard to believe. Disasters come and go, I thought, aware that it was a bizarre thought for me at my age and I'd had my small share of dramatic events and managed to survive. Big business was another matter, though, and out of my league.

I thought of the offer I'd turned down, to go away with Daniel; twice. A dream-come-true holiday with no strings attached, paid for, as a guest of the family, a tenuous relationship based on passion.

"Come back with me to Trinidad," he'd said. "You'll love it. I'll teach you to sail."

"No. I've things to do," I'd said. I needed to make my mark without diversion or help.

That was before I knew about Madoc Marine. Now I had even more reason to learn these very new ropes. Would Daniel have known his buyer was intending to offer me the management post and chuck me in at the deep end? Was it to see if I'd fail, or to give me a chance to succeed? Had they discussed me in a private conversation between them?

I felt like a puppet when I thought about it in those terms, and had to convince myself firmly that I was still in charge of my own destiny. But white leather sofas or not, this flat didn't feel like home. In fact, nowhere felt like home anymore; my residence temporary or under threat, uncertain, insubstantial, transient. I sat on the bed, and wished I was elsewhere.

The wardrobe in the bedroom was full of Helen's clothes and only a few of mine. Some of the evening tops and smart trousers from her selection of 'clothes for important occasions' kept in Wales, I'd borrowed at her Nain's insistence. My hand paused at the little black dress and jacket worn for my first date with Daniel; then it moved on, to flick through the rest of the hangers, the memories a mixture of longing and regret.

After her Nain died, Helen said I was to take her and her Nain's clothes to the charity shops, but to keep anything I wanted for myself. It was a strange task to sort them out; to wear Helen's expensive, formal outfits seemed fine, and surprisingly, I'd kept the long black, wool coat belonging to Helen's Nain; a present from her husband, never worn, and lent to me to impress my solicitor. I decided that she would have wanted me to keep that. Helen said she had no need for her spare clothes where she worked, doctoring in the most appalling places on earth and didn't want them mouldering in an empty house. I'd felt uncomfortable, going to the house on my own to collect them, and asked David to accompany me, as his firm of solicitors was handling the estate.

I stood back with the wardrobe door open and stared at the clothes with mixed feelings. Memories flitted through my mind; of the first interview with my solicitor, the elderly Mr Gerald Hughes with his neck like a wrinkled tortoise, and the shock when I first learned of my inheritance. "Smart jacket," Helen's Nain had said, "and no nose-stud. Play the game, Cassie. It won't hurt. He's very conventional." My hand returned to the little black dress and thoughts of Daniel. I could still feel his hands on my skin as he slipped the straps off my shoulders. I shivered with the memory, shut the wardrobe door, and turned the key. Nothing in there would do for today.

On this occasion, I had nothing to gain by towing the line in dress-code and nothing to lose by not; besides which, I had no problem finding black for the occasion. But there was a limit to my bloody-mindedness. I rooted around in a still unpacked suitcase and pulled out black jeans, a black, leather jacket and a skinny-rib jumper. More importantly, Helen's Nain had been a strong individual; 'her own person,' as Helen described her. This time it was about identity; mine and hers.

The summer of hard work in the yard had toned up my muscles; the jeans fitted like a glove, the jacket rather unconventional for a formal Welsh memorial service, the mirror said, as I checked the diamond stud in my nose, brushed my hair hard until it shone, laced up my polished Doc Martens and clattered downstairs to face Denise. She looked up from the screen and made a face. The door whispered shut and I set off for Borth-y-Gest.

CHAPTER 4

It was always difficult to pass Helen's Nain's house. The Bed and Breakfast sign had faded and the rooms were now empty and cold. So much warmth, so much kindness finally gone from behind the bay windows, and only the end-of-summer geraniums in the hanging baskets were left to show that anyone had ever lived here.

Further round the bay, where residents had worn themselves out with dead-heading summer plants, I knew the wilted ones would soon be replaced with winter pansies, miniature daffodils, and trailing ivies. Spring was forever just round the corner when you're a gardener, Helen's Nain used to say. I'd ask Helen if I should plant up the hanging baskets for the summer. I didn't know her plans for the house.

I cut across the car-park and up the path, glanced briefly at *Tai Pilots*, which was now almost not mine anymore, and in the last stages of the exchange of contracts. I didn't know who'd bought it; a company, the estate agent said. I didn't care about it, never had, and disliked it even to the point of sheer hate and if the money allowed me to do what I wanted with the Boat Shed, I wasn't bothered whether it became another holiday-let or not, despite the local feeling.

It was a two-edged sword, the argument of local houses for local people. I got that, but I also knew how much the place depended on tourism. No easy decision, I knew, but I had to survive, and if my great-uncle wanted his classic boatyard to survive and flourish, that's the way it was going to be. I would do my best, and the house would pay for it.

I stopped and leaned over the wall that separated the road from the rocks below. The tide was out and the sand-banks were now high and dry, a dull brown in the miserable, morning light, and the water ran flat and grey in the river channels. An uninspiring, autumn landscape, but I dredged up pictures of it in its summer garb, with sparkling blue sea and golden sand. It helped.

"It'll be summer before you know it," said a welcome voice behind me. I hadn't expected to see Mark, obviously absent from his Deputy Harbour Master's duties for the morning.

"Bit of a miserable day for it, yeah? Mrs Parry was a friend of my Nain's," he explained. "We all used to play down here in the holidays when we were kids. Helen as well."

"I didn't know," I said. "Well, why would I?"

We walked on together and joined the black-coated throng, more-or-less socially-distanced. The headland was running out of space, but the Welsh rules were only moderately adhered to here, where everyone knew everyone else. People were careful, mostly, apart from the one I tried not to think about. Common sense took precedence over rules after a summer of lockdown, which was now only gradually easing.

The immediate family stood with the minister in the churchyard, grouped around a small area set aside for memorial stones. It was solid rock under the soil up here and there were only a few traditional graves, but the more recent, small memorial stones were splashed with colourful posies and the grass around had been recently trimmed.

I stayed on the edge of the group with my back to the sea and near the edge of the cliff, and with only a few minutes until the service, looked around. I nodded briefly to Helen over the sea of heads. We would catch up afterwards. A few of the others I recognised as owners of small, rowing dinghies and sailing boats moored in the bay.

And then, there she was. The two, white-haired ladies, Gwen and Gwennan, stood together; the tall, thin sharp one with the short hair and pointed nose, still had the look of grim disapproval firmly fixed on her face. I wondered if she had another expression in which to face the world, or was this a permanent feature? Her friend, the marshmallow, was shorter and rounder, with white waves in her hair, her soft, pink cheeks, and bright, disingenuous eyes. She looked up as I scanned the group, and caught my eye. She had the grace to look down, which was just as well. I could almost feel the barbs of my dislike hurtling across to her. Any common sense she might have had back in the summer, had been swallowed by her desperate need for company and gossip. She was to blame for Helen's Nain's death and she knew it. I couldn't forgive her.

It was a short service, sad and uplifting at the same time, a few words added by Helen, whose happy holidays with her grandparents, were seemingly not replicated in her own mother's childhood memories, from what she'd told me. Nothing to do with the home and parenting; Helen's mother had wanted to be out in the big, wide world from an early age. At least I understood what it meant to have a distant relationship with one's mother.

I'd thought Helen's mother cold and dismissive when I first met her, after Helen's Nain had been diagnosed with Parkinson's. She was glad to have someone else, me in this case, to take over her mother's care. She shot back to London as though old age and its problems were infectious.

I was curious to know how she'd taken the news when her mother's will had been read out. The house and its contents had been left to her grand-daughter; Helen's parents had received nothing. But then, Helen's parents were successful, private consultants in their own right; they didn't need money, Helen had said. Even so… We had a lot to talk about.

The service ended and I watched the group, some of whom had known Helen's Nain all her life; an acceptance of life and death and continuity showed in the nod of a head, the touch on a shoulder, a quiet whisper, a group respectful and comforting for those left behind.

For an outsider like myself, despite my Welsh roots, I felt only a tenuous connection through my long-dead relatives, their ashes at one with the churchyards, both here and up on the hill in the graveyard above Black Rock Sands, but I couldn't feel it deep-down. It needed shared history to achieve that.

The *Seaview* hosted the wake on the green outside, masks used only when people went inside to refill glasses and refresh plates with sandwiches and amazing cake. A man I knew vaguely, touched my arm.

"I hear you've sold *Tai Pilots*."

"Yes," I said.

"You're not going to live in it, then?"

"No."

He drained his glass and studied my face for a second.

"Shame, all that history. The house was in your family a long time."

That was one way of showing disapproval, I thought, mildly annoyed with the lack of sensitivity.

"Your great-uncle would have been disappointed."

"No, he wouldn't," I said, straight to his face. "He hated it in the end. He went to live in the Boat Shed, I was told. If you'd had to bury all your children and your wife and then live in that house with memories of them, you'd be glad to see the back of it, too."

"Right, yes," he said, and cleared his throat. "Probably." He glanced down at my Doc Martens and then at the stud in my nose. I couldn't figure out the expression on his face.

"If you'll excuse me," I said, "I've got a boatyard to run." Rude and unnecessary. Too bad.

I said a polite goodbye to Helen's parents.

"Do keep in touch," her mother said. "If you're in London, visiting your mother…" and delved into her handbag for a business card. I looked at her beautifully made-up face, manicured hands and nails and couldn't imagine her changing a bed or washing an ancient incontinent. Had she ever done that, I wondered? I just couldn't see her as a caring doctor.

Helen said that competent medical and nursing staff did the work, and she and her husband just raked in the profits. Still, it was a successful private hospital so they were doing something right. It must be difficult for Helen, I thought, who chose to work hands-on in poverty-stricken, mosquito-infested parts of the world. Did she do it to atone for her parents' materialistic approach to medicine? I wouldn't ask; that was too personal.

We'd agreed to meet on our own that afternoon while her parents were busy in Helen's Nain's house, removing whatever small possessions that might be precious to them. She walked out of the café with me and we stood under the awning outside. The drizzle had turned to rain. I was cold and damp and sad, my feelings reflected in the low-tide grey mud over the wall in the bay.

"They can take what they want from the house," said Helen, "but I can't imagine there's anything that would meet their tastes. Just a thought, though. Is there anything you would like, Cassie? You take precedence, if you think of something. You spent so much time there and cared for her so well. A memento, I mean apart from…" She stopped in mid-sentence. I hardly noticed the hesitancy. "The rest of the house contents can stay for the moment. I can't get my head round it. See you later."

Helen's Nain's house, transformed into a Bed and Breakfast after her husband died, was stuffed with old-fashioned, dark-wood furniture and pictures of local landscapes. The kitchen cupboards were crammed with cooking utensils and pots, baking tins and bowls, and blue and white willow-pattern plates adorned the shelves on the dresser. The clocks that had once ticked away the years, were now silent, centre-stage on the mantlepieces in the front rooms. And, of course, there was the precious barometer in the hall.

She'd always known when there was to be change in the weather, tapped the clock-face, set the hands every day and was rarely wrong in her predictions. I considered whether it would be too much to ask for; it was hardly a small thing. Besides which, I reminded myself, I didn't even have a home to put it in. It was all appropriate for a traditional Bed and Breakfast, and that was all.

I walked up the steps and down the path to the boatyards, stood in-between the two sets of gates and leaned on the fence that backed onto the harbour. My new and extended boatyard domain lay either side of me, new and old, both tainted with difficult histories and uncertain futures. I hesitated, cold, then walked towards the warmer one. The door had scarcely shut behind me, before Denise said, "Arnie's coming for the first proper meeting on Friday evening after we've shut up shop. He's bringing Ben with him and a film for him to watch while we talk. Oh, and fish and chips. Okay?"

I didn't reply.

"Sorry." Her voice softened. "How was it?"

"Sad," I said.

Our first proper, business meeting. Fine, excellent, at last, I thought, and at least I would finally know what he expected me to achieve in the next year, under what conditions and how long I could use his apartment to live in.

I left Denise with orders and invoices and disappeared up to the flat to change, hung the leather jacket, on a hanger this time, and brushed my hand over the little black dress again; the two articles of clothing that seemed to define my fluctuating identities. Stick a pair of overalls between them and that would really screw my head up. I put work clothes on, looked at the list of jobs and decided I wouldn't do any of them today; out of respect. Denise just nodded when I said I was going to the Boat Shed for few hours, to talk to Helen. She'd asked to meet there, rather than a pub; at least we could be quiet and uninterrupted. There was so much to talk about.

I fed the fish and wiped the counter with a polishing cloth, restored the gleam to the old, oak work-top and lit the fire. The Boat Shed crackled into life, the cold air dispelled in minutes with the heat from the stove and I washed a couple of mugs ready for coffee. Then I pulled out a couple of tumblers from the shelf under the counter, washed them, polished them up with kitchen towel and put them on the window-sill beside the kettle.

An errant spider had made a winter home in one corner of the window. I watched it scuttle in and out of its web and decided to leave it there. Not much point in us both becoming homeless. I knew that my occupation of Madoc Marine would only be temporary and unless the planning department okayed the outline new build for the Boat Shed, I'd be out of a home again. New caravan? Flat in town? The contract for *Tai Pilots* was about to be signed and although I'd burned my bridges there, I'd had no intention of living in it; not ever.

I pored over the drawings until the door opened. Nobody ever knocked; it was a shop after all. Mark stood there in his smart coat, his wet hair pushed back off his forehead. He still looked tired, the new baby an excuse, but I had a feeling there was something more than that, more wear and tear from the added responsibility of supporting his boss; Will Roberts's wife had died. Mark was only my age, but looked older, I thought.

"Kettle on? Thought I'd pop in just to see if you're okay. Funerals an' that. You were fond of the old lady, I know."

I nodded. He plonked himself down in the spare chair.

"These your plans?" and picked the folder up from the table and studied the drawings as the kettle boiled.

"Put in an appeal, yeah?"

I handed him a coffee.

"It's the cliff-face at the back. They won't consider an appeal until the loose stuff has been stabilised and I can't get that done until *Tai Pilots* is sold and the money is in the bank."

"Well, that won't be long. It's going through, okay, isn't it? Biscuits?"

"And I'll need a mortgage to fund all this hospitality I extend to all and sundry," I said, and handed him the tin.

He laughed and dunked a biscuit in his coffee. A pang of something indefinable shot though me; another man, another time.

"I know this guy who works for a rock company. Gabions and stuff, stabilising cliffs. He'd give you a quote, at least. I like the drawings, Cass. House on stilts and workshops down below. Concrete pillars, yeah? Cladding on the house? Like a log cabin. You can't leave all the chandlery at sea level, though. Not after the flooding last time. You'd never get insurance."

"Well, I had this idea," I said, "being as I can't get the timber easily anymore, so Hugh says. I'm up against the big suppliers and climate change. So, I thought, I'd set up as a hub, for finding rare bits and pieces, run the business virtually, and keep the conditions of the inheritance."

"You mean, like a broker?"

"Sort of. What do you think?"

"Yeah, I get it, but isn't it already being done? And you don't know that much. You've only just started on all this classic boat stuff, and you've got next door to think about now."

"That won't be forever, Mark. I know it won't. Don't even know if I'd want it to. Anyway, I know a fid from a baggy wrinkle and blocks from cleats. I can learn. What do you think?"

"I think you're bonkers," he said, "but you'll do it anyway, won't you?"

"Probably," I said, and closed the biscuit tin. He left, and I waited for Helen.

"To your Nain," I said. "Helen's Nain," and handed her a tumbler. The light from the fire caught the amber liquid and it glowed gold in the glass. We drank and I refilled the glasses. She sat and stared at the fire.

"Did you always call her that?" she asked. "It's such a mouthful."

"I tried 'Joan' and I tried 'Nain'," I said, "but neither sounded right. She was quite happy with it."

She nodded and sipped her drink, slouched in the chair with her legs outstretched and her head bowed over. Miserable, I thought. At one time I would never have asked, especially since the last time we met, the Christmas before Covid dug its heels into our lives, she'd arrived with Hannah, her new partner and was happy and cheerful.

But the year seemed to have changed people, myself included, and it seemed nonsensical to pussy-foot around potentially upsetting issues. Too many people had been affected one way or another. How stupid to let it fester, to not share it. Sharing helped. Hugh taught me that. I'd have to ask her, when the time was right.

"I have something for you," she said. She put her glass down on the counter and pulled out a Tesco bag from her pocket. It was folded over and over into a small parcel and fixed with sticky tape.

"Couldn't find any posh paper," she said, "but I needed to get it out of the house before my mother found it."

I pulled off the tape and unwrapped the small box. It was as I remembered; the blue velvet covering soft in my hand. I pressed the catch and knew exactly what was in it. I was the last person to have closed it. I don't think Helen's Nain would have checked when I took it back. Why would she? It was lent to me out of love, worn with love and left around my neck in the act of love. I took it out of its nest of satin and draped the choker across my palm, the tiny white pearls a startling contrast to the black velvet.

"Nain willed it to you," Helen said. "Mother knew that, but I brought it to you, now, just in case… you know."

What a terrible accusation to make about one's mother. I put it back in the box, snapped the clasp shut and wondered if I would ever wear it again.

"You were fond of Nain, weren't you?"

I nodded. "It was a proper home," I said, "even though she was on her own. One of those houses full of warmth and care. She was always there, kettle on and fresh baking on the table. Every time I visited her, I felt wrapped in a cocoon so I could go back out stronger to face things."

"Were things that bad?"

"At times."

I'd said enough. To describe her Nain as she died from Covid, was not on the agenda.

Then we talked. Of course, I told her about Daniel and there was so much to say. But not about the choker; that was bound up with an intimacy too private, too special to be shared, commented on, or laughed about.

"Will you change your mind?" she asked, "about going to Trinidad? All that sun and sea and a wealthy family to boot. Sailing and champagne on the foredeck. I can see it now… and he's asked you twice and left the options open."

I shook my head. "It would seem like running away, especially now. I need to make some success of all this first. I still don't understand why he's asked me, cash-poor and scruffy as I am most of the time. Maybe he's got a whole harem of women out there and I'd just be Number Twenty-Six or whatever, and I can't leave this place until it's fixed, or re-built. Maybe next year, if…"

The rain had turned to a downpour, and the familiar clatter of small stones dislodged from the cliff behind the shed bounced on the tin roof above us.

"I see what you mean," she said, looking up "But you did have a relationship. Something special?"

"At the time, yes, I thought so. Then when he came back, after the lock-down, I wasn't sure. Just passion and too much to drink. But there was something. I hadn't had time to get the balance right and there were moments when I felt in danger of being… eroded? Men like him take charge as a matter of course, I'm beginning to find. Not equal enough. We're in touch, still. It'll keep."

I opened the fire-door and chucked in some sticks and a log. There was a magic about the first sparks, a hint of flame, hypnotic; our silence, watchful. The kindling caught; reds and oranges and yellows, a flash of copper-blue. I turned the air-flow down and the log settled to a hot-white glow as the flames slowed and gentled, flickered and danced over the hot wood.

"Now your turn."

But she was silent.

"You look utterly miserable," I said. "Are you?"

It was a brave, personal, whisky-fuelled question.

She didn't answer.

"Was it the service? She was your Nain after all, and I know how much you loved her. You're allowed to be upset you know. Just because you're a medic and see death all the time, doesn't mean you're impervious to it."

"No, it's not that," she said, at last. "No. I can manage that." She lifted her head. "Hannah and I split up. She finished it. Only last week. By email. For good."

"Oh," I said, shocked at what I considered an unforgivable way to end a relationship. Not my place to comment. She didn't need that. But I wanted to know.

"Why?"

"Why? Because she didn't love me. I thought she did and she lied. She had other partners all over the place, I found out, just by a chance comment. Jetting all over the place with the WHO breeds a huge network of people who bump into each other all the time. Gossip gets back," she said, "so the misery is more about betrayal than loss. It hurts."

"Yeah, I bet it does," I said. "I didn't realise it was so serious."

"You thought it was just a gay fling, did you?"

"I don't know what I thought. You were both all over the world in different places, so I must admit I couldn't see how you could ever settle down anywhere."

"What, and have a nice house and babies? Maybe that's what I wanted and I've certainly seen enough orphaned children desperate for a home. That wouldn't be a problem. But only if I had someone to share it with. Maybe it got to me, but she wasn't interested."

It was bold, but I asked anyway. "So, was it the end of a dream of settling down that's got to you so badly?"

"No," she said. "I loved her," and held out her glass.

The rain drummed on the roof and we sat in silence, separated by our own thoughts. I wondered if I might never see her again. A shared confidence, but still passing ships. Then she told me.

"I've had it with clinics and disease and awful poverty. Sick of children's sunken eyes that blink through the flies and stare at me in my sleep; sick of the swollen bellies and stick-legs. So much death and misery, despite all the efforts. I'm burned out, Cass. Going to start a new job next month," she said. "In Australia. Something different. Do you remember what I told you when we were eating ice-cream in Criccieth? I know it was a while ago."

I hadn't forgotten.

"I bet you're going into pathology. Are you?"

"One of the big hospitals in Sydney has offered me an internship. I need to do the training, but yes, that's what I'm going to do. New start, new country. Find out why people die rather than watch them go through the agonies. Besides which, investigative stuff highlights all sorts of issues, like diet or pollution. It's just that it'll distance me from the real thing."

"Just dead people, then," I said. "But you'd still have to deal with families. Death and bereavement. I saw a bit of that in London; all part of the course to toughen us up; burns and drowning and car crashes. And I've watched *Silent Witness*. Could you do all that? All those desperate people in the throes of grief?"

"Yep. And the bodies don't need to be fed."

I thought it sounded callous, the way she said it but tried to visualise the awful images she'd painted and how she had to face it day after day, the need like a bottomless pit.

"I get it," I said, after a while. "Really, I do. You're no good to anyone if you're falling apart. I wish you all the luck in the world."

A burst of heavier rain on the roof made any further talk impossible. It subsided into a patter.

"Can I ask a great favour? I won't be offended if you say 'no.' I would love to have your Nain's barometer. I know I haven't a proper home for it yet, but I will. It's very much a part of her."

"Of course. You can come down tomorrow and take what you want. Mum's back to London in the morning, thank God. Anything else?"

"Well, yes, actually."

I waited for the caustic comments.

"Her jelly moulds, especially the rabbit one. Oh, and the recipe for her brownies. It's in a book in the dresser drawer."

She burst out laughing.

"Good God, Cassie. The rabbit jelly-mould? I remember that from when I was a kid. Chocolate blancmange rabbit on a bed of green jelly. You're not getting all domesticated, are you?"

"So? I can learn to strip an engine as well as make cakes and puddings. They're not mutually exclusive," and topped up the glasses. "Anyway, she made posh chocolate mousse for the guests' kids. I thought I'd have a go. Arnie's bringing his youngest, Ben, with him on Friday. That's all."

"Can you do that?"

"What?"

"Strip an engine?"

"No, don't be daft. Arnie's found me a mechanic, but at least I can learn some of the names of parts. Sounds good on the phone… 'certainly Mr Frobisher, and would you like your impeller changed as well?' Anyway, it would ruin my nails, as Denise is fond of saying."

She took a quick glance at my hands "What nails?"

The tension passed, the unhappiness out in the open, a marginal return to a sense of humour, our individual lives laid bare and our plans on the table. Instead of looking back, we were both looking ahead to our separate futures, without even realising what had happened. But her Nain would connect us; always. She put the empty glass on the counter and stood up.

"I'll see you tomorrow. Come about two. I'll be there and I can guarantee mum will have gone."

It was nearly dark when I locked the door and made my way to the welcome bright lights and warm showroom of Madoc Marine. A man sat behind my desk opposite Denise.

He got up as I opened the office door.

"Hi. This is Steve Lewis," said Denise, with a wave of her hand. "From Rock Solutions. We both lived in Blaenau for a bit. Friend of my dad's. He's older than me. You can tell. Had a good gossip, though," and carried on typing.

He held out his hand and grinned. "She always was a cheeky madam. Mark mentioned you needed some advice. Bit of a rock-fall, yeah? I'm on my way home, so thought I'd call in. You don't mind? Haven't seen Denise for years. Shall I make an appointment?"

He was quite a bit taller than me; a gaunt, craggy face with a hooked nose and high cheekbones; almost as though he was carved out of the materials he worked with, dark hair with streaks of grey brushed back off his forehead and an evening shadow on his chin. He had to stoop a little to talk to my face and I lifted my head up to meet his eyes; grey and clear.

"Thursday?"

"Fine. Morning, it'll have to be, as I'll need the light," he said.

He waved to Denise and we walked through the showroom to the front door.

"I heard about you taking over the yard before Covid," he said.

"They were talking about it in the pub. Hell of a rundown place it's been over the years. You've got your work cut out. Is it right you've taken over as manager here? As well as the other place?"

He shook his head as though he hardly believed it.

"Looks like it," I said, uneasy by the thought of being discussed in the pub.

"Both yards, then?"

"About ten o'clock," I said, not in the mood for a discussion.

He drove off. The headlights picked out the rain as it slanted in from the sea and glistened wetly on the cliff-face opposite, a wall of slate that rose one hundred feet up to the Garth, its quarried slabs now under my feet, blasted and hacked out to form the base of the old Cwmorthin wharf, as it was. I stared up into the blackness and tried not to think about rock-fall onto the road, let alone onto the back of the Boat Shed, the cliff less steep but loose and crumbling. The comfort of expertise I'd set in motion accompanied the soft hiss of the door as it closed behind me and the lights drew me in. I didn't dare think of the cost.

"I need to buy some things ready for Ben when he comes with his dad on Friday," I said to Denise, as she closed the computer down for the night. "He's only five. He won't be occupied all through our meeting with just a film. Bet he's seen them all anyway. And I know Arnie's bringing fish and chips but kids nibble, don't they? What do they eat and drink, anyway? Sweets? Pop? Flavoured water? Help me out here, will you?"

She stood up.

"You make him sound like a pet dog. Do him a favour. Buy some fresh orange juice, fizzy water, a tall glass and some straws and a packet of cocktail umbrellas and offer him a Mediterranean Sunset. He'll love it. Oh, and some black grapes and obscene-footfall- strawberries from Peru. If he doesn't like it, tough. But he will. Kids eat too much crap these days."

"You can talk," I said, and pointed at the chocolate wrappers and plastic bottles in the bin.

"My problem," she said. "See you tomorrow."

She zipped up an expensive sailing jacket and put the hood up.

"That's stock," I said. "Three hundred pounds worth."

"Old stock," she said. "There's a mark on the cuff. 'Night."

I took the pick-up and drove to Tesco, my head full of Helen's visit and news and the sadness I felt already at the thought of the empty house. She hadn't mentioned it, but I wondered if she would ask me to look after it for when she came back to visit, or turned it into a holiday-let. I could manage that, I thought, and perhaps get someone to do the change-overs?

The sight of Angela at the till and the basket of appropriate items for Ben's amusement brought me to my senses. She raised an eyebrow at the contents of the basket until I explained.

"I've still got Tomas's games at home," she said. "Jigsaw puzzles and stuff. I couldn't bear to part with them. Do you think Ben would…?" Her eyes filled. Briefly. She was a tough cookie and carried on pricing the goods; tough enough to offer her dead son's toys to another child. I checked behind and there was no-one waiting.

"Could we have a talk about next year?" I asked. "I need to start plans for the snack-bar."

I packed the shopping away.

"Shall I bring the toys down to the yard on Friday?" she asked. "I haven't seen Ben since he was a baby."

"You know Arnie pretty well, though?" I asked. "He used to buy his lobster and smoked salmon from you when you ran the snack-bar for my uncle, didn't he? Bet you never thought Arnie' buy Madoc Marine. You were as surprised as the rest of us when Denise brought him over to tell us."

"God, yes. Couldn't forget those tattoos. I thought he looked a bit sad underneath all that enthusiasm, though. He must have pots of money to afford this yard. And that cow of a wife. I remember her alright. Only really saw her once at a distance, but I remember that shrill voice as she shrieked at that spotty child, Jason, to go away and play somewhere else. She only had time for those twins and their jet-skis."

"They're not living together now," I said. "Do you remember when he said he'd thrown her out after the twins were arrested? Or maybe she just left. Arnie looks after Ben during the week, but he goes to his mum some weekends, he told me. Seems to be a reasonably amicable, child-sharing arrangement."

"Amicable? Her? Don't you believe it." She looked thoughtful. "Bet he's a good dad. Bet she's not much of a mother. Arch-bitch, I'd call her. See you Friday. About seven."

I picked up the flash-light and walked over to lock the Boat Shed and shut the yard gates for the night. The early evening darkness was as funereal as the rest of the day, and the instinct to be tucked up inside with light and warmth became more acute as I checked the boat cradles and ran my hand over the smooth surface of *Capella's* hull. The rain had persisted all day; puddles had formed in the new gravel and I picked my way between them and round to the back of the shed. A fresh fall of pebbles and soil had slipped down the rock-face into the gap and piled up, not quite touching the galvanised sheet-metal of the back wall.

The smoke-house was still separated from the debris, but I knew it wouldn't take much for the space to fill with a bigger landslip. It was only a large, filing cabinet after all, big enough to walk into, with the fire and racks at the back. Solidly built, with heavy-duty steel, the floor had worn thin in places where it joined the walls. The catch on the double doors was unreliable; sometimes it shut and sometimes it didn't; it needed a new one, but that was not on the priority list. Much more satisfactory, was the wooden bar that slipped through the handles, the old tiller from the chandlery that Hugh had once picked up and wielded like a baseball-bat to threaten my intruder, Jason. The doors swung open easily when I pulled the bar out, shone my torch inside and leaned against the wall.

The last, and only time I'd experimented with it, had been the Christmas before Covid struck. Helen's Nain had given her seal of approval for the smoked salmon and the gravadlax I'd made in her kitchen. I still had some oak and applewood chippings. I would do it again, and walked back through the yard, wet through from the heavy rain, but with a sense of purpose. But I needed more than that to lift my spirits.

I hadn't got used to being on my own in Madoc Marine. It was only a hop and skip from my caravan in the boatyard, but I'd felt secure there, with the big gates and the security lock and nothing much to interest anyone. Here, I was responsible for tens of thousands of pounds worth of powerboats outside and some expensive clothing and boat-gear inside, all covered by CCTV linked to a security company, just in case. But no amount of surveillance covered me and my fears. Arnie laughed at me and said he'd bring one of his guard dogs, if I wanted.

"Dogs?" I asked. "I don't like dogs much. You know that, Arnie. What would I do with a dog? You couldn't leave it outside in all weathers, and all that barking or yapping or whatever. No thanks. I'll get over it."

"What about my best Doberman? She's called Princess. You'd love her. Next time I come up, I'll bring her along for the ride."

"No, ta," I said, "don't even think about it."

I put the hood up on my jacket, locked the gates to both yards in the dark, switched all the main lights off in the showroom, set the alarm system and checked that the cameras and lights worked, and fled upstairs to the apartment. With the TV on and dinner in the oven, I moved from window to window and pulled the blinds down. Outside, the rain hurled itself against the glass, the spotlights in the yard flashed on briefly and illuminated a scene I was glad to shut out.

CHAPTER 5

I couldn't settle. Disturbed and jittery, I switched from channel to channel on the TV as the wind picked up and howled through the boatyards below. My mother phoned with queries about Christmas. Was I going to come to London? What for, I nearly asked? Then I thought of the alternative; here, on my own, just me and two bloody boatyards in the rain. I rang back.

"Yes," I said, "and I'll bring the best smoked salmon you've ever tasted."

Trish was ecstatic. I phoned her, lounged on the white leather sofa, which was as inviting as a concrete slab until covered with Indian throws from a craft fair at the Canolfan, and thought long and hard about the day. A flicker of resolve had been rekindled by the Rock Engineering guy, the gossip about my coping abilities, the news of Helen going away to start a new life, and the imminent business meeting with Arnie on Friday. I reached for a notepad and pen and started a list. He wouldn't like it.

It rained all night and drizzled the following morning. I started to clear the ashes from the smoke-house and scraped down the racks with a wire brush, ready for the first batch of salmon on its way from Scotland.

At two o'clock, I walked over to Borth-y-Gest to meet Helen.

"I'm really sorry," she said, upset and angry. "Mother's taken the barometer. I left a note. Sometimes, I can't believe she's my mother at all. I said you wanted it. Also, I didn't tell you yesterday…"

The doorbell rang. She opened the door to the same estate-agent who had sold *Tai Pilots* for me.

"Hi, Cassie," surprised to see me there.

The silence was profound. He looked at Helen and back to me.

"I was just about to tell you," Helen said. "I couldn't yesterday. I hadn't decided finally. Not until last night. Sorry."

"I'll go," I said, stunned. I should have guessed. How stupid of me. It would fund her new life, as *Tai Pilots* would fund mine. It was her property after all.

"Never mind the barometer. Can I have the other things?" I asked, and put my hand on her arm. "It's okay. Really."

The jelly moulds, one made of heavy glass and the other two, light metal, were in a cupboard in the dresser, dusty with lack of use, and the recipe book was in its remembered drawer. I found an old shopping bag and piled them in. Then I took one of her favourite decorated tea-pots off the dresser shelf and added it carefully to the bag. The oystercatchers painted beak-to-tail around the pot, turned their red beaks and beady eyes to the light and I tucked an old tea-towel around them.

"Pannad?" I asked. "New home?"

The kitchen was cold and quiet as I packed and took a last look around, closed my eyes and saw her again as she filled the kettle and piled warm brownies onto a plate. Through the open door, I could hear Helen and the estate agent.

"God knows there's always been a big enough queue of prospective buyers for properties here," he said, "but it's all gone a bit crazy since Covid. I won't say name your price, but don't be too hasty to accept the first bid. Anyway, first come, first served if the money's up front. I've got a buyer who's had their eye on this place for years. Consider it sold; at a price we need to discuss first."

How much? And to whom?

I said goodbye to Helen, and wished her luck. We didn't hug, just touched each other on the arm, and I walked through the car-park, past *Tai Pilots*, sad and neglected but not for much longer, up to the pill-box on the headland and sat on a bench. Two dead and empty houses, two more holiday homes, two anonymous buyers. None of my business, after all. I held the bag with the jelly moulds and precious tea-pot tight against my chest and walked slowly back through the bay and up the steps in a grip of something indefinable; another loss, another small grief. Move on, girl, I said to myself. Think of the money.

Thursday, and Steve Lewis arrived in a battered, long wheel-base Land Rover. The colour of the paint was indistinguishable from the rock-dust that coated it from bumper to bumper; the only clear space was where the wipers had cleared an arc on the windscreen. Ladders were strapped to the roof-rack and machines and tools were vaguely visible through the windows. A large dog sat in the passenger seat.

"He won't care if you don't like him," said the man. "It's whether he likes you that matters. Where I go, he goes."

I stood still as he unclipped the dog, pulled a harness over its head and it jumped from the seat to the gravel on the yard. He shut the passenger door and said one word. The dog sat, in one fluid effortless motion, onto the gravel. The head, as though carved out of granite, remained still, aloof, the eyes fixed on its master; a black and tan velvet statue, motionless, alert, waiting.

"Right, let's get on, shall we?"

He nodded to the dog, and it trotted over to the harbour wall where it stood with front paws on the edge. It looked out over the river towards Ballast Island, head lifted high, then he lowered it and scanned the water below.

"Won't it jump? Does it have a name? What is it?"

"Jackson," he said. "He's a Rottveiler and no, he won't jump. He's too bright for that. You don't like dogs, do you?"

"Is it that obvious?"

"As the nose on your face," he said. "No worries. He won't care. He'll just ignore you."

He slid the ladder off the roof-rack, whistled the dog away from the edge and it turned and peed up against one of the wooden chocks under *Annie*. He carried the ladder past the snack-bar, cleared some of the debris away from the back wall with a shovel and placed the top of the ladder against it, stepped onto the bottom rung and tested his weight on the loose rubbish beneath.

Up and over onto the flat area below the cliff, he pulled up the ladder and dragged it over to the base of the rock-face, partially obscured by dense ivy, then climbed up and disappeared into the thicket. Soil and stones clattered down and the bigger ones bounced over the wall and hit the back of the shed. I went back inside. The picture of my bank balance in free-fall floated in front of me as I cleaned the glass on the fish-tank, lit the fire and tried not to think of the verdict. There was nothing else I could do, except wait.

I threw on an old coat, put the hood up against the drizzle that had set in from the sea, walked over to the harbour wall and sat on a mooring bollard. The dog was nowhere to be seen. If I couldn't see it, I convinced myself, I wouldn't worry about it, reassured by its master's testimonies. This wasn't Rosie, Emily's ball of very-sweet but attention-seeking yappy, fidgeting fluff who I tolerated but had no attachment to. This was a large, strong, self-contained creature, with rippling muscles under a glossy coat and, as its master said, would make its own choices. The man trusted his dog and I trusted the man. I didn't have to like it, but I had no need to fear it, either.

The tide had turned and the water gathered pace below me, the grey surface broken in places by swirls of twigs and leaves from the persistent, heavy rain on the Traeth. I'd taken Emily home to her farm above the banks of the Glaslyn on the previous Saturday. Her father had moved all his sheep off the marsh and onto higher ground and housed the pregnant ewes in the barns. Days of heavy rain had flooded the low levels as far as the foothills and I'd driven back on the Beddgelert road and stopped on the bridge to watch the spectacle.

Torrents of water hurtled down from Snowdon to join the Glaslyn, into the Aberglaslyn Pass and culminated in a roar of tumbled white water as it poured over the boulders, under the stone bridge and out onto the flood plain, the outlines of half-drowned, river-bank willow emerging black through the water with little reference to the natural course of the river. It had burst its banks days before, and the waters had spread out in a silver sheet, until blocked in its rush to the sea by the Cob, stretched across the Traeth from Boston Lodge to Ynys Towyn.

I'd driven back though town and parked outside Cob Records, walked through the footpath at the base of Yynys Towyn and stood above the lock-gates. The flood waters surged through into the harbour, swished past the few yachts left on the pontoons for the winter and scoured out the river bed for the deeper moorings, just as it had done when the harbour was first constructed two hundred years ago.

I closed my eyes and saw the scene clearly, as on a summer's day; the white sand and grassy edges of the river high and dry as the river glided obediently through its banks, the cattle like statues in the shallows, and in the distance, Cnicht and the Moelwyns soared a hazy-grey into the sky. It would be spring and summer again soon, but for now, it seemed the rain would never stop and the river would never run clear again and sparkle in the sun. That was four days ago and still it rained. I stared vacantly, immersed in its unwelcome greyness below me.

I didn't hear the pad of paws on gravel, as much as felt the presence behind me. I held my breath. On that morning during the summer, when I discovered my great-uncle's pet lobster dead in the Boat Shed, I had a strong feeling of an unmistakable absence of life that had nothing to do with sound or sight. It was simply an absence. Now, at that moment, I had that same feeling but this time, the presence of another creature, close to me, living and breathing; no sound, no smell, no warning.

The dog appeared by my side, stood for a second with its front paws set firmly on the edge, then, with that smooth, unruffled action, lowered its backside and sat down. Its head remained still, the chin slightly lifted, the mouth firmly shut, the eyes fixed on the island. I might as well not have existed. I let out my breath, not realising I'd held it. We sat, motionless, and the river ran slowly below us and out to sea. Then, with a slow movement on the beach opposite, the ponderous beat of a heron's wings disturbed the air; black, stick-legs hung down from its body and sloped backward as it flapped along the old wooden piles and settled on the mud further down the island.

"Heron," I said, surprised by the sound of my own voice, but then I used to talk to Neifion in his tank; a regular morning briefing which helped me keep my thoughts in order. In the absence of anyone close to share problems with, I just did. It seemed perfectly natural. Bonkers, Jason had said. The dog watched. I stole a look at its head, still too wary to move, and it opened its mouth slightly so I could see black gums and pink tongue.

"The thing is," I said, "you're not at all like Rosie. She's the only other dog I've ever been close to; since I was bitten, that is."

I pushed back my cuff.

"See?"

The scar on my wrist was still white, even after all those years.

"But you," I said, and turned properly towards him, reached out, tentatively touched the velvet head, and studied the way the tan markings contrasted with the black. It didn't mind, just lifted its chin a little higher. "You're quite ugly, aren't you? Also rather magnificent, in a funny sort of way. A bit special, aren't you? I bet you'd look after those you chose to."

It trotted beside me back to the Boat Shed and I filled Rosie's old water bowl and put it by the step, where it drank deeply, sat with its head slightly to one side with ears lifted, listening.

"Should you be a 'he' rather than an 'it'? And at what point?" I mused.

The ladder clattered against the roof-rack of the Land Rover.

"I think your boss is done," I said, "Want to come in?"

But he sat outside and waited. The door opened and I switched the kettle on. Steve Lewis wiped his feet on the grubby mat, came around the counter and sat down in the chair by the fire, as though he'd been there before, easy-going, and comfortable. The dog stayed outside.

"Cosy," he said, warming his hands and looking at the drawings on the stool. "These your plans? Nice."

I handed him a mug of coffee and put the biscuit tin on the counter.

"Help yourself. Mark takes all the chocolate ones."

He reached into the tin and took two biscuits.

"What else is in this shed, besides the chandlery?" he asked, and looked behind him.

I showed him the room with the model ships.

"About thirty altogether," I said, when I could see he'd started counting. "Ten large ones, like *Evelyn* here and *Fleetwing*, about ten middle-sized ones and some smaller ones, even tiny rowing dinghies and a replica of the pilot boat. I can't decide what to do with them."

"Valuable?"

"Don't know. I've had so much to do, I just shut the door on them. I'll get round to it."

He nodded, picked up a tiny sailor from *Evelyn's* deck and held it in a grubby palm.

"Amazing," he said, and put it back gently. I shut the door behind him and he sat back down, cradled his mug and stared at the fire.

I was desperate for the verdict, but like his dog, he would not be rushed.

"Right," he said. "This is how it is. The original rock-fall you told me about from last winter, above where your caravan was parked, that was a drainage problem; simply too much vegetation had collected on a shelf and the water couldn't run off. All these heavy down- pours don't help."

"Right. I can see that," I said. "But this recent stuff? The soil and stones seem to be coming from much higher up the cliff. It just tumbles down onto that flat area and stones are bouncing up and over the wall. Is the wall going to collapse with the weight?"

I could hear the alarm in my voice.

"It's a possibility. The drainage pipes need to be found and cleared. The water should be running free into the system behind the shed but there's no sign of pipes. It's all bogged down behind the wall and can't run off."

"But that doesn't explain the rock-falls from the top, does it? I mean, why is it doing that after all these years? It was quarried out for the old wharf a long time ago, and hasn't been a problem since, not that I've heard of."

He drank his coffee and put the mug on the counter, leaned forward and stroked his nose, quiet and thoughtful, then reached for a small rucksack he'd put on the floor beside him.

“There’s a huge boulder, an overhang, underneath all that growth up there that looks unstable. That’s one problem. But this is the sticky bit,” he said. “I don’t know what to make of it.”

He delved into his pocket and pulled out a pair of work gloves, opened the bag and took out four objects, covered in dirt with fragments of dead bracken and nettles clinging to the ends. He laid them out on the floor and brushed the dirt off with a cloth from his pocket.

“And?” I asked, impatient but curious enough to wait.

He lifted two objects, one about twelve inches long, the other much bigger.” These are crowbars.”

“I know that,” I said. “And that’s a stone hammer. And that’s a cold chisel. I’m not completely ignorant. But I don’t understand?”

“Miss Jones…” he said.

“‘Cassie,’ please,” I said, exasperated.

“I found these at the top of the cliff on a ledge above an overhanging boulder. There’s one like it that came down recently, into a yard by the Yacht Club.”

“Yes, I’ve seen it, but…”

“What I’m saying, is this is a police matter. Someone who thinks they know what they’re doing has deliberately, or is in the process of, weakening the rock at the top which is already unstable and loose. It could cause a landslide. Even if it broke off naturally and just tumbled down the cliff, the weight on that sodden ground would put huge pressure on the land and the retaining wall at the bottom.”

Ice-fingers of fear crept into my gut; denial and uncertainty progressed to sheer disbelief augmented by the stirrings of anger and impending shock. Why?

“But why would anyone want to do that? To help it along, is that what you’re saying? And this stuff. Why leave it? And how would they get up there? They’d have to have access from the top and the land’s private up there."

"Too public? Someone scared them off, perhaps. The job of chipping away at the rock would have to be done a bit at a time. This slate splits easily with pressure from a crowbar at the right point. With cataclysmic results, I have to say, if it came down in one piece, like the one up the road."

"But wouldn't it just land at the bottom of the cliff?"

"It might, but the ground's sodden and if it caught on the rock below, it might be projected further out and land in the middle of that sodden ground. The pressure on the retaining wall would be enormous."

"The Boat Shed?" I asked, in a small voice.

"Flattened."

The burning log in the fire flamed its last and collapsed in the ash.

"Phone the police," he said. "Do it now."

He sat and waited for me, too shocked to make sense of his words.

"But who in their right mind could hate me enough to even think about doing something like that? All that drugs stuff has been and gone. I haven't upset anyone. It's like something out of a movie. Things don't happen like that in real life."

I pulled myself together. We went back outside and I looked up and studied the cliff-face. A small conifer poked its nose out of the clumps of ivy and an oak tree, skeletal in its winter garb, perched precariously on the skyline. Thickets of brambles intertwined with the wispy, dead heads of willow-herb and bamboo plants planted and now populating the flat land, which was a quagmire of soft mud. The cliff-face itself seemed so much closer to the back of the Boat Shed and the retaining wall, than it had before. A trick of the light? My lack of attention? Or was it simply that I'd never looked through Steve Lewis's eyes before. I now understood his concern.

"Before I phone the police, I need to know the result of your scrabbling around up there. If the cliff-face is unstable anyway and only needs a shove to bring it all down, can you and your company fix it? And the drainage and anything else to save the yard. It's going to be my home as well as a business. I need to know for the planning permission. Can you guarantee you can fix it, like bolts and gabions and stuff? How much, Mr Lewis?"

He scratched his head.

"I'll need to go back to the office, work it out and send you a quote. And you need to phone the police."

"Yes, I know," I said. "I will. But I can't wait for a quote. You do this all the time. You must have a reasonable idea. I must know. More or less. I must know whether I'd be wasting your time and my money, if there's another agenda at work I can't even begin to imagine. I will find out, though. The police will find out. Cost. Please?"

"Give me twenty minutes," he said, "and I'll do my best."

The dog had settled itself under the porch to the front door. This time, when I wandered over to the harbour wall, he stayed where he was. There was nothing to see, nothing to occupy my mind, except the gnawing anxiety that, again, I was in a situation over my head. The man emerged from the back of the shed with a clip-board.

"The snack-bar and that cabinet smoke-house thing will have to be moved for access. All the debris this side of the wall will need to be scraped away to enable the digger to get in. The water-logged soil the other side of the wall will need to be dug out, removed into skips and the drainage pipes replaced. Then the cliff-face, netted and bolted after that large chunk has been broken up and removed. The caravan can stay where it is."

He ticked items as he spoke, grave and business-like.

"At least with all the work going on," he added, "any criminal activity would be impossible. And pointless. The top would be secured and there would be no access. I guarantee that."

It was only late morning, but a grey gloom descended on the yard and shrouded Ballast Island in mist. The smoke from the chimney-pot rose lazily above the tin roof of the Boat Shed, once a sign of warmth and welcome, despite its shabby appearance. Now it felt like a mockery.

"I suggest I liaise with colleagues in the planning office and the building inspector to see if the recommendations we make would meet their requirements. It might seem a big deal, but we do it all the time. You'd be surprised where folk want to build properties. That way, there are no nasty surprises."

I glanced up at the cliff-face.

"Would you have to strip all that ivy as well?" thinking of the amount of rubbish.

"Yes, and scale all the loose rock away," he said.

He opened the Land Rover door and put the clip-board on the seat. When he turned around, he stooped over and peered into my face, a searching look of concern, as though he hadn't quite believed I was listening.

"It's not the rock, love," he said. "That's all manageable. That's what we do and it needs to be done as soon as possible. But the threat to you, that's something else. I know you'll hate me saying it, but you're young, female, and vulnerable. There's something nasty out there and I don't like it. If you were my daughter, I'd be very afraid for you."

He ran his hand over his face. "Phone the police, Miss Jones. Please. As soon as I've gone. We couldn't start work until there's been an investigation, anyway. They'll need those tools and a statement. We'll also need a reasonable weather forecast; we can't work in torrential rain."

Jackson left his post by the front door to the shed, loped over and sat down with his flank close against my leg. Where had the dog-fear gone?

Replaced by something more sinister? I could feel his body heat though my jeans, sensed his head directly below my hand. I placed my hand on his skull, as though for strength, but Steve Lewis had not finished yet.

"There is a possibility that the yard could be closed, or at least out of bounds to the public for safety until the work is carried out."

"Do you mean it's in imminent danger? I didn't think you meant that. I thought you meant in the future. The weather, I mean, not the other stuff, the threat, if that's what it is." My voice tailed off. Hadn't I been listening or only hearing what I wanted to hear?

"More heavy rainfall, like the last few weeks could be dangerous. If I were you, I would move all those models out of the shed and anything else of value. Some of those planks, maybe? That's good hard-wood. And tools. Can you get someone to help?"

"No, I can manage, but to move the snack-bar and smoke-house in case there's a fall? They've never been moved. I need them for the business. I can't risk them. Not those."

The dog seemed to acknowledge the panic and pressed his head up against my hand.

"I'll make some calls," he said.

How long is a minute? A frozen tableau in time; two people and one dog; the question waited, hovered unspoken in the damp air.

"So, how much?" I asked, very quietly.

"Forty thousand."

CHAPTER 6

"The police said they'd send someone this afternoon," I told Denise, when she'd stopped fussing about my white face and shaky hands, put a coffee and a chocolate bar in front of me, sat on the desk and fiddled with her hair, "and not a word to anyone about this, okay? No texts. Nothing. I just need to get on and move this stuff. It's just a natural event if anyone asks and they'll see all the activity anyway, if I'm given the go-ahead."

"Okay. I'll put a notice on the door, close the office and help. We'll be to and fro with the models. It's dead quiet here, anyway. You can't do all that by yourself."

She switched off the computer, checked the answer phone, disappeared into the cloakroom, and returned with the expensive sailing jacket in her arms and a pile of dust-sheets which she dumped on the floor by my feet.

"I hope you'll write that jacket off and claim against insurance, or something," I said. "What are these for?" looking at the dust-sheets.

"Pads for the model boats in the back of the pick-up, and the insurance claim is already done for the coat. Damaged cuff in transit, besides which, if I'm going to carry out duties above my pay-grade, I'll need to be properly dressed against the weather."

She stared at me, one arm through the jacket sleeve.

"You weren't seriously thinking of carrying the models over, one by one, were you?"

Thinking? I couldn't think. A sudden urgency to check on the sale of *Tai Pilots* blocked all the practicalities of clearing the Boat Shed. I needed the money. I rang the receptionist at the solicitors.

"Any day, now, Miss Jones. There shouldn't be any problems. Contracts are exchanged and there are no hold-ups with the buyers. Maybe end of next week."

The *Evelyn* was the first to go into the pick-up. The model was three feet long, three feet high to the top of the masts and included the stand with its brass plaque. I lifted it off the shelf and carried it through the shed like a basket of eggs. The tiny spars and rigging were so fragile, the sails made from canvas, but frayed in places where the sheets had been attached. I knew if the sails and running rigging parted company, I hadn't the knowledge to mend them accurately.

I took a picture of each ship with my phone before relieving the tiny sailors from their deck-chores. I put them in an envelope with the name of each ship written on the front and sellotaped them to the hulls. Denise stood in the back of the pickup, tucked each ship into a nest of dust sheets and bunched up the material so they stood upright. When the ten large ships were onboard, I drove slowly to the showroom and unloaded them into the annex at the back of the showroom.

I emptied each shelf of cleaning materials and clothing items, piled the stock on the floor and placed the large models on the shelves. Denise stood back.

"Looks like a bloody museum. Hardly state of the art, modern high-tech, powerboat gear, is it? What's Mr Blackwell going to say, and where are we going to put all this stuff for sale?"

"Don't know, don't care," I said. "They've got to come out of the Boat Shed. We can make some new shelves with the planks of hard-wood. Nobody wants to buy them. Then we can move the ships onto them and make a special feature. Anyway, it's all part of the diversification project."

"What project? You never said anything about a project. What are you cooking up, Cass?"

"You'll see," I said. "Wait till Friday. It'll be fine."

The police car drove into the yard that afternoon and stopped by the pick-up. I stood on the step with a replica of the eighteen-foot pilot-boat in one hand and the steam-ship Rebecca in the other.

"What's the problem, Cassie?" Lyn asked, as she shut the passenger door, police hat pulled down firmly on her head of short hair, bright eyes scanning the yard, as her partner Jim's lanky figure slid out of the passenger seat, a familiar comfort from their support in the summer and the help they gave to catch the drugs gang. I knew them both, knew them well enough to make coffee and offer the remnants of the biscuit tin.

"Thought you'd have had enough excitement for one year," she said, and they took down the details, bagged the tools and scratched their heads.

"It doesn't seem related to the County Lines thing," Jim said. "We'll try and get a match off the tools, but anyone up to no-good would wear gloves, I reckon. Have you any idea what this could be about?"

I shook my head.

Lyn opened the car door, turned and met my eyes.

"Is this about you or the yard? Think about it. Any personal vendettas you haven't considered? We'll be in touch. If the work on the cliff goes ahead, that'll be a good thing. Phone if you're concerned about anything out of the ordinary. We'll ask the patrol car to keep an eye open. They usually do the rounds down here at weekends in the summer, anyway."

Friday evening and Arnie, Denise and I sat round a table in the showroom. The spotlights had been dimmed and focused on the table, but even in the shadows, the lights picked out the gleam of the white hull and stainless-steel fittings of the powerboat in the middle of the showroom floor. The office was now dark and shut up for the night with the answer-phone on. There would be no distractions, I'd decided, while I laid out plans for Madoc Marine; with trepidation, misgivings, and a dose of bloody-mindedness. I hadn't told Arnie about his foul-mouthed client, Mr Robinson There was nothing to tell. He was still in Pwllheli, after all.

Who did I think I was? In my preparation for this meeting, I had written lists of ideas, despite being an inexperienced, ex-journalist of no standing whatsoever with no business sense or experience. Who was I to tell a successful businessman he needed to look at things differently? I could be signing my death warrant. But somehow, simply because of all the doubts, I felt that the ideas that flooded my mind were justified, different, progressive, and imaginative, unsullied by years of status-quo business dealings, perhaps a way forward in uncertain times.

Maybe it was the generation gap; Arnie was at least twenty years older than me, but seemed older than that. I recognised the wear and tear, the responsibility of care looking after Ben, his huge scrap business, so Hugh had told me, and the emotional trauma with the split from his wife over the two older sons in prison. If I could help make up for all that and his kindnesses to me, by suggesting something to make the boating world sit up and take notice, and be part of something different in this part of Wales, I had nothing to lose. Except the Boat Shed. I put it out of my mind for the moment as Denise cleared away the chip-papers and brought in coffee.

I handed out folders to Arnie and Denise, vaguely aware of the soundtrack from Peter Rabbit in the flat above us, and Angela's voice and footsteps. I blessed her for being there. She'd brought Tomas's toys and games as promised and had stayed.

"I've nothing else on," she'd said, "beside which, I can tell Ben about all the mischief Jason and Tomas used to get up to," and they'd gone upstairs hand in hand.

I watched Arnie as he reached for the folder placed in front of him. I watched his huge hand flip the cover open, reach for his glasses in a case on the table and stroke his moustache as he read through the introduction. I don't know you, I thought. I don't know you at all. Queasiness settled on my stomach.

"Talk me through, bab. I'm listening."

I talked: I talked him through the installation of solar panels and a small wind turbine for helping to power the yard, the replacement of traditional cleaning chemicals with eco-friendly ones, the thoroughness and certification of emission checks on engines and a second-hand clothing shop for good-quality, foul-weather gear.

I talked him through the idea of setting up a jet-ski course for safety on the water with professional tuition, to be ran as a franchise, with use of the Boat Shed's slip-way to extend launching times and store jet-skis in the yard; the snack-bar and smoke-house, to provide food using local, farm produce as well as freshly-caught lobster and crab in high quality, snack-cuisine and take-aways.

He listened without interruption, his elbows on the table, his chin rested on one large fist, turned the pages as requested, and then sat back in his chair.

"An eco-friendly yard. I get that, Cassie, but how the hell do you match all that up with these fuel guzzlers out there?" and he waved his hand at the dark window.

"I can't quote figures," I said. "But surely, these energy concerns can't not affect the leisure industry, eventually. It would be stupid to think that an expensive pastime like powerboating would be excluded. That's why we need to think about diversifying."

He sighed. Was it a patronising sigh, from one who was extremely wealthy?

"There'll always be money around, bab. This is a powerboat yard. The rich will always be rich."

"Yes, I know that, but it's not so much for the moneyed ones, and don't tell me wealthy people don't care about the environment. They'd like to think they're doing their bit as well as having a good time. It's the cost of the resources for ordinary people, Arnie. Not everyone who wants to play in the sea is loaded. And it's about selling ideas, a different way of having fun on the water with low-key supervision and training; back to basics with a new twist."

He narrowed his eyes.

"You're talking about an amalgamation of the yards, aren't you? To save your skin as well as looking after mine. Is that what you're up to?"

Denise scraped her chair back and glanced up, unsure of the atmosphere; a strained silence in the dark showroom, the TV faint upstairs, the rain against the window, his eyes on my face.

He shut the folder and pushed his chair back to stand up. I'd got it wrong. He'd misunderstood.

"No," I said, panicked. "Not a business amalgamation. Sorry. I didn't think you'd presume that. Mine's never going to be anything but a failure as a working yard. I know that. But it could be an asset to Madoc Marine if the facilities are shared, my yard leased to you, maybe, as an income for both of us."

"Not for sale, then?" he asked. "Not what you're offering? You said you wanted to use the yard to build a home, as well as a business. Make yourself clear. Cassie."

There was an edge to his voice I hadn't heard before. Hugh had told me he was probably a millionaire. He must have been more than that to have bought this place outright and still own his scrap business. I'd got that wrong as well.

I glanced at Denise. She'd said nothing. Frightened, intimidated by her new boss? I should have known better. She turned towards me

"I think you'd better tell Mr Blackwell about the dangerous rock-face," she said. "And the rest of it. Also, maybe," and she turned to face her boss, "there are certain points Mr Blackwell would wish to clarify. The future, and plans for himself, perhaps?" and she held his gaze.

I knew she was more than just a secretary; I just hadn't known how much more.

He pulled himself back to the table, placed both fists either side of the folder, threw his head back and laughed, a deep, belly laugh that reverberated through the showroom.

"I knew I'd picked you two for a good reason," he said, when he'd wiped his eyes. "Good God, what a pair."

What future was Denise hinting at? She knew, or guessed, something I didn't.

"Right," he said. "Cards on the table. My plan involves a move away from the Midlands. The scrap business will be sold eventually; for the moment I'm waiting to see how things progress; for a year, if you like. The intention is to move here permanently, live upstairs, send Ben to a good school, and let him grow up by the sea. This will be my livelihood, Cassie and yes, I'm interested in your plans, but not sufficiently to jeopardise my future business. All these ideas will cost money, with no immediate reward."

"There are grants available," I said, "and things like advertising and a new web-site don't cost a fortune. If I can afford the work to stabilise the cliff-face and the planning permission is granted, it'd be a fine project, to use both yards, classic and modern high-tech. I could finance some of it, anyway, possibly an extension to the slipway; the food outlet I've already got. If I can't afford the new-build Boat Shed or they refuse permission as a residence, I'll just have to refurbish the old one as a chandlery, and find somewhere else to live."

The very thought of refusal stopped me. I shuffled some papers to hide the doubt I knew was imprinted on my face. It was quiet in the showroom for a few minutes.

"What about the conditions of your inheritance?" he asked. "Weren't you supposed to retain the use of the yard for classic boats? As for the slipway, I don't think so, bab. I know how much it cost for the main one in the harbour and that was a few years back. Not in your league."

"Well, I don't know that, do I? It's just an idea. As far as the conditions are concerned, it didn't specify how much of the yard was to be used. Anyway, a few clinker-built rowing dinghies and skiffs for hire might do the trick with the solicitors; classic designs made in wood, maybe."

It suddenly became very clear to me. I owned the land. It was worth a fortune, so I was told, but only if it was safe and usable. I had to prove that or be left with nothing; no home, no income, no career, nothing. I might as well join Pete, my vagrant acquaintance, on the streets of Pwllheli and peddle drugs, or find a job on a newspaper and live in London. I shook my head at the thought.

"I'll think about it over the weekend," Arnie said. He stuffed the folder down his coat and stood up. "I'll call on my way home on Sunday."

"By the way," said Denise. "Your manager has been busy." She reached down under the table and lifted the framed certificates up and onto the table.

He looked at them, looked at me and reached out his hand.

"Well done," he said, with a slightly bemused look, as though he didn't really see what he was looking at. His huge fist enveloped my hand. He scratched his head with the other. "Well done."

Angela brought Ben downstairs. I walked them to the car and Arnie strapped Ben in.

"Just to let you know," he said, " that me and Shelly are giving it another go. She's been back for a while now. For Ben's sake, really. We're getting on okay. Nice to have her back, isn't it son? And I had to be away on business last weekend. See you Sunday," and drove off.

Really? Leopards changing spots? Just like that?

Denise turned off the lights. "If she's got herself moved back into the family home, you can bet your life there's a reason. Maybe she's realised which side her bread's buttered, but she'll still be a bitch. Maybe…"

"Maybe what?"

"Maybe he's frightened of her, that's why he took her back," she said.

"Frightened of what? I can't imagine Arnie being frightened of anything, but keep your enemies close, you mean? To keep an eye on her?"

"Something like that. See you Monday. You didn't tell him about the boat models in the shop, did you? Or about Mr Robinson."

"No. Not the best time, was it?"

She shook her head, put her hood up and ducked into the rain. The door closed softly behind her.

"I'll run you home," I said to Angela. "It's pouring out there. Sounded as though you and Ben were getting on okay."

"He's a great kid. Pretty happy with his own company, I'd say. Mind you, from what he told me, I think he must have to be."

“What do you mean? He’s in school and he’s got his mum back home, Arnie said. I bet he gets loads of attention.”

The headlights shone against the wet cliff-face as we drove out of the yard, the rain water running in rivulets down the gullies in the rock.

“I wasn’t sure whether I should mention it, Cass,” she said, as we bumped over the cobbles by the Pen Cei. “I mean, it’s none of my business and maybe I got it wrong, but…”

“But what?”

“Well, I said to Ben, it must be lovely having your mum home at weekends, if your dad needs to go away. Then he said, Jenny’s there, and I said, I thought your mum’s name was Shelly. He said, yes, it is, but she goes out with her friends and Jenny stays. She’s nice, he said. We watch films and she reads me a story at bedtime.”

“So, mum goes out at night, then?” wondering why, when Arnie was away on business. “Surely she could go out during the week, when he’s there?”

“That’s what I thought, selfish cow. Anyway, that’s not it. It’s what he said after. I wasn’t sure if I’d got it right, or even if he was making it up.”

I turned off the main road down to Borth-y-Gest. The lights from the café twinkled in the rain but the bay was dark and uninviting. I drove up Mersey Street and stopped by her front door.

“Tell me.”

“Ben said… he said that last weekend, Jenny was sick and couldn’t baby-sit, so his mum had to stay in. She said she was going to watch a grown-up film on Netflix and put him to bed early and he was to go straight to sleep. He said she was cross, and he played on his phone under the bed clothes for a bit, and looked at a picture book with his torch and went to sleep.

‘Then he said he heard a car door shut, and voices outside the house woke him up. He said he'd just learned his numbers and how to tell the time in school so he switched his torch on and shone it on the clock; it pointed to three o'clock on the little hand. He heard the front door close and his mum's shoes click on the wooden floor in the hall. The door to his room opened and he pretended to be asleep in case he got into trouble."

I switched the wipers off and turned to her, the words stuck in my throat as I realised the enormity of what she'd told me. If it was true.

"Do you think she left him on his own all night? I can hardly believe that. She wouldn't, she couldn't. He's only five. Can he really tell the time?"

"We played a game, so I could check it out. Spot on, with all the numbers. He's a bright boy. Also, he made me promise not to tell. He was asleep, so he didn't even know she'd gone out. He said he didn't mind, really. He wasn't scared."

"Christ," I said. "That's not the point. He's bound to defend his mum, isn't he? Arnie'd kill her. What do we do?"

"I've chewed it over all evening. I can't tell Mr Blackwell or Ben would never forgive me, even for telling you. The easiest thing would be for Ben to tell his dad himself. Maybe set up a conversation where he would tell the truth without realising it."

"Trip him up, you mean? That's a bit unfair."

"So's leaving a five-year old on his own. That's neglect. Suppose there'd been a fire or a robbery?"

I stared at the windscreen and switched the wipers back on. She opened the car door.

"Leave it with you," she said. "You decide what's best."

I started the engine and drove slowly back to the yard, contemplating the nature of decisions and their consequences. Ben was safe with his dad for now, tucked up in the static caravan next to Black Rock Sands, asleep to the sound of breaking surf as it pounded the North Bank. A restless sea to complement a restless situation. I didn't know what to do. The answer lay in work; the decision would arrive of its own accord by Sunday, when Arnie returned with his verdict.

The weekend was quiet, with no customers, no phone calls, nothing to disturb my methodical organisation of the model room. All the small models were lined up in plastic storage boxes in single layers; the larger models filled the shelves at the back of the glass counter. The overall effect of clothing, life-jackets, cleaning and painting materials, ropes and stainless-steel fittings and a selection of classic, wooden model ships looked totally incongruous, and Arnie would have a fit if he saw it now. I just needed time to fit it into separate areas and order some more moveable racks for the outdoor gear.

In fact, nothing less than a complete makeover of the whole room would do; a small, maritime history area with typed details of all the models, separated from the retail section by a screen. Not everyone who owned a powerboat would have been to the Maritime Museum, I reckoned; I wasn't stealing their act, just adding to it, especially as some of the ships had been built on the land where the yards now stood.

Full of wild ideas, I stood back and studied the room, enthusiasm mixed with anxiety. But then, he had put me in charge. I shut the door firmly; he had no need to look inside in the short visit on Sunday, and I turned my mind to the more serious matter of Ben. I could no more let it lie than fly to the moon, but I could mitigate the consequences, if handled carefully.

On Sunday afternoon, Arnie arrived. I shut the door to the backroom and the chaos in the shop; now was not the time to discuss the appropriate use of retail space. We went upstairs, where Ben opened the toy-box Angela had left, and his dad scooted him to the far end of the lounge to play. There was no argument; this was a dad whose word was law, I thought, but he ruffled his son's hair, bent over him, and kissed the top of his head, and I remembered his gentleness when Ben was just a babe-in-arms, cradled in those huge muscles with his dummy in his dad's mouth.

The file he'd taken away to read lay open on the coffee table, with each page detached and separated, pencil notes in the margins and a new sheet with a summary. My anxiety increased a hundred-fold as he talked through the proposals, with additional information he must have gleaned from the Internet over the weekend. He lost me in a world of business investment and projections, left me behind, humble and humiliated to think I could discuss my ideas with a millionaire who had developed and owned the biggest reclamation works in the Midlands. Just a scrappie? That's how I'd thought of him. I kept very quiet and shrank further into my pathetic little shell while he talked.

"So that's how it is, bab," he said.

I looked up from the papers, not sure what he meant, blitzed by all the information, and confused as to whether he approved of any of it; 'ifs' and 'buts' all round.

"You've got one year to prove that your ideas are valid, retain and increase customer footfall and hold your own with the finances. I don't expect a profit, neither do I want to see a deficit. But overall, I like your ideas, particularly the eco-side and the energy saving ones. I'll make ten thousand pounds available for you to develop those areas and if you can apply for grant aid, all the better. No more than that. One year, Cassie, then I'm taking over. The business must be in good shape and if you can put your mark on it, all the better for you in the future."

Stunned, I prised Ben from a jigsaw puzzle and we walked down the stairs into the showroom. Arnie stood and looked around.

"About as far removed as you can get from a scrapyard," he said. "All clean and white. Love it, don't we, son?"

"Before you go," I said. "Is it okay if I shut the showroom and yard for the Christmas break? I want to go to London and see my mother and friends. I won't get a chance in the spring. Denise says she'll be on call for the few days."

"No problem. I thought I'd bring Ben up after Christmas, though the van's cold this time of year. It's a bit of a small space for him with the days so short. They shut the site after New Year, so it'll be the last visit."

I didn't have to think. "Use the apartment while I'm away," I said. "It is yours, after all. Ben will like that, nice and warm and a bit of room to run around. I'll make the beds up in the spare rooms. Then you can be caretaker and I won't have to worry about it while I'm out clubbing."

He smoothed his moustache. "Won't you mind me in your home?"

"No, really. It still feels like a holiday flat," I said. "You're welcome any time, especially if you need to come up just for a night to negotiate a sale. You did say you'd broker any big sales we make, didn't you? Like that Sea Ray. We might have an interested customer and that's way over my pay-grade, just yet."

He laughed, wished me good luck with my rock-fall issue, and the planning department, not the slightest bit perturbed by my seemingly gargantuan problem and the possibility of the Boat Shed being demolished. I'd said nothing about the tools Steve had found and the insidious threat, even though it was in the hands of the police, but perhaps that wouldn't bother him either; a tough guy used to a tough life. It wasn't his problem, had nothing to do with him and didn't jeopardise Madoc Marine, so what was the point in telling him? It wasn't until he lifted Ben on to the booster seat and strapped him in, that I remembered. Oh God, should I tell him what Angela had told me? Shouldn't I? It was too late. Ben waved through the window and the car disappeared down the road.

I was right. The decision made itself in a curious way. Relieved that

I hadn't stirred up a hornets' nest at a time and place where there was no control over the results and concerned at the same time for Ben, I went back inside. Perhaps a carefully worded text to Arnie, I thought; just something Ben had said to Angela and she was worried in case she'd misunderstood. Then Arnie could take it upon himself to ask questions, find out the truth, as he would. I would not want to be in Shelly's shoes, if Ben was right.

I'd never forgotten something that Jason had told me about his dad, Arnie. When told his twin sons were pilfering from the business to fund their drugs habit, he'd turned the office upside down, wrecked it, hurled desks around, would have mangled his sons if they hadn't fled. No, I would not want to be Shelly; arch-bitch, as Denise called her. The ramifications of it all spoilt my good humour for the rest of the day. Would there be a divorce? Would there be custody issues for Ben? Money? Property? Don't even think it, girl. Arnie will know what to do. It'd probably never happen again. Maybe they'd turn out to be just a normal, happy family. Not my business, I convinced myself.

Next stop, I needed to move the smoke-house to safety and prepare some salmon for Christmas. If the council decided to close the yard while the work was being done, I'd move it over into Madoc Marine, I thought. Just shift a few powerboats around. Plenty of space. Arnie wouldn't mind.

CHAPTER 7

"The good news is," said Steve Lewis on the phone on Monday, as I was lighting the fire in the Boat Shed, "the planning officer is now aware of the work we're going to do and will bear it in mind for the appeal. He seemed quite positive. We'll need to move that smoke-house and the snack-bar before work starts and the yard's out of bounds to the general public for the moment. I've organised a fork-lift for this afternoon for the smoke-house and I'll tow the snack-bar out with the Land Rover, so at least you can get on with your smoked salmon. Bags some of the first lot. Also, we can start work on the rock next week if you and the weather give the go-ahead."

Please God, let the contracts be exchanged this week, I prayed, and chewed a finger-nail which I promised myself never to do again in times of stress. I had enough money to pay for some of the work out of the last of my trust fund, but I'd be living on bread and water after that if I wanted to go ahead with plans for rebuilding the Boat Shed.

Will Roberts turned up in the yard to discuss dates, so that we didn't clash for the last of the lift-outs and rescued me from my angst. His Harbour Master's jumper was hidden by the duffel coat he wore in cold weather, a wisp of hay clung to his sleeve and there was mud on his boots, unlike him, usually so immaculate; good habits from his naval service, I imagined. He still looked tired.

His wife had been buried quietly, in a Blaenau churchyard, near the farm. She had been ill for such a long time. He was not a man to whom you could ask personal questions; a formal man, with a stiff upper-lip, a wry sense of humour and a short fuse with idiots.

I offered my condolences, the response an abrupt nod of acknowledgment. He didn't object when I ushered him into the Boat Shed and sat him down by the fire, out of the cold.

"Pannad?" I asked.

He nodded and took out his notebook. Business over biscuits and coffee was so much easier. On the way out, he leaned out of the driver's window.

"Congratulations, by the way, Miss Jones. I saw those pieces of paper on the wall in your office. It's comforting to know there is now less likelihood of you damaging my harbour wall. I presume you had a lesson in bow-thrusters? And did you resolve your issue of the hypothetical client with the unsafe boat?"

I didn't need to answer. He knew perfectly well what had happened.

By late afternoon on Friday, the yard was a mess. I couldn't bear to look at it and walked into town to pick up the beautiful, whole salmon I'd ordered from the fishmonger. I disappeared into the apartment kitchen, cut it into two fillets and started the preparation for smoking. Sugared, salted and vacuum-packed, it could sit in the fridge all day as the recipe said, then I would rinse it and dry it until Saturday evening and the first smoke. It could cook gently all night, rest for Sunday and smoke again Sunday night. More rest, and then on Tuesday, I would make the first, smoked salmon sandwich for Steve Lewis. I wrote all the times down beside the recipe.

The smoke-house had been lifted and moved next to the caravan and the snack-bar had been towed to the other side of the gate nearer the edge of the harbour wall. The gravel surface had been churned into the underlying mud, soft and wet with the incessant rain, and was criss-crossed with tyre tracks. Jackson said hello briefly, a nudge of his nose against my jeans, and wandered around out of the way of the vehicles, peed up against *Capella's* cradle and lay down on the harbour wall out of the way. Been there, done that, know where to go, his expression said.

I stood back and surveyed my boatyard in horror.

"It'll get worse before it gets better," Steve said, "especially if you get the final go-ahead from planning and decide to demolish the Boat Shed. That'll be messy again for a bit. Don't fret. By the time we've finished, it'll be safe to start your new build, whatever you decide on. Have you?"

"What?"

"Have you decided?"

"I'm waiting for exchange of contracts," I said. "And to see what I can afford when you've finished putting pins in my rock."

He patted me on the shoulder. I didn't mind; any comfort was welcome. He picked up his shovel, whistled the dog into the Land Rover and followed the fork-lift out of the gate. I shut and locked the gates behind me.

"The solicitor said to ring back before five," Denise said, back in the office. "You stink of fish."

"Go home," I said. I owed her some time, made the call and was glad I was on my own to consider the news. If it had been bad news, I wouldn't have wanted company.

Deal complete, money in the bank, *Tai Pilots* gone forever, decisions to be made. I sat back in the chair, sick with relief and felt I needed to celebrate, but the empty showroom mocked me with silence. It was Friday night and the weight on my shoulders had lightened, but not disappeared as I thought it would, and there was no-one to share it with, to explain to, just to talk about it, for God's sake. What was wrong with me? I couldn't think of anyone who could really listen and understand, without throwing in their pennyworth of ideas, telling me what was best. Maybe I didn't need anyone at all and cheered myself up with a large vodka and tonic and a long look at the salmon marinading in the fridge. Now, that was exciting.

Saturday, and I took the salmon into the snack-bar, placed the two sides on the newly-wiped rack from the smoke-house and shut the door firmly against marauding gulls while I prepared the fire. Outside, I threw the salmon head over the harbour wall. The gulls swooped down from nowhere, tore it to pieces in mid-air and squabbled long after it was gone.

The bags of oak and apple wood-chips had been stored in the Boat Shed, and I wheeled a bag of each over to the smoke-house in the barrow. They took hold easily with some kindling, and smouldered happily in the metal sheep-trough Emily's dad had given me.

My great-uncle had made the fire loose on the floor, but it was messy and this seemed a better idea. While the fire settled itself down, I ventured around the back of the Boat Shed, looked with newly-informed eyes at the cliff-face and dreaded to think how many skips of rubbish would have to be removed. There had been no further, natural falls of rock or soil, but then it hadn't rained hard for a few days.

I stood on the harbour wall and took stock of the yard trying to visualise the space without a building, then with a new building, then with a refurbished shed, much as it was now. I gave up, piled some more chippings on the fire, carried the rack from the snack-bar and placed it high up on its supports and shut the door. The wooden pole slid happily through the door handles with a tight fit, the whole cabinet sealed and safe, apart from the small air-vent. I blew a kiss at it, shut the gates behind me but didn't lock them. I reasoned that there was nothing to steal any more, and I needed to check on the fire later in the dark; it would be easier without the padlock.

Happy and satisfied with the day's work and over feeling sorry for my lonely self, went to *The Ship* that night. There was no music, but the pub was full of regulars, some of whom I was on nodding terms with, but the isolation I'd felt in the showroom returned when Mark arrived with his mates, mouthed 'Hi' and disappeared into the other bar. I sat on a stool with a drink, but without the music there seemed little point in being there, unless in someone else's eyes, I was there for a pick-up. I mused on the fact that, had I been a bloke, the thought probably wouldn't even have entered the equation.

I finished the drink and wove my way through the crowd to the front door. Something about the couple who sat under the window stopped me; a woman with short, black hair and a man with a face like a boxer, or a bouncer, both well-used, fortyish, I guessed; him with a bashed nose and pock-marked skin and her, with hair black enough to fit Denise's description of my prospective client.

As she turned sideways in her seat to look at me, I caught a glimpse of long, black, high-heeled boots and a short skirt. A white, quilted coat hung over the back of the bench. They both looked straight at me; I smiled, briefly, thinking if I was right, they would know who I was; most people who frequented the local boatyards seemed to know me these days, I thought ruefully, and left. Besides which, if she'd been the woman in the marina, she'd have recognised me anyway.

Fine rain born in on the sea-breeze dampened my face and hair. I pulled my hood up, left the comforting reflection of the street-lights on the wet cobbles, walked past Madoc Yacht Club and into the lane. It was dark and deserted and the cliff-face loomed wet and black to my right; a hundred feet of jagged slate covered with thick ivy, all the way up to the Garth and the road and houses built along the top.

The huge boulder, reckoned to weigh about sixty tons, that had fallen only recently, lay at the foot of the cliff in a private boatyard, where it had trashed an old boat and trailer, and now lay like a dead thing, the debris poking out from underneath and just visible through the security fence. The thought of a disaster like that happening to the Boat Shed began to freak me out.

I walked faster, imagining dangers the other side of the boatyard walls and menacing figures lurking in the shadows. I stopped, turned around a couple of times and listened for imaginary footsteps. My jacket collar rustled against my hair when I turned my head, and the rain, heavy now, pattered on the hood, confusing the sounds; I desperately wanted to be tucked up warm and safe in the apartment. The tell-tale tap of rigging against masts in the yachts over the wall, heralded yet another system of stormy weather. I'd walked down that lane many times in the dark, and always marvelled at the difference between here and city life at night, with its lonely alleyways and parks; places no-one in their right mind would go on their own, but this was the first time here that I'd felt uncomfortable, frankly scared, and for no good reason.

I needed to check the salmon in the smoke-house and stoke up the wood-chippings before bed, but the temptation to bolt into Madoc Marine overwhelmed me. I unlocked the gate and locked it behind me, leaned against it, wiped the rain from my face and struggled to summon up the courage to walk down through the ranks of sleeping powerboats to the Boat Shed, but I wasn't going to let my nerves ruin the first batch of salmon.

The security spotlights flashed on in the first half of the yard, then clicked off to darkness as I reached the bottom gates and fumbled in my pocket for my phone, switched on the light, unlocked them, and crossed the car-parking area to the Boat Shed gates. The one gate swung open easily and I pushed it shut behind me. The motion sensor on the security light illuminated the track and tyre-marks from the vehicles and I picked my way carefully the few feet from the gate to the smoke-house to avoid the worst of the puddles.

A wisp of fishy smoke from the air vent rose straight up, before being blown into tatters as the wind gusted through the yard; one of those small but meaningful gusts, I recognised now as the precursor to a gale. The wooden bar, the dinghy tiller, slid so easily out from its snug fit through the door-handles, that I wondered if it needed a new catch at all.

I propped one door back with a piece of slate jammed into the gravel, pulled the front of my jacket collar over my mouth against the smoke and stepped inside. The torch lit up the glowing wood-chips ready for replenishing, and I shone the beam on the rack above, touched the barely-warm salmon with a fingertip and wished it well. Perfect. So far.

The wood-chips, stored in the caravan next door, were in heavy bags and I mixed up some oak and apple in a bucket and carried it back into the smoke-house. The wind caught the caravan door I'd left open and banged it shut, and the security light came on briefly and flicked off. It was going to be a rough night and I looked around nervously, expecting to see something, a spooky feeling of a presence, as I'd felt when Jackson had crept up by my side. I wished he was here now.

With the gust of wind, the anxiety, and the rush I was in, the meagre beam from the torch in one hand and the bucket and trowel in the other, I don't honestly remember the exact sequence of events. I tripped on the step, fell on my knees onto the floor of the smoke-house and landed in the scatter of wood-chips that tipped out of the bucket. Some landed in the fire and started to smoulder. The trowel clanged against the metal trough in front of me and the phone flew out of my hand. The light died.

Then the door behind me banged shut.

Through dark and smoke, I scrabbled for the phone, burned my hand on the hot metal and kicked the door with booted feet. Was this the one time the catch decided to function? Maybe it had been released by the move on the fork-lift and this time, it had locked solid. There was no handle on the inside; why would there be? The whole thing was ancient, anyway. I kicked at the doors and coughed, turned round to try a different angle with my back against the hot trough, smelled the jacket fabric as it began to smoulder and the heat seeped through to my skin.

I needed my phone. The floor was covered in wood-chips and it would have landed somewhere soft. With a flicker of optimism, I started at one end on hands and knees and raked through every square inch as best I could in the dark, feeling the first flutters of panic.

Then through the wood-smoke, rose the noxious smell of burning plastic; it had to be the phone. The fumes caught the back of my throat and made my eyes stream and my stomach heave. I couldn't get away from it, shouted and banged the metal walls with the trowel and kicked with my feet. The only air-vent was high up on the wall, but the smoke was drawn towards it. I tried to find a chink in the floor where I thought the metal was thin, bashed the trowel into it until my palm was blistered and raw. Then I sat, slumped against the door, and waited for inspiration.

Nauseous and sweating with the heat, I kicked until my legs ached and shouted until my throat was raw. I coughed a bit, but most of the smoke curled lazily upwards and the wind dragged it through the chimney. I closed my eyes with the thought that, ironically, I wouldn't die of cold or starvation. The wind moaned outside and rattled the doors, as if mocking me. Somebody would come. I was warm, and then sleepy. It wasn't so bad, after all.

Cold mud under my head and sharp stones in my back, torch-light and voices. I coughed, someone pushed me onto my side, hands underneath my shoulders and sat me up coughing uncontrollably, gates crashed open, then headlights and uniforms and radios.

"I couldn't get out," I heard myself say, over and over through the spasms. "I kicked and kicked. The catch was old. It should have broken. I don't get it. I don't understand," propped up in the mud in the rain, soaked through and crying and coughing, until I thought my ribs would break. "How did you find me?"

I didn't know the guy from the patrol car. He crouched down, his face close to mine, his expression serious.

"The yard was on our list for later, just for a check, being Saturday night," he said. "We usually drive down anyway, but I believe you'd reported something odd last week."

He said, just coincidentally, there was an anonymous call and they were asked to divert and investigate straight away. Something suspicious in the yard, the caller said. That was all. The gate wasn't padlocked.

"Being a nosy pair of coppers, we saw the smoke," he said, chatty with relief, and to comfort me, I thought, "and being fond of smoked salmon, we thought we'd better check. My wife used to buy it off your great-uncle and she heard you were starting the smoke-house up again."

I stared at him through mud-streaked eyes. There was more.

"Miss Jones… Cassie," serious now, and he picked up an object from the mud by his side; the dinghy tiller I used for securing the door through the door. "This is not good. Someone put this through the handles. You're lucky to be alive. They say thirty minutes for carbon monoxide poisoning. The fact that we were contacted might mean someone just wanted to give you a fright. Maybe a joke? It was a close call, love."

"Some fucking joke," I said, in-between the coughs, anger dispelling the shock. "That'd be bad enough. It could have killed me."

He squeezed my shoulder, mentioned statements and prints from the tiller. They'd be in touch when I'd recovered.

I'd never considered an A& E department would be anything but tedious and unpleasant, but they were efficient, kind and concerned, stuffed me full of oxygen, drained oceans of blood from my arm, and allowed me to make a phone call. I was certainly not going to call my mother or anyone else who might make a fuss, but I was very clear in my call to Denise; no gossip.

"The salmon's ruined with the fumes from the phone when it burned up. The fish will have to be binned. The fire-brigade had to come and put the fire out. It'll be all round Port by now, but not the details."

I coughed and coughed but she waited patiently. My tongue ran away with me.

"They'll probably say the fire was out of control or some such rubbish. I'm too scared to even think about what happened. It's too horrible. I mean, why? Who? Look, just leave the Boat Shed yard locked and fend off any questions. I need a new phone but it'll have to wait."

"When they throw you out, I'll come and get you. No arguments. Shall I tell Arnie?"

"No. Yes. I don't know. You decide."

"Somebody's got it in for you, Cass. You need all the help you can get. He needs to know. Just in case…"

"What?"

"In case it's something to do with him."

"Don't be ridiculous," I said. "No reason. He's a good guy and nobody knew I was there, or even planning to be there. Especially not Arnie, miles away in Dudley. Sorry." I cut her off and coughed until I was exhausted.

CHAPTER 8

Despite all the investigations there were no answers. It seemed a continuation of the underlying fear that had never really gone away; a dark, unnatural creature that lurked in the perimeters of my mind, scorned all those things one was supposed to do at the age of twenty-two, like parties and fun, shopping with friends, films and clubs and gossip over coffee.

The smoke-house stood empty and the only evidence of the event was a pool of black water where the fire crew had hosed the chippings out onto the mud.

"We've put fires out here before, I seem to remember," the fire-officer said, when he called by a few days later. "You know you can buy smoked salmon in Tesco? It's so much easier."

I was too tired and dispirited to laugh, managed a wan smile, and wandered around while the digger began to scrape away at the loose debris between the Boat Shed and the retaining wall.

"I can't say how long we'll be able to work," Steve Lewis said. "We can't operate in heavy rain, but we'll make a start."

I'd told him about the incident in the smoke-house. I had to; he'd found the crowbars, after all.

"Are you going to be able to start with the smoking again?" asked Steve Lewis. "I can't imagine how you could even go into that cupboard again. You must have been terrified."

He was appalled, especially after his concern about the tools he'd found. I shook my head. I couldn't face the thought of going through all that fish preparation again and didn't know if he was right and whether I'd find the courage to go back into that dark, smoky cabinet. One of the projects I'd so looked forward to, had crashed around me.

"Why don't you go away for a bit, while we get on with the digging? Get over that cough," he said.

"I can't. Not until Christmas. I'm paid to look after next door. It's no good running away. I'll just have to be more careful until I can figure out why someone wants me out of here that badly."

He leaned on his shovel and looked hard at me. "Why don't you just sell the place? With the work done up on the rock, it'll be worth a fair bit. This is no life for a young lass."

If those words had been spoken by David Hughes, I would have bristled, despite the hours at sea and the amicable relationship we'd established. From Steve Lewis, a tough, rugged, capable man, I guessed that the care and concern on his face, even in his voice, came from life experience; difficult people and shady dealings. I knew nothing of his background, but he emanated an aura of confidence and reliability; a man one wouldn't mess with. I didn't mind his suggestion one bit, but a feeling of strength returned; strength from the care from others. I knew about that and had forgotten. But there it was, just a flicker, but it was there.

"I'll think about it," I said. "But I'm not giving up that easily. But thanks, really. I appreciate your concern. Besides which, I promised you some of the first batch of salmon."

I hadn't seen or heard from Hugh for a couple of weeks. *Capella* lay comfortably in her new cradle and the weather had been too wet for work on the hull. Even the operation on the cliff-face had come to a halt and the digger had been reassigned to another job. The ground behind the wall was saturated, a swamp impossible to work on. I tried not to think about the weight of water held in the mud. The rock-face above glistened where little streams found their way through the crevasses, washed the slate black and trickled down, slowly, inexorably, to the sump at the bottom.

I tried not to imagine the first signs of disaster, as water seeped between the stones in the retaining wall and started to wash away the ancient mortar, the tell-tale bulge as the pressure increased and it finally giving way to collapse against the back wall of the Boat Shed. The old, galvanised sheeting would give way, the roof timbers would be unsupported and then…

Hugh texted me from the engine-sheds to say he'd been busy at weekends and was involved with the construction of a new carriage, a replica of the original Ashbury Brake, and attention to detail was paramount. That suited him, I thought, with his funny OCD ways and I texted him back to ask if we could meet for coffee. I needed to tell him about the rock-fall and the smoke-house, and somehow thought his way of thinking might help to unravel the problem. I'd chosen to regard the incident as a problem rather than a threat to my life in order to stop the danger of it spiralling into paralysing fear. What else was there to do, except carry on? The police had checked the tools and the dinghy tiller for finger-prints, to no avail, and there had been no further incidents.

The smoke-house had produced its first batch of salmon and I honed my skills for slicing it into delicate portions with the help of the local fishmonger, who offered to sell it for me until the yard was open again. I cut my finger twice, sported blue plasters with pride, vacuum-packed and froze the remainder after giving a generous portion to Steve, as promised. It was simply excellent, but perhaps a trifle more apple in the wood-chips next time; I wanted it to be perfect for the Christmas batch to take to London. Denise tutted at my new occupation and said there was work to be done in the yard and she couldn't believe the smell of fish that transferred itself from my hands onto the office furniture.

The first boxes of eco-friendly cleaning materials arrived and were displayed in the newly re-organised shop. The model ships had been reunited with their crews of busy sailors retrieved from the labelled envelopes. I typed and laminated a short history of each ship, put shelves up and bought a divider to separate the room into old and new.

"Arnie's not going to like it," Denise said, when I mentioned the plan for second-hand outdoor clothing; wet suits, life-jackets and expensive foul-weather gear. "Where's the profit in that?"

"Children have a habit of growing," I said. "More family-friendly ideas bring in more customers."

"You mean catering for the families at the lower-end of the budget? Isn't that part of your plan for the Boat Shed yard? Low budget being-on-the-water plan? Kayaks and rowing dinghies?"

"It might be."

She shook her head. "He won't like it," she said. "Bit of a cheek if you ask me, using this showroom to promote your stuff."

"No, it's not. It's part of the joint venture. People start small, get their kids hooked on the sea and the next thing they're buying Sea Rays or jet-skis. Makes sense to me."

"I wonder if you've got any sense at all, sometimes, what with smoking fish and nearly getting yourself fried."

"That wasn't my fault." This felt like the beginning of an uncomfortable discussion. We never argued. Change the subject, Cass. Denise had been worried sick about me.

"I won't do anything grand without discussing it with you first, I promise. Well, not too grand."

She made a face, and flounced out with a wave of her hand in dismissal. It was okay between us, I thought, and left to meet Hugh for the coffee I'd suggested.

Cappuccino for me and camomile tea for him. He'd taken his beanie off and his bald pate shone in the lights. The steam fogged his glasses and he took them off to wipe them clean, but didn't take his eyes off my face while I told him of the recent events; most unlike him, I remembered, and realised, for whatever reason, he was able to talk to me face-to-face without the nervous habits I was so used to.

"Is everything alright with you?" I asked, a little curious about the change in his demeanour.

"Very well, Miss Cassie, very well indeed. I'm sorry to hear about your troubles."

After his openness and words of wisdom to me, only a couple of months ago, I felt I could be as open with him as he was with me, despite the minor breakdown he'd suffered after the storm damage to his yacht. On reflection, we'd both seen each other's weaknesses. But Hugh had a way of picking out the essentials in a complex problem; that's why he was good at his job, so I was told, and that was why I wanted his advice; objective advice.

"What exactly do you wish me to focus on?" he asked. "It seems that the sale of *Tai Pilots* has been successful and allowed you, financially at least, to continue with submitting your plans for the Boat Shed. Also, your new position with David Hughes' training has given you some status in your new position as manager. That was a wise move and extremely thoughtful of him."

I'd gabbled away in a torrent of words, mixing up all the financial and house information with the potential rock-fall and the threat it posed. I found it difficult to explain about the smoke-house; the words caught in my throat and I had to stop. He sat quietly and didn't break the silence while I gained some composure, surprised how the re-telling had upset me.

"That is indeed truly dreadful. I hope you are recovered physically? Now what, exactly, would you like me to consider?" he asked, again.

I sat back in my chair and thought I ought to be able to think this through by myself, but I couldn't; it was too personal, too painful.

"Someone has a plan I know nothing about," I said. "When I first started to renovate the Boat Shed, any unpleasantness was connected to the drugs and Doug Peterson, but it never became a physical threat, just threatening words about my nosiness. This is different, Hugh. I want to brave it out and carry on, but deep down, I'm watching everyone I know for duplicity, hypocrisy, hidden agendas…. it must be serious if my life was threatened, and I don't believe it was a joke; more someone's after-thought of a plan to scare me, then a sudden panic over the consequences. Hence the heads-up to the police. Or I'd be dead."

He steepled his hands and stared into the empty mug. I waited.

"Think of a chain," he said. "Connecting links to everyone you know who has associations with the yard."

"Which yard?"

"Both, I think. Who would gain by your removal?"

"That's a polite way of putting it. Nobody. I haven't made a will, if that's what you mean. I suppose it would be sold. Should I? Make a will? I'm only twenty-two. David never mentioned it."

"Perhaps you never asked. Perhaps you were not very approachable."

I stared at him in astonishment. He would never have spoken to me like that before.

"Miss Cassie, let us suppose the Boat Shed yard becomes untenable due to land-slippage, rock-falls, whatever, and too expensive to repair, or even unrepairable in the long run. Let us suppose that your appeal to the planning permission for residence or rebuild, is turned down. You would be left with the yard, just a piece of land, and the value would be affected, would it not?"

"I've thought of that, obviously, except for the slipway, don't forget."

"So, if it were for sale at a vastly reduced cost, who would benefit from the purchase of the land with no need of the building?"

"I've thought of that as well. Not Arnie, never Arnie. He couldn't be the person he is and have such an underhand plan. He might want the yard because of the slipway but he'd never go to those lengths. Not to threaten me, or actually kill me for it."

I shook my head vehemently, felt sick at the thought. No, it was not to be considered.

"Shall I replenish the drinks?"

I nodded, chewed the inside of my cheek, stared out of the window at people on the pavement with their pushchairs and shopping bags; just normal folk going about their lives.

"Mr Blackwell has a wife, if I remember correctly?" Hugh asked. "Quite a sharp lady," he said as he placed coffee and a slice of carrot cake in front of me.

I nodded and smiled my thanks. More surprises.

"That's one way of describing her," I said. "Shelly. I only met her once; not the most loving of mothers. Denise calls her the arch-bitch on account of the way she spoke to Jason, her own son, in front of his brothers. You knew Jason, of course you did, I forgot you were using the yard well before I moved here. He used to knock around with little Tomas, he told me, despite their age differences."

Hugh nodded. "So sad. Such a terrible death for a child."

"I got the impression," I said, "Shelly didn't much care for either of her younger sons; Ben was only a baby but she complained he was too heavy to hold and couldn't wait to hand him over to his dad. She was horrible to Jason; he was even dressed in his brothers' hand-me-downs. He was a spotty, sensitive, teenager and didn't deserve being ridiculed in front of other people, especially strangers. But then I was only seventeen and didn't know much about children and maternal instincts; still don't.

'Anyway, she and Arnie split up after the twins were sent to prison; he said he'd thrown her out after she refused to acknowledge they'd committed serious crimes. Arnie never divorced her. Now, he tells me, she's moved back in, for Ben's sake, and they're getting on well. I find it hard to believe, after all that happened. I don't get it."

"I think if they'd been going through a divorce," Hugh said, he wouldn't have been able to buy Madoc Marine at the same time. Not in either of their interests. Property is usually the most acrimonious of issues, alongside custody of children. Which brings me to an uncomfortable thought."

I looked at Hugh with new eyes. Who was this person who had previously been only interested in the perfect renovation of an old yacht and obsessed with steam-engines?

"How come you know about this stuff, Hugh?"

I swear he blushed. He said he'd met someone. They talked a lot.

"I can't imagine any common ground between a wind-turbine engineer and a marriage-guidance counsellor," I said, and laughed, pleased for him. "Oh." The penny dropped. "The railway?"

He nodded.

"Well, that's great," I said. "How lovely. I knew something had changed. You're happy, aren't you?"

He smiled, squeezed the teabag with the back of his tea-spoon, placed it carefully on the saucer, looked up and met my eyes.

"How long were Arnie's twins sent down for?"

"Seven years."

"So, they'll already have served time on remand and then there's always the possibility of early release, bearing in mind the over-crowding in our prisons."

A cold wave of fear spread from my stomach and made my scalp prickle; a fear tucked away in a closed box; seven years was so far off I hadn't needed to think about it.

"I heard they were quite violent towards their brother," he said.

"They beat him up. He told his dad they'd been dealing drugs, selling the firm's car parts on the quiet. Arnie went berserk. Shelly sided with the twins. He said they couldn't live together after that until she'd come to her senses. It was ages ago. I don't remember the details. Arnie said she'd been more amicable since they were sent to prison and said she accepted they were a bad lot and deserved what they got. That's what she said, if you can believe it. Now Arnie says she's changed. True, or is he just gullible?"

He sipped his tea and his glasses misted up again. He took them off and wiped them.

"And am I right in saying the twins were aware you'd informed the police of the drugs landing?"

"Only helped to confirm it. I think the NCI and police already knew."

I sat like a stone and waited. I thought I knew what he was going to say but couldn't see the connection.

"I don't think this has gone away, Miss Cassie. These are purely my thoughts, you understand, but here's the possible scenario. If, and only if, Mr Blackwell's wife, Shelly, having now engineered herself back into their happy home with renewed marital status, found reasonable grounds to instigate divorce proceedings, all the properties owned by him or jointly, would be considered in the settlement."

"Yes, obviously, but why would she do that now? And what would constitute reasonable grounds? It would have to be something big if she was going to screw most of his business out of him and win big style."

"I think she'd do it now, because if the twins were released early, it brings the time-scale forward. Also, bear in mind, many of these difficult divorce cases take time, especially when properties are involved; years sometimes. She could be looking ahead to set up some security for the three of them; you said she appeared disinterested in the younger boys. If she decided to make a bid for Madoc Marine, a lucrative business proposition, it might be considered in her favour."

"What? And take it away from Arnie? Is that possible? It's his dream for the future. She couldn't do that, Hugh, could she?"

He stirred the tea, round and round and the teaspoon clinked against the mug; more like his old behaviour, I thought irrelevantly, but he was deep in thought, and forgiven.

"Not only that, it would not be in her best interests to have the Boat Shed still owned by yourself; you were a significant link in her sons' arrest. Oh no," he shook his head, "she would most definitely not want you there. If you could be persuaded to sell it, by fair means or foul, any buyer, or divorcee in this case, would gain access to the slipway. I remember Doug Peterson applied to Cadw to build one for Madoc Marine and was turned down. That won't change."

"But this is all pie-in-the-sky, Hugh. They're not divorced. There's no indication of it that I can see. You said yourself he wouldn't instigate divorce proceedings whilst he was in the process of buying Madoc Marine. But I suppose that's all completed now and they're back together. The only…"

I stopped. I couldn't share the conversation Angela had with Ben about being left on his own until the small hours. Besides which, I hadn't mentioned it to Arnie and was still hoping that the incident would not be repeated. If he did find out, lost his temper, and confronted her, would it result in violence? A likely possibility, but then, the boot would be on the wrong foot. Custody of Ben would be a separate issue.

"What could Arnie possibly do so wrong to justify her setting the ball rolling after all these months?"

He shrugged. "Maybe she's waited and plotted; still doing it. She must have known he was planning to buy Madoc Marine as soon as it came on the market. To set divorce proceedings in motion, she would need time to acquire and collect proof or time to fabricate evidence. Perhaps an affair? Adultery?"

"No, I can't see that. They're getting on okay, so he says. And are you suggesting the business with the tools and the smoke-house are connected to Shelly? To scare me off? Or worse? I don't believe it. It doesn't make sense."

"Oh, I think it does," he said. "It's a strong possibility. I can talk it over with my partner, hypothetically of course, if you would permit me? He's seen his fair share of acrimonious divorces where property is a major issue, he tells me. As for an affair, there is a saying, 'Hell hath no fury like a woman scorned.'"

"Shelly cheated on? Scorned, by Arnie? Would she care that much? For another woman? Who?"

"That's the whole point," he said. "Depends who it is," and looked at me meaningfully.

A man rapped on the window; a kind face and cheerful smile, with a red and yellow striped scarf round his neck. He pointed to his watch.

"Do excuse me. I must go."

He held out his hand, the grip strong and firm. Not the Hugh I remembered at all.

"I hope it's been useful, if not pleasant to consider. They're just my thoughts, of course. I'll ring you when I've talked it over with Alistair. He's not a lawyer but he's very knowledgeable. Take great care, Miss Cassie. Leave no cause for conjecture."

I sat, stunned, stared at the crumbs of the carrot cake and the rim of froth inside the mug, and wanted to laugh hysterically at the preposterous idea of a fling with Arnie, twenty years my senior, a beefy scrap-merchant from Dudley, millionaire or not.

I lifted my head as the couple met up and walked past the window; Hugh not much taller than me, a little man with myopic eyes and his bald head now covered with the beanie, and his friend, a tall, thin beanpole of a man; small and tall, an unlikely pair, but I could see their affection for each other, their closeness, even through the glass. They waved and disappeared.

Cause for conjecture? Ridiculous. I walked back through town, considering how many times Arnie and I had ever been together; a few, always in the yard with others present or at the meeting with Denise. This was nonsense. The nonsense grew to disbelief, grew through anxiety to anger, to the beginnings of outrage. I felt as though I'd been projected into the set of a shabby soap-opera and the sordid minutiae of other people's shitty behaviour. The railings around the harbour wall outside Madoc Yacht Club dripped with yet more rain, but I leaned on the top one and looked down at the few yachts left after the lift-outs, tucked up safely in the corner out of the tide and the winter river.

I swept away the curtain of misery for a few precious moments, conjured up another picture of a summer's day and a white hull cutting through blue water, the thrill of the speed, the wheel responsive and the taut sails bellied out bright and white in the sun over the wide, wide sea; no people, no conversation, no lies, no subterfuge; out there, what you see is what you get and all the happiness that bubbles up, is channelled into the simple task of pitting one's wits against the wind and the water. I pushed back from the rail, a decisive action and stood for a moment, rock-solid in the rain. I would tell no-one, absolutely no-one. I would sell the Boat Shed and walk away.

I kept the decision tucked into my coat, where it kept me warm all the way back to Madoc Marine. Denise sat with her feet up on the desk, a chocolate bar in one hand and the screen-saver denoting no work.

"Got five minutes?" she asked.

"I might have. Not exactly snowed under with customers, are we?"

She scrunched up the wrapper and dropped it in the bin, took her feet off the desk and tapped the keyboard. Google Earth came up.

"You know I said to remind me to talk to you about your solicitor?"

"David Hughes? He's not my solicitor anymore," I said. "The inheritance stuff is all finished with now. Anyway, it was his father I dealt with."

"He's just your sailing friend, then?"

"That was a one-off training thing," I said, annoyed. "So what?"

"So, what do you know about him?"

"As far as I know, his mother does his ironing and makes apple pies to impress his crew on the boat. Which he owns. Oh, and he's got a sister called Heidi and she's a geologist. I met her once; she crews for him sometimes. And he's got a degree in English, so we swap poetry and Shakespeare quotes. And he likes everything his own way. And he has flings with girls who own expensive cars. You told me that."

"Quite a lot then," she said. "But do you know where he lives?"

I shrugged, assumed he still lived at home and never thought to ask where; it was none of my business. Truthfully, I'd never been interested. She swivelled the screen round.

"Good God," I said.

A large, country house, accessed by a long drive, filled the screen. Somewhere obscure in the middle of the Lleyn Peninsula, it was surrounded by farmland, the area served by a network of narrow lanes that linked the north and the south coast. It was flanked by numerous outbuildings built in stone and slate, and from what we could make out, it looked as though it had been there a very long time. The estate around it was extensive; fields dotted with sheep, large areas of woodland and a small river meandering its way through to a lake in the grounds; not exactly *Pemberley*, but very impressive.

"Wonder if it's listed," Denise said. "Look at those chimneys." She zoomed in further. I was uncomfortable, spying on David's family home. If I hadn't known him, it wouldn't have mattered, but I did, and it felt intrusive.

"I know solicitors earn good money," she said, "but that is a serious family pile. Bet it's worth a couple of million."

I sat back in my own chair, surprised and bemused and against my better judgement, curious as well. I wondered how a small firm of solicitors had created so much wealth. Then I tried to equate it with the people who lived there; old Mr Gerald Hughes and his wife, his son David, and David's sister Heidi; ordinary folk. They would have grown up there, but I'd never had any indication that he spent his childhood in such exclusive surroundings.

"What made you look it up?" I asked.

"Dunno, really. I was bored and a couple of days ago my brother said he'd seen that flashy car around, you know, the one he was picked up in by the girl-friend outside his office? I checked out the address, just curious to see if he was rich, with his socialising in company with flashy cars and the yacht club and that."

"He's only got an Audi and it's not new and the girl-friend, well, that was months ago. Anyway, from the way he spoke, she wasn't an item anymore."

"You asked him?"

"Not really. Just said I hoped his girlfriend was alright after the lockdown. He just dismissed it, quite abruptly, if I remember. Maybe a one-night stand. Not my business."

"So, what do you think? Living in a place like that?"

"Lucky man." I didn't want to discuss it, or him, at that moment.

She switched off the computer. It was home-time and I wanted to be on my own, to consider the decision I'd made and what to do with my life next; poor little rich girl with money and no home; no job either. Maybe I'd change my mind. David Hughes and his family residence, at that moment, were irrelevant.

"Know what?" she said, as she zipped up the expensive sailing jacket she'd purloined from stock. Good thing Arnie hadn't seen it. "What I said to you before, about him?"

"What?"

"I said you're an idiot if you don't do something about it. He obviously cares about you and he's a nice guy. Now we know he's minted. Bet you he lives in a converted barn on the estate and he'll inherit the whole damn lot when his folks die. Not to mention the business."

I picked up the rubbish-bin full of sweet papers and threw the contents at her.

"Now you'll have to clear it all up. See you Monday," and she laughed and disappeared through the door.

CHAPTER 9

November. The Christmas break in London seemed a long way off. My birthday came and went, a vague affair I was not the slightest bit interested in, at the grand age of twenty-three with no social life in which to celebrate, although Denise bought cake and my mother sent me money. I had money of my own in the bank since the sale of *Tai Pilots* and could afford new streaks in my hair now, and a manicure, but hadn't bothered for ages.

My mood was as grey as the weather, which was relentlessly dull and wet. Drizzle, interspersed with heavy rain, lasted for two to three days at a time, and continued to flood the Traeth as far as the eye could see, from the Cob to the foothills. Mr Gilbert said he and the other farmers worried if the salt marsh would ever recover in time for the spring grazing. It was a bit extreme, he said, even for Wales.

I'd called in to the farm one weekend to say hello and had hoped to see Emily. She'd stopped visiting me on Saturdays, having recovered from her salutary experiences at *Tai Pilots* and understandably preferred the company of her friends to me. I crossed tentative fingers and hoped she made the right choices, but her mum and dad seemed relaxed and easy about her whereabouts. Rosie, a growing, pretty ball of apricot fluff, leapt out of her basket by the kitchen Rayburn and hurled herself at my legs. I picked her up, made a fuss as she licked my ears, thinking that I'd never be able to say hello to my new Rottveiler friend in that way, and put her down gently. Jackson would eat her for breakfast, if they ever chanced to meet. I remembered Mr Gilbert's warnings to his daughter about owning an expensive puppy as a pet and the responsibility it carried.

"Well, you know how it is," said her mother. "All teenagers want is money and food, in that order. Parents and pets take a back seat."

"Rosie will be used for breeding," said her dad. "She won't be wasted. We're not daft. Emily will go off to college and leave home, eventually. We knew that, but young girls wanting pets need to learn about responsibility. After all that worry that she'd caused us and then after we said 'yes' to Rosie, she wasn't allowed out on Saturdays for a month and had to work on the farm as well. She was pretty good, too. Earned her colours, as they say."

Mrs Gilbert put tea and biscuits on the table, then touched my forearm with a warm hand. "If it hadn't been for you, cariad, God knows what would have happened to her."

Her father cleared his throat, his way of thanking me; a natural reticence from a farmer more used to animals than people, I thought.

"Have you seen Will Roberts since the funeral?" I asked. "He looks terribly tired. I was worried when he called in last. His farm's a lonely place to be, up there in the hills. I know he'd got used to being on his own when his wife was in the home, but at least he could visit her when they eased the rules. I think it was a major part of his day, just being with her. Mark helped him out at work; he looks tired as well."

It was warm and comfortable in their kitchen; like Helen's Nain's, I thought sadly, except that in this one, the smell of baking mingled with the earthy smell of wet dog and damp coats.

"Now then," Mrs Gilbert said, breaking the moment, "what are you doing with yourself this Christmas, apart from dwelling on sick and dying folk, and running a business? You're far too young for much of that," and she looked up at her husband, as he struggled with his wax jacket. It was streaked with mud and a thread of orange baler-twine hung out of one pocket. "Isn't she, love?"

He nodded. "You're welcome here, you know," he said. "Can't spend Christmas on your own in that place. It's a dead hole in the winter, down there in those yards."

"We've never asked," Emily's mum said, "but have you got family to go to, cariad?"

The days ticked by and I packed a case ready for London, raided Helen's wardrobe, then wasted some time on the Internet, in the name of retail therapy. Work had ceased completely on the rock-face and Steve Lewis inspected the gloopy mud at the base of the cliff and said it was in the lap of the gods; he couldn't control the weather. It rained and rained, and on the news, they showed pictures of flood waters where rivers had burst their banks, washed away bridges and caused landslips on roads and railways up and down the country.

I opened the door to the showroom, ready for lunch and Denise shot out of her chair and ran to the office door.

"You'll never guess what?"

"What?" unimpressed by her enthusiasm.

"That woman. She's coming back on Saturday to make an offer on the Sea Ray."

I stared at her.

"But she wants to negotiate with Arnie, not you. She asked if you were the boss or the manager, so I told her. I reckon she knew. You're not offended?"

"God, no. That's brilliant," I said, brightening up. "Arnie and I had already agreed that he'd deal with any big sales. I'll call him."

Even down the phone, I could hear the throb of heavy machinery in the Dudley scrap-yard, the clanging, banging and grinding of steel, as used and unwanted possessions were cut up and crushed. I heard him shut the site-office door so he could hear me.

"That's great, bab. I can come up Friday night and stay just for the Saturday morning, then I'll need to get back for Ben. He goes swimming with his friend and parents on a Saturday morning. They'll' hang on to him for the afternoon. I've done it for them a few times. Nothing like two rowdy five-year olds on a Saturday afternoon. Film and a Big Mac is the answer. Don't suppose I could beg a bed for the night? It'll save me going to the van. Take the covers off the Sea Ray and give it a wipe down. Okay?"

As if I needed to be told.

Filtered through the excitement of a potentially big sale, I wondered how I would feel sharing my space with a man old enough to be my father and whom I hardly knew; I mean, really knew, like whether he peed accurately into the toilet bowl, or dribbled on the floor and then left the toilet seat up, or had unpleasant table manners and slurped his soup, or ate like a pig in a trough. I'd only ever seen him eat a burger outside the snack-bar, and that didn't count.

Entertaining a stranger at my own table and sharing my home was different. I began to wish I'd never offered him a room. With Daniel, the niceness of manners had never crossed my mind. Nor with David, on his boat. But then, I reassured myself, I'd seen how Ben behaved and how his dad corrected him. It was only one night after all and Arnie could get to know the apartment while I was there, reminding myself he was going to stay there while I was away for the Christmas break. Good plan.

The only man I'd ever shared a house with had been my dad, and it was such a big house that I had no sense of being uncomfortably confined in a small space with him 'cluttering the place up' as Millie was fond of saying. When he came home from his overseas trips, he left coats slung on the backs of chairs in the lounge, dumped bags on the hall floor and spread books and papers on the coffee tables, even the dining table. His laptop migrated to all flat surfaces in turn, with working notes spread around it, even though he had an office in one of the small bedrooms off the third landing. My parents had their own bathroom, so pee habits were never an issue and Millie cleaned the downstairs cloakroom toilet with a fervency prompted by the dinner invitations to numerous visitors from the academic world.

The other thought that crept erroneously into my head was one of curiosity about Arnie's static caravan. I'd walked through the site, which was neat and well-kept, but an overall impression of the statics, even the large ones, didn't equate with Arnie's supposed wealth. Why not a proper house, a second home with grounds? Or at least a posh chalet? I'd ask him.

"Post for you," Denise shouted up the stairs. "Packages. I've signed for them."

The dress I'd ordered was short enough to be 'almost indecent' Denise said, as I paraded my purchases up and down on the showroom floor. Low neck and long sleeves, in the glitziest silver, the material clung to me 'like the skin of one of those salmon' and she appraised my clubbing finery with a mixture of approval and disbelief at the transformation. The boots, also in silver, had high heels and a stretchy softness that moulded itself over my knees and half-way up my thighs.

"Wow," she said, her voice raised to reach me at the far end of the showroom, and picked up her phone. "Facebook…This is how a boatyard manager should look," and posted it.

One hand on hip, I sashayed passed her by the office door and along to the showroom entrance. Will Roberts emerged from the shadows, and the door whispered shut behind him. Rain glistened on his coat and dripped on the tiled floor; his jaw would have dropped if he'd been a lesser man. I stopped in front of him; there was nowhere else to go.

"Clubbing. For Christmas," I said, not sure whether to be embarrassed or to laugh it off.

He studied me from top to toe, his head on one side, as though analysing the suitability of apparel for sea-going adventures.

"I hope you've thermal underwear? Very nice, Miss Jones. I presume, as it's all over Facebook now, you'll be hoping your client numbers increase dramatically," he said with a glimmer of a smile as Denise shepherded him into the office and put the kettle on.

"I just called to inquire after your health since that unfortunate incident in the smoke-house. Got yourself locked in, did you?"

"Yes, but I'm fine, thanks. I was just a bit careless." Change the subject, Cassie. "Could you possibly keep an eye on the place while I'm away?" I asked. "I mean, if you're around at all. I know it's cheeky, but Mr Blackwell will be staying for the week after Christmas, so it's only for a few days."

"What about you, Mr Roberts?" Denise asked. She was never afraid to ask difficult questions and I knew she couldn't bear to think of him on his own any more than I could, but she had more nerve.

"I've been invited to the Gilberts for Christmas lunch," he said, his head up and some punch in his voice. "Very good of them. Bill and I are going to discuss fruit trees."

"Fruit trees?"

"For an orchard on his land. Commercial, you know. Bit of diversification. Apples and pears and so on."

I knew they'd get on. So pleased, so relieved.

"Do they come with partridges? You know, in the pear trees," Denise said, as he looked blankly at her. "It is Christmas, after all."

He finished his coffee and stood up, a burly, solid presence in the small office space. It was hard to think of him as distressed or vulnerable, but a closer look at the craggy face revealed a dullness in his eyes, a sagging of the jawline, as though he'd been punched and had all the stuffing knocked out of him.

"Have you considered how to feed the goldfish while you're away, Miss Jones?" he asked, on his way out.

Had I? I'd moved the model ships, as advised in case of a landslip. The fish-tank in the Boat Shed should have been moved but was big and heavy and I knew I couldn't manage it by myself. The fish needed to be caught and the tank emptied. I'd quietly shelved the idea, found other things to do and ignored my conscience. As for feeding them…

"Yes, of course," I said. "It's all under control. Have a lovely Christmas Day with the Gilberts."

Denise gave me a derisory glance when I returned from the front door.

"You'll have to do it, Cass. Not in that dress, though. Don't ask me to help. Right, I'm off, now."

I planned how to do it that evening. The following morning, I drove the pickup into the Boat Shed yard and parked it outside the door. I'd got as far as netting the fish; the ten, beautiful, fish that Emily had chosen with such care, and transferred them to a bucket of fresh water in the passenger footwell. Then I drained the tank.

It was still raining and the hose only reached to the middle of the yard and the trickle of water added to the mud outside. The tank, four feet by two feet of dirty glass, stared at me disparagingly; the lack of care evident in the green algae around the edges and a faint smell of decomposing fish poo hovered in the cold air. The wheel-barrow left by Steve Lewis was a fortunate find. I hosed it down and wheeled it into the shed, past the counter and tight up to the tank-stand.

Inch by precarious, heavy inch, I slid the tank down off the stand into the barrow, balanced it across the top, front to back and wheeled it carefully to the door and out to the pickup, where I'd unlatched the tailgate at the back to slide it in. Then I stood in the mud, like an idiot, with the awful realisation that the floor of the Toyota was too high. I couldn't lift it up, not even one edge.

I sat down on the tailgate and wiped the rain off my face, the image of my clubbing, silver finery as far removed as it could possibly be from this sorry state. Who could I ring to help, without suffering humiliation, stuck in the pouring rain and mud a week before Christmas and not yet packed? Not David, in his smart, leather jacket berating me with predictable scathing comments; not Will Roberts, to whom I'd lied; not Arnie in Dudley, or Hugh, out in the Irish Sea fixing wind turbines. But it was nothing to do with gender roles, I consoled myself, I just needed a big, strong bloke to lift the bloody thing.

I didn't hear Steve Lewis's Land Rover; he'd left it outside the gate.

"Finished with that barrow, have you?" he asked, one end of the tank already lifted like a feather in his strong hands, into the back of the pickup. I could have hugged him, but he wasn't a huggable sort of a man.

The fish liked their new home in the showroom, where the tank looked good on a low table by the side of the Chaparral powerboat. Incongruous, maybe, but 'fish and boats go together,' I said to Denise.

"They're goldfish. Arnie won't like it," she said.

"Tough. He's going to have to feed them for a week, so he might as well have them over here. Besides which, it adds an exotic feel to the showroom. I think I'll buy some house-plants as well. After Christmas."

Friday evening, and Arnie finished a second, small helping of the lasagne I'd cooked and cleared the salad on his plate. His manners were impeccable and he ate frugally and delicately, against all my expectations.

"Nice dressing," he said.

"Angela's recipe; lots of citrus."

"She's good, isn't she?"

"Yes," I said. " She hasn't anyone to cook for now and that bastard Gareth would never have appreciated what she could do, anyway. She told me once she'd missed all her opportunities in life and says she's too old to stand the pace in catering. What a waste. She's a lovely lady."

He nodded and opened a second bottle of Rioja. The conversation was light and chatty and we studiously avoided all the trauma that had brought us to the same place. Then I remembered my curiosity about the holiday caravan. The wine helped; it was a personal question.

"Your static?" I asked. "It's the same one you've had for years, you said. Did you ever think to upgrade, you know, buy a property, or one of those posh chalets?"

He placed his knife and fork down, gently, side by side, picked up the napkin and wiped his black moustache discreetly, the white streaks near his mouth more dominant now. He shook his head.

"Good question, bab. It was the first one Shelly and I owned, before the twins were even thought of. In Abersoch, that was. Good times, they were, first love and all that, and we discovered the sea and boating. We had an old powerboat for water-skiing. She was good at it, too. Then the twins and Jason came along and we stopped coming up so much while they were little. I just kept the van as it was. Then the twins got to be arsy teenagers."

He topped up the glasses. I cleared the plates and put fruit salad and a cheesecake on the table.

"So, it was easier for you to spend time up here again?" I prompted.

"Don't know about easier. More expensive, that's for sure. The twins turned into demanding brats and she just encouraged them. Jet-skis, better jet-skis, designer clothes, all the trimmings. For them, anyway. Jason got the leftovers, but he was never that bothered."

We were on uncomfortable ground now; the very recent present. I thought he'd stop talking, but then he didn't. He needed to talk, desperately. Despite our age differences, it didn't seem to matter; perhaps it helped. There was no hidden agenda. I needed to listen, and understand, and answer questions that had lurked in the back of my mind since I was seventeen and first met this dysfunctional family, a strange mixture of likeable and decidedly unpleasant people. Shut up and listen, girl.

"It all changed after that," he went on. "She was more into clothes and the club at Pwllheli, all that socialising and stuff with the moneyed, powerboat clique. The twins had their own lives, moved the jet-skis here to Port; I didn't know why, at the time, and they spent most of their weekends doing their own thing. Her an' all.

'At home, the business was thriving, the yard was open every weekend and I was that busy, I rarely came up with them. Jason stayed at home with me, sometimes. Quiet lad, he was; still is. He wasn't happy up here with his brothers taking the piss out of him. Used to play with little Tomas.

'When baby Ben was announced, fifteen years after Jason, Shelly threw a wobbler, practically disowned him, even when he was still in the womb. Handed him over to me, she did, plastered herself in makeup and skimpy clothes, forty years old trying to look twenty. I think I lost control then. She and the twins ganged up on me. I was too involved in work to do much about it. Had to earn the cash to pay the bills they ran up."

I had an uncomfortable moment as I remembered my dad doing just that for my mother; just pay the bills and don't ask questions. It was too much trouble.

“That was when I first met you,” I said.

“That’s right, and that’s when it all went badly wrong. Still can’t believe that they were in so deep with drugs and I never knew. I can’t forgive her for protecting them, but she’s changed so much, it doesn’t seem to matter now. She must have known about the drugs, then; all that time spent partying with Doug Peterson and his mates…” and he stopped in mid-sentence. Enough.

“Anyway, forgive and forget,” he said. “Better get to bed and think about tomorrow. Thanks for the meal. I enjoyed it.”

I had listened and learned, but the questions in my head were still unanswered, just fuelled with renewed curiosity. He had been good company and hadn’t spoilt the convivial atmosphere with anger over his family disappointment and had kept his emotions in check. He was the third man this week I wanted to hug: Steve Lewis, to thank him for his practical, un-fussy help, Will Roberts, to offer comfort for terrible grief and Arnie, for the acknowledgement that it was okay for a big bruiser of a man to be sad. I was humbled he felt he could share it with me. He hadn’t left the toilet seat up, either.

CHAPTER 10

'Conjecture' woke me at three in the morning, or was it the faint sound of an engine? The road outside was in darkness and I rolled back into bed under the warm duvet with Hugh's last words about Arnie's wife resounding in my ears; 'give no cause for conjecture,' he'd said. Well, how ridiculous is that, I thought, as Arnie was the boss, only making a visit to meet a client and stay in his own apartment; hardly basis for an affair, by anyone's standards and I went back to sleep.

"Your client's here," I said to him after breakfast, and watched through the window as her car came to a stop outside the showroom door, and yes, she was the same woman I'd seen in *The Ship*.

The stairs to the apartment were accessed through a door from the showroom. Another door at the top of the stairs led directly into the lounge. Arnie reached the bottom of the stairs quickly, for such a big man, and opened the bottom door. With one foot on the top stair, I was about to follow him down, with thoughts of courtesy, by introducing myself. I couldn't see her for Arnie's bulk in the doorway and she couldn't see me at the top of the stairs.

"Hiya," said the woman in a high, girly voice. "You the boss?

Thought that girl lived up there."

That girl? Me? Rude bitch. Don't reply, Arnie, please. I couldn't hear if he had, but tried to imagine the look on his face.

I retreated to the lounge and watched them through the window as they walked down the yard to the Sea Ray. His frame towered over her petite figure; skinny legs cased in tight jeans and white trainers on her feet, with a fluorescent stripe on the heels, and the white, quilted coat. As manager, I'd have to meet her sooner or later if she bought the boat, and contemplated whether my instant dislike would translate into a smack in the mouth. They disappeared up the steps into the Sea Ray. I ran downstairs to the office and banged the door behind me.

"What's got under your skin?" Denise asked, barely glancing up from the screen at my face. "Yeah, right," she agreed. "She reminds me of that wife of his. Out of the same stable, I reckon. Still chewing gum like last time, and stinks of fags. Are you going to join them?"

I shook my head, still seething. "I need to calm down first. She called me 'that girl,' like I was a bloody housemaid or something. I'll have to be pleasant, won't I?"

"Absolutely," she said. "The customer is always right, Cassie," and she wagged her finger at me.

"Fuck that," I said, cross, but knew she was right and pinched one of her chocolate bars.

They were gone ages and I fed the fish that Arnie had surprisingly approved of, polished the stainless-steel fittings on the Chaparral and washed the coffee mugs.

Then they came back. We shook hands; long, blue nails and her hand tiny and cold like a dead fish, her eyes hard and calculating, a milky brown defined with black eye-liner. She had a tight mouth and pointed nose, upturned at the end. She wasn't pretty, the short black hair contrasting with remnants of a fake tan and foundation caked on too thick. She tipped her head on one side, as though measuring up the situation. And me.

I did well; firm handshake, head up, good eye contact and a welcoming smile. Then she ignored me and turned to Arnie.

"I'll be in touch. I'll need to talk to my partner, first."

She caught my glance with a questioning look on my face, I supposed. She relented.

"Come into some money, love, but he makes the decisions. Likes to bargain, he does."

So why did he send you, I asked myself? Did he think Arnie would be a soft touch? I don't think so.

"See ya," she said, shifted her gum to the other cheek, and left.

We gathered in the office.

"Well?"

"Cheeky cow tried to knock me down ten thousand." He could barely contain himself. "She must think I'm nuts. I said three, at most. Can't imagine we'll see her again. Time-waster," and hauled himself out of the chair. "That's business, Cass. I'll be on my way, now," and that was that.

He slid into the driver's seat, turned to me, and tugged at his moustache, which he did when he was thinking.

"I swear I know her from somewhere," he said, "but for the life of me, I couldn't say where. Have a good Christmas in London. I'll bring Ben up after Boxing Day. Don't you worry, bab, I'll look after the place, feed the fish, and keep it clean and tidy."

But I wasn't so sure. Not about Arnie and Ben inhabiting my home; but about her, and not just the faint aroma of stale cigarette smoke and peppermint gum. She'd left behind a taint, a trail of something insubstantial, something that didn't ring true, something unsettling, the way she looked at us, as though gathering details; the purchase of the powerboat an irrelevant charade.

I caught the bus to Bangor, then the train to Llandudno, Crewe, and finally Euston; a relatively seamless journey it turned out, despite the changes. I'd set off, ridiculously excited, like a child, and could scarcely believe I'd ever been a Londoner, worked and lived in a city, travelled widely and never turned a hair at being away from home, up the road, abroad, wherever.

I left the sea behind, cold in its winter garb and the mountains capped with recent snow, glued my nose to the carriage window and stared at the once-familiar landscape as the Midlands rushed by; towns, villages, roofs and bedroom windows, washing-lines and swings, scrap-yards and warehouses, buses and wagons; all flew past, an essence of humanity in a three-hour journey.

The tired green of fields was divided by the black, stark outlines of trees and hedges, minimal punctuations in the sprawling outskirts of Rugby, Coventry, Northampton, and Milton Keynes, and melded finally into one great, urban sprawl as I approached London. I wasn't impressed and lost my excitement temporarily in the sheer greyness of it all. Then I thought of my best friend Trish, the chatty swap of gossip and intimacies, but only some, and a warm welcome to their lovely house, my home as well, I supposed, and clubbing and music and friends.

"You have had your jabs, haven't you? Negative test? No matter, stand in the other queue and I'll slip you my phone down the line. We do it all the time. No big deal. Nobody notices."

Trish emerged from the shower and towelled her hair dry. I'd abandoned my mother's apartment upstairs to get ready for the night out. I couldn't think of it as my home; it was her space, after all, and I was just passing through.

So, these were the Covid restrictions for socialising in England. I hadn't thought to check; we were practically locked down in Wales, yet again. No matter. I wasn't going to abide by the rules and miss out, and reasoned I was young and fit and would survive if I caught it; unlike Helen's Nain. That was still too close to set aside completely and after an uncomfortable pang of sadness, I decided it was a calculated risk and worth it. I couldn't wait, poured myself into the silver dress and boots and savoured the look on my mother's face when Trish and I appeared in the lounge to wait for the taxi; she'd only seen me in overalls in the last year.

Despite the barrage of questions from my mother, Trish and her mother Felicity, over dinner, breakfast, lunch and in-between, I concentrated my answers on the side of enthusiasm and optimism about the business, the successful sale of *Tai Pilots* to fund the Boat Shed, my sailing tuition with David, and avoided information about rock-falls, and smoke-house doors that mysteriously shut by themselves, and new clients I didn't like. Boyfriends, too.

"That bloke David?" Trish asked. "He sounds like a good catch." They were disappointed.

"We're having a Boxing Day drinks party here," Felicity said, as she topped up the champagne glasses, except mother's, over dinner the night before. "All my favourite, wealthy clients, will be here, darling. Perhaps we'll find you a new man."

The XOYO, Trish's favourite club, a reasonable taxi drive from Hackney and worth every penny, welcomed us with open arms and a cursory glance at the phone. The club bounced with fun and loud music, charged extortionate prices for drinks and I lost myself, happily, in the beat, the heat, the bodies and too much alcohol. In a break, I left Trish with her friends and excused myself, with a sudden weariness I couldn't explain.

The' shush' of the door in the Ladies blocked out the music. The mirror watched, as a slim, silver figure emerged from the cubicle; appraised the bob of glossy, purple-streaked dark hair, the flushed face, and a sudden glint where the light caught the diamond stud in her nose. She washed her hands, and looked up to brush her hair, the lift of the arms slow and reluctant, as though the brush was too heavy, or she just couldn't be bothered.

But the reflection in the mirror wavered, morphed, the silver dress transformed into a figure in a red sailing jacket with the hood up, and wisps of black hair escaped and plastered a tanned face. She tilted her head to one side, listened to the sound of the wind in the rigging and watched for the shiver in the white sails, licked the salt from a wet hand and turned the wheel; just a fraction, just enough, to bring the bow off the wind, feel the speed pick up and turned to watch the wake cream out like a broad ribbon behind her.

"Hey, are you okay?" A girl at the next basin peered anxiously into my face.

In the mirror, the images merged, a surrealist reflection that shifted in and out of reality until the red jacket disappeared entirely.

"Fine," I said. "Thanks," but had to steady myself against the vanity unit. Too much to drink? Or what?

"Your phone's pinged," the girl said. "Didn't you hear it?"

The brush still in my hand, I ran it through my hair, hand shaky and brain confused, put it in my bag, pulled out the phone and read the text. From Daniel.

'In London, last minute arrangement. Can I come and see you in Wales?"

'No need. In London now." It was a dreadful cliché, I'd learned that in school, but my heart gave a lurch. Then my stomach threatened to follow suit. Too much to drink, after all.

'Fantastic. Address please, and will send Uber.'

I downed a glass of water at the bar, shouted in Trish's ear that I'd be back in the morning and not to worry, picked up Helen's Nain's coat from reception and stood outside in the freezing cold. I didn't care, just thanked the Welsh sheep for the wool and the high collar. No toothbrush, no other clothes and I couldn't have cared less.

The black coat lay on the back of the settee, in a comfortable sitting room, small, like the rest of the little mews house. Only a lucrative business could afford a place like this in London, I thought, though it had been in the family for years and used as a headquarters for the marinas in early days. He looked jet-lagged and travel-worn, but tanned, lean and just as gorgeous as ever, hugged me hard and offered champagne.

"Can I have tea?" I asked, and texted my mother and Trish, while the kettle boiled.

Too tired, too much to talk about, we just went to sleep, curled up like spoons. It was fine.

"A strange thing happened," I said in the morning, propped up on feather pillows with toast and tea he'd brought in on a tray, and told him about the image in the mirror.

"Perhaps it was just the drink," I said. "I'm not used to that level of abuse anymore."

"Perhaps it was an identity crisis."

"Bollocks," I said. "Now tell me what you're doing here in the middle of winter. Visiting friends, you said. Really?"

He put the tray on the floor, turned over in bed, his face close to mine, and touched the stud in my nose.

"God, I've missed you," he said. "Everyone else I know is so polite." I'd missed him, too; body and mind, but mostly body. Much later, we talked.

"We haven't sold any of the marinas. Mixture of Covid and global worries about future energy costs and the effects on us; specifically, powerboats. The board has decided to take all the marinas off the market, change tack to the marketing of 'green' marinas, for a start, as far as we can."

"But that's what I'm doing," I said, surprised and excited. "Arnie's given the go-ahead for some changes and some cash to get us started. I've ordered eco-cleaning stuff and put in for a grant for solar panels. It's not much, but it might appeal to some of the more thoughtful clients." But not that one with the gum, I thought.

"Well, that's interesting. We can swap ideas."

Don't pinch mine, I thought, selfishly.

"So, I've been reinstated as UK manager again," he said. "And thought I'd spend Christmas with friends and do the round trip of the businesses over the next month or so."

We stayed in bed until lunchtime. I didn't want to go back to the house and face the questions.

"I'll run you home. You can't go on the tube, or a taxi in daylight, looking like that. Anyway, the Porsche needs a run."

"You'd have to meet my mother. And Felicity. And Trish."

"I'll just drop you off," he said. "I have to meet friends later."

But Trish was waiting.

"You must come in," she said, through the driver's window, "whoever you are," barely masking the awe on her face as he unfurled his beautiful body from the seat and stood, head and shoulders above her in the road. Trish, who had never been one to mince her words, looked at me and said, "You bloody dark horse, you," and shooed us inside.

"You simply must invite him for drinks on Boxing Day, Cassie," said Felicity when he'd driven off after tea and a polite chat. "He's just exquisite, and of course, he might meet some interesting and useful people."

He was already acquainted with the businesses of at least three of the guests, and I heard him chat comfortably in Spanish, French, even used a smattering of German. He was the dark horse, not me. I didn't know he was multilingual, but then, why would I? But Spanish, I should have realised, was no surprise. My mother was quietly impressed with his attention towards her and charmed nearly speechless by the end of the afternoon; I was relieved she drank only sparkling water these days; she would have been impossibly behaved on champagne.

"So, what's he like in bed, then?" asked Trish, continuing her speculation about Daniel. I hadn't told her much. "I mean, is he more than a good screw, or what? And you said he'd invited you to Trinidad twice for sailing and that, and learning about the business. You're bonkers if you don't pick up on it."

"He's just a friend," I said. "I've got things to do and I want to do them on my own. I think he might be a bit controlling. Just the odd hint. We're friends, in and out of bed, and that's all, Trish."

"He's just charming," my mother finally managed, after supper. "Are you…"

But I was already loading up the dishwasher.

We spent one more day together, tucked up in bed with the heating full on and champagne on ice, for lunch. It rained solidly all day but we didn't care. The one o'clock news was filled with stories of Storm Bella, with floods and collapsed bridges in Yorkshire and the Lake District, and some rail services were out of commission. North Wales had experienced heavy rain in the mountains and the rivers were at bursting point after the heavy rain before Christmas. I relegated my Boat Shed and landslips into the 'things I can do nothing about' box in my head, and shut the lid; very firmly.

He took me out to dinner that night and I told him about my sailing tuition with David. The restaurant clatter receded into the background, as I relived that last sail of the year in Tremadog Bay, screaming along at nine knots with my hands on the wheel, in complete control, and laughing out loud to the sea and the sky.

"That's it, though," he said, complete understanding in his eyes. "Now you get it. That's what it's like. That's your real self you saw in the mirror. That's what really makes you tick."

He was serious. "You must do more sailing when the summer comes. As well as everything else, like running two businesses. You've such a lot to look forward to. The Boat Shed will be renovated or rebuilt, Angela will produce wonderful food with your smoked salmon and Arnie's cash flow will go through the roof with sales and yard fees from your new, discerning clients. But you can and you must sail. There's nothing like it," and we finished the meal in complete accord, with light-hearted tales of his childhood, sailing adventures; a Swallows and Amazons in the West Indies

It was nine-thirty in the morning when my phone pinged, my early morning well-being shattered, with a simple message from Arnie.

'You need to come home.'

CHAPTER 11

Gone. Flattened. Demolished. The Boat Shed lay in a heap of twisted beams and rusty roof sheets, not a top-down demolition, more of a back-to-front swipe, as though a cardboard model had been erected, then deliberately deconstructed by judiciously pulled strings, like a reversed ship-in-a-bottle. The space between the back of the shed and the retaining wall was obliterated, filled with mud and the tangled remains of vegetation; twigs and branches from the willow trees, leaves from the bamboo plants that had been once planted to fill up the space and soak up the water, and stones that had once been the wall.

In the late afternoon gloom, I could barely make out the dark shape of the huge boulder that had finally detached itself from the top of the cliff and tumbled down into the swamp at the bottom; it had bashed into overhanging ledges and fallen away from the cliff, away from the base and nearer the wall, as Steve Lewis had feared. There would be no need, now, to commission anyone for the demolition of the Boat Shed. It was no consolation.

My throat tightened; any words squashed in disbelief. Arnie put his arm round my shoulders, while Daniel, as shocked as I was, and tired from the driving, shook his head and wandered around the yard.

"Just a building, bab," Arnie said, "just an old building. Come on, now. There's nothing you can do."

He locked the gate and they escorted me, closely, one each side, a protective cloak of care, back to the showroom. I slipped out from their warmth to the cloakroom, caught a glimpse in the mirror of an ashen face and black shadows under puffy eyes of shock. I sloshed cold water on my face and felt better, but shaky, and joined them in the office, where hot tea and biscuits were already on the desk and Denise was there, rising from her chair to hug me.

What was there to say? We sipped in silence, standing, until Ben burst into the office, thrust a piece of paper, a picture of the Boat Shed with its shabby, red front door, into my hand, and hugged my legs.

"It's for you," he said. "I drawed it from memory. It's a big mess over there, Cassie. Can I watch the digger when it comes?"

"Drew," I said. "Not 'drawed' and yes, it is a big mess. Thank you. The colours are lovely and I like the seagull sitting on the bin. Diggers might have to wait."

That'll do, I thought. The whole scenario could have been a nauseating cliché from an American disaster movie, but there is nothing like a child's interpretation of situations to bring you to your senses. Then I was ready for the details. Daniel grouped chairs around the desk.

"Ben and me were having breakfast," Arnie said, "then there was a thud outside from somewhere, a big thud, and the mugs on the table shook. Couldn't see anything from the window, but I guessed something was up. We grabbed coats and ran down the yard and stood this side of the gates. The rock was already down, but bits of stuff, stones and pebbles and soil from the cliff above was still falling. It was the way the mud had started to move that got me. It was still moving when I unlocked the gate, then we kept well back…"

The security light outside in the yard flickered on and the front door opened. Steve Lewis strode up the showroom to the office. Jackson nosed his way in behind him and lowered his haunches to the floor, his coat wet, as much part of the group as a dog could be.

"I only just got the message. I came straight down," and dragged up a chair. "I'm listening."

"… like an avalanche, it was. It flowed up to the top of the wall, then over the top of the wall, and then the stones started to break loose and the wall bulged. Then it disappeared beneath it. Like liquid shit, and it kept on coming, right up to the back wall of the shed." He looked at me, as if to confirm I could bear to hear it. I nodded.

"It was like a lava flow, Cass. It just oozed up to the back wall, piled up and then the metal sheets just crumpled inwards and the roof timbers came down. The rest followed, like a pack of cards."

The dog was as stunned and silent as the rest of us.

I knew that nothing much happened in that dead week between Christmas and New Year. Insurance companies were inundated with requests for assessment; there was flood damage up and down the country, but by the end of January, my frustration had turned to anger. The clearing up couldn't be started until the assessor had been, but David, without any request from me, took it upon himself to contact them directly; 'old friends and favours' he said.

"There's no reason the planning appeal should be compromised," Steve Lewis said. "The weather's just done the job for you. What's down, can't come down again, can it?"

No, I thought, but that wasn't all I'd worried about, but I couldn't share it. Neither could I share the decision I'd made about selling the whole damn place.

It was useless now to even think about it, that moment of wonderful optimism I'd felt when I decided to just walk away. With what? Nothing, now, I supposed, with a dangerous piece of ground and an expensive mess to clear up. There was a sour taste in my mouth and I could scarcely believe how quickly all my plans and visions seemed to melt away. I'd known the rock-fall was a probability, but I hadn't bargained on the visual shock of the reality. Had it been helped on its way, or had it just been the rain? I'd never know, but I constantly looked over my shoulder again for odd events to happen, strangers to appear for no reason, and any natural resilience I'd had to unpleasantness or conflict seemed to fade away in the drab weeks before spring.

Daniel disappeared on his UK business and said he'd call me from Holyhead on return from Scotland. Holyhead? I thought the plans for a new marina had been ditched; he hadn't said. We might have shared a bed, and passion, and fun, but he didn't share information about business deals. I didn't care. I was way out of his league.

January ended and the assessor came and went. I waited for his verdict. I hadn't bargained on an insurance claim, but even a small contribution would help. David said the terms of the policy were complicated, but the insurance guy okayed the clearance of the boatyard and the digger arrived over February half-term.

More rain from Storm Christoph at the end of January, and a continuation of dull, wet weather in Wales, added to the morass of debris to be cleared. The mud dripped off the bucket of the digger, like wet slurry, and trickled through the base of the skip. I could barely look at the mess. Steve said that as soon as the mud and the remnants of the Boat Shed were cleared, they'd start strengthening the cliff-face. The winter storms had been extreme in other parts of the country, with flooding in Yorkshire and Manchester and snow and ice down south, but here, it had just rained; every bloody day, it seemed, but not torrential, and I worried even more that the rock-fall hadn't been an act of nature.

Arnie took a few days off at school half-term, and he and Ben stayed at the caravan now the site was open, but spent every day at Madoc Marine. Ben had freedom to come and go in the apartment but was strictly forbidden to be in the yard on his own. I watched his dad lay down the law when they arrived, his jacket sleeve pushed up and his tattooed arm bare as he pointed out the dangers; I didn't think I'd disobey him, either. There was no sign of Shelly. I didn't feel I could ask Arnie about his wife, despite his confidences during the evening we'd spent together, but over a game of Snakes and Ladders upstairs, one wet afternoon, I asked Ben, quite casually, how his mum was.

"She's alright. Gone to Majorca," he said, "and I've won the game."

The positive action and progress in the yard had a strange effect on me. With the uncertainty of my ability to pay for the clearance and stay solvent, and the planning appeal still in abeyance, I'd temporarily shelved thoughts of selling and running away. Like everyone else, I concentrated on preparation for the spring lift-in, a major event in the calendar for boat owners. As the remnants of the shed disappeared in the skip and the mud was scraped away, the space in the yard opened old possibilities and I could see my dream building once more.

"Aren't you upset?" Denise asked, as the last skip was collected and driven away. The digger followed.

"Actually, no," I said. Confusion set in. One minute it had been an important part of my life, the next minute, demolished. Did I really want to sell the yard, gifted to me out of the blue, and the only thing I'd ever owned? In fact, it had been the only place that had felt like home for a long time. But, I reasoned, it was the people who called in for a pannad, and a warm by the fire, who made it special; 'only a building' Arnie had said, and the people were still there and part of my life. I could do it all again. Nothing more unpleasant had happened, no insidious threats, no suspicions, no conflicts; just the anticipation of spring round the corner, a stirring in the air, and the blackbirds starting to sing again.

"Have you seen the tide-heights for the end of the week?" Denise asked one Monday morning in late March. "And the weather forecast? Looks like the equinox could be interesting. We need to check the pontoon risers. Don't get tides that high very often. Look."

I looked. I agreed. Only occasionally, did a high spring-tide spill over the top of the harbour wall into the boatyards and only when the peak of the tide coincided with a south-westerly gale. High seas, spawned by low pressure systems out in the Atlantic, could drive big waves down the estuary, despite the protection of the bar and the shallow waters inside. I'd seen it all before, but not when I'd been responsible for someone else's property. Did she mean a squirt of WD40 on the risers? I rang Don, recovered from Covid and back at work in Pwllheli Marina.

"Right," he said. "I'll come and check, but I don't think you need to worry. The pontoons have coped with gales before. I'd be more worried about the river if I lived in Port. I was talking to Will Roberts this morning. You know he's responsible for checks on the sluice- gates? It's part of the NRW's safety-net for flooding. Can't stop work and tell you now. I'll explain tomorrow."

I knew the sluice-gates. You couldn't live here and not know them. Without them, the harbour wouldn't exist, and the Glaslyn would have continued to run its course wherever it pleased, bashing into the back of the Cob, and destroying all the work William Maddocks had spent the best part of his life building. After storms and breaches of the new embankment two hundred years ago, something had to be done about the diversion of the river, which ideally should have been in place before the building of the Cob. Even I could see that but then I thought, we can all be wise in hindsight; even clever folk.

I'd walked over the walkway above the sluice many times, and peered down in awe as the Glaslyn rushed through from the Traeth, under the bridge into the harbour, then out to sea. The original, massive wooden sluice gates had been backed up in 1964, by new, steel ones, based on the same principal of pivots and counterweights, but these ones had an electricity supply from a generator. I still didn't get it.

I was glad to see Don the following morning and I realised how much I'd missed him; without him, the yard couldn't function. I thought of asking Arnie if I could give him a pay rise, just to ensure he didn't desert me.

The rafts of four pontoons, joined and laid end to end, lay against Madoc Marine's harbour wall. Steel plates had been drilled into the wall and risers attached to enable the pontoons to slide up and down with the rise and fall of the tides. Accessed by a ramp from the yard, they'd been put in by Doug Peterson to encourage the powerboat owners to berth their boats at Madoc Marine, instead of moving to the marina in Pwllheli.

The step-on, step-off culture had rapidly taken over from mid-river moorings; no more wet journeys across the water in inflatable dinghies, no more clambering up the side of boats, electricity and water on tap, and the berths were fully booked for the summer; hopefully not with the delightful Mr Robinson, from whom I'd heard nothing. I'd ask Don about him. He'd know how much damage had been done to the powerboat's engine and the owner's bank balance. Lots, I hoped.

"So, what did Will Roberts tell you that was so interesting?" I asked Don, and handed him up a spanner. He tightened up bolts, checked the risers and climbed down the ladder to the pontoon.

"He said the river levels are so high, and the flooding so bad on the Traeth, he's concerned about a tide-lock on Thursday; there's a high spring-tide forecast, and a hell of a gale behind it."

He packed his tools back into the bag.

"The risers are all good, Cassie," glancing up at the wall above us. "They've survived bad storms before. At least there are no boats moored up. That's when it gets sticky."

"Yeah, I know all about that," I said, and remembered how I watched *Annie* during a storm, as she rose ever higher up the wall until she nearly became beached in the yard. Only the mooring ropes and the timely fall of the tide kept her from disaster. "What's this tide-lock that Mr Roberts is worried about?"

Predictions about climate change and rising sea levels were not, as most folk supposed, the only concern for the town of Porthmadog; the risk of serious flooding not just from the sea, but from the increased winter rainfall constantly filling the rivers above their normal levels was also very worrying.

Will Roberts had been talking to the North Wales manager for Natural Resources Wales. They were collecting data for a future public consultation on flood risk management, but were beginning to bite their nails and wondering if their feared predictions for a major flood event could be about to happen this week, never mind in two hundred years.

"It could never happen, or it could happen tomorrow, they told him," Don said.

"What could happen, exactly?" I asked, none the wiser.

"The sluice gates open to let the river run out, when the tide's falling, yeah?"

"Scours out the harbour," I said. I'd seen the water rush under the bridge and into the harbour at a scary rate after heavy rain in the mountains, too fast and dangerous sometimes, for even an outboard engine to push against it.

"Well," he said, "it seems that in an extreme event, if the tide is high and stays high, and there's an unusual amount of water on the Traeth to drain away, as it should, it can't. See? On account of the tide on the other side. Stalemate, you might say."

"In time for what? Wouldn't it just flow over the dyke into Llyn Bach?"

"And what's at the top end of Llyn Bach?"

"Oh, right," I said. "The sluice-gate that drains into Y Cwt. But that goes into the old canal channel. It's quite deep."

"Maybe not deep enough, they said, for the extreme rainfall we seem to be getting. They don't know. Not only that… and this is the bad bit. If the water couldn't get through the sluice gates because of the tide, it might naturally find its way around the side and back of the dyke; it's all flat ground, just reclaimed marsh."

"Okay. So? It was all marsh once, wasn't it?"

"Yes, but what's round there now?"

This guessing game was beginning to annoy me. Then I thought about it.

"The Industrial Estate and oh, right, I get it; the sewage pumping station… and the sub-station for Port. Not to mention the business units, and if Y Cwt over-flowed, the streets and houses and shops as well. Could that really happen? I mean, is it just scaremongering?"

"It's only a projection. They're already gathering data for the whole of the Welsh coast. We're just a part of it. Should they spend more money on coastal defences here, on the off-chance it might happen? Anyway, that's all I know. Keep your fingers crossed it doesn't."

"But it might," I said.

"Pigs might fly, climate change sceptics would say."

We started back up the ramp. "By the way, your client, Mr Robinson, plans to come back to Madoc Marine in a few weeks. I fixed his engine."

"Was it expensive?" I asked.

"Very."

"Good. Wonder if he'll be able to afford to buy some manners."

I hadn't heard from Hugh for a while. He'd been sent to the east coast of Scotland as part of a team advising on a new wind-farm in the North Sea, but I'd messaged him about the sad end to the Boat Shed; just the facts, and reassured him that his little yacht, *Capella*, was untouched and safe. I also messaged Paul to tell him his yacht was undamaged. He was in Dublin and working for his father. The return text was a little unsettling. 'Will phone end of month for a chat. Think I've sold the boat. So sorry about the shed. Build another.'

Well, thanks for that. I thought. One boat down halved my income from the yard.

Hugh said nothing in his text of his warning shot across the bows, over coffee that day, about my giving 'no cause for 'conjecture'. My concerns, and his advice, now seemed rather extreme and Arnie's presence at Madoc Marine over half-term had been perfectly justified; he was the owner, after all. Neither had there been any sign of the gum-chewing client, whose presence had made me so uneasy.

Then she turned up; no phone-call, no warning, but this time brought the bouncer with her. Denise called me in from the yard.

"We want to buy the boat," she said, to Denise, and gave 'that girl' as I'd been referred to, a cursory glance. "The Sea Ray. We'll take Arnie up on his offer. Let him know, will you? You can do the paperwork, can't you? Bank transfer."

"I'll take you through the paperwork," I said, determined not to be side-lined. "There's quite a lot to consider with change of ownership; informing the authorities, ship's registration, finance checks and so on. It's not like going to Tesco," I couldn't resist adding.

Her head came up sharply. The bouncer shuffled his feet.

"Are you saying we haven't got the money? He's got the money.

He'll pay," she said. "But it's my boat."

Oh joy, I thought, now I've upset her. Spiky cow. Now I'll really have to know what I'm doing.

"If you can come back in the morning, I'll have all the documents ready," I said. "It would have helped if you could have let us know ahead of time."

"Can't do tomorrow. It'll have to be Saturday."

"That's fine," I said, in an unpractised, conciliatory voice. "I'll make sure it's all ready for you. It'll give you time to sort out the bank transfer, as well. Denise has the details."

"Can we launch it on Saturday, then?"

"Probably not," I said. "I'm afraid there's a forecast for a gale at the end of the week. Also, our mechanic will need to give the engines a service and give it a general check-over. In a few weeks, when the weather settles down, it can be lifted in with the other boats. Would you want to berth it here?"

"Yeah, 'course. On one of those pontoon things, with electric and stuff."

"I'll have to check…"

Denise nodded. "I'll put your name down, then, shall I? Mrs…"

"Miss, and it's Tracy Downs. Ta. See you Saturday." She turned to go, then turned back.

"Lives here some of the time, does he?" she said to me. "Arnie, I mean. Saw him in your flat the last time I was here. Friends, are you?"

I stared at her. Arch-bitch, Denise called Arnie's wife. This one wasn't far removed from that. Trouble-maker, I wondered? What's your agenda, miss? I'd keep that to myself, I decided.

"He's my boss, Miss Downs, and he lives in Dudley. Goodbye," and walked away.

The bouncer hadn't said a word.

"Help," I said to Denise, when I saw the car disappear out of the yard.

"No probs. You've got work to do. Your first brokerage. You can do it all and I'll check it for you. Better ring Arnie and tell him."

The gale blew in as predicted on Thursday and the high, equinoctial tide peaked alarmingly with scarcely a space under the road bridge. The swell carried in as far as the inner harbour, lifting and twisting the Yacht Club pontoons. Wavelets broke against the parapets of the road bridge, and the sea flooded through into Llyn Bach as it always did, but the levels rose higher, abnormally higher, on the other side. Locals, including me, congregated to watch, wellies and hoods up against the rain, heavy in bursts, and then a continuous barrage of water. If it hadn't been for the fascination of a potential disaster, none of us would have been away from our homes. But we watched in fascination, as humans do, when a crisis unfolds; the mind-numbing awfulness of the unthinkable.

Will Roberts spent the crucial hour at slack high-water between his office, the bridge, and the sluice-gates. Out over the Traeth, a sheet of water covered the ground as far as the eye could see and flowed towards the Cob as the mountains poured more rainwater into the river and down to the flood-plain. The banks of the Glaslyn had been indistinguishable for weeks, but now, as the water-level began to encroach on the bicycle track that had been built below the road across the Cob, I understood what Don had meant about timing. Would the tide fall in time for the gates to open? Would it equalise? Could the gates cope with this amount of water? They always had, I reasoned, in the two hundred-odd years since they were built, old and new.

But this early-spring event had a life of its own. The sky darkened and a wall of rain poured from the sky in torrents, the mountain ranges obliterated in dark clouds. It crashed down on our covered heads, filtered through expensive wet-weather coats, splashed up and over boots, a deluge of water that made breathing difficult and talking impossible. Phones were relegated to pockets and one by one the crowd dispersed; beaten down, cowed by the sheer force; a monsoon, out of place, belonging in another country.

I flattened myself against the stone wall of the railway track. It rained, without any break, for an hour, but I waited, mesmerized by the sheer power of it. I could only imagine the crashing of water high up on the hills, as it gushed and cascaded its way down the rocks and gullies.

Finally, the black skies blew into tatters in the wind, the gloom lifted a fraction and I made my way over to the back of Cob Records, stopped and watched Will Roberts as he stood at the entrance to the walkway. I could hear the roar of the river as it rushed through the gates, and saw the dark line on the banks of Llyn Bach where the tide had started to recede. He nodded his head to himself, as though satisfied, and turned around. I felt that my presence was intrusive, lifted my hand briefly and left.

"Scaremongering?" I said to Denise, the following morning over toast. "I think it was a pretty close-call. Not the perfect storm this time, but who knows, next time round? Thank God it's nearly summer. What's this?" and she handed me a post-it.

"The phone call from Mr Robinson. I thought I'd write it down so you can see what a changed man he is."

The note asked me for half of the engine repair costs, being as how my mechanic defaulted on his promise to complete the work. Also, he'd like his berth on the pontoon reinstated for the season.

"I think Arnie can deal with this," I said. "Remind me to charge my phone so I can video the meeting. Arnie's bigger than him. I can't face it."

"There's post for you, as well. Gwynedd County Council, it says."

I froze, took it upstairs and shut the door.

'We are pleased to inform that your appeal planning application for the replacement of the retail outlet, the Boat Shed, has been granted. However, the application for a new build as a place of residence has been refused. Please contact the office for details and information regarding building regulations.'

I sat on the settee, unsure whether I was surprised, disappointed, philosophical, even angry; it just complicated my already confused thoughts about the future. A faint knock on the door and Denise walked in.

"I couldn't wait for you to come back down. It's the appeal decision, isn't it? What does it say?"

"Says, I haven't anywhere to live after the summer. Need a lodger?"

But the autumn was a way off and strangely, I wasn't surprised or disappointed. I started to think about the Boat Shed differently, in a positive light, and all my misgivings paled into insignificance as the pace of spring gathered in the wings, and I knew I wouldn't have time to think about big issues; like my future. When the bigger boats were all lifted in, then I could relax and deal with the regular requests for 'Launch and Go' at the weekends; the smaller powerboats and jet skis would keep me busy.

"Then what will you do when Arnie wants to move in?" Denise asked.

"He's got to sell his business first. It might never happen."

"But if it did, he'd bring that cow of a wife with him," she said, eyes wide open with horror, "now that she's moved back in with him. I hadn't thought of that. I'll be looking for work elsewhere, Cassie. I can't stand her."

"And I can't believe they're back together," I said. "Let's wait and see. Now I've got to face the charming Miss Downs. Talk me through the paperwork again."

She arrived on Saturday morning with the bouncer in tow, reasonably pleasant but still chewing gum. It was Denise's weekend off so we sat in the office on our own, of which I was glad. It was suddenly very important I managed this transaction without a back-up. It would add to my street-cred, and I knew she'd gossip if I made a mistake. The innuendos that she'd made regarding Arnie seemed never to have existed.

I made coffee in the best mugs, and put biscuits on a matching plate; Denise's little touch. We finished the paperwork, she signed her name and he filled in his banking details.

"We can't hand over the keys until the money has cleared," I said, "as in all boat transactions, but would you like to have another look around your boat, in case you think of any questions I can help you with?" I asked.

They looked uncertainly at each other.

"That's mean. I thought we could sleep on it tonight," she said.

"No, I'm sorry. That's not the way it works. Next week when the finance is completed, you can have access to it, but even then, we don't insure for owners sleeping on their boats in the yard. I'm afraid you'll have to wait until it's on the water. You're welcome to work on it during the day, of course."

"So, we'll have to pay to stay somewhere tonight, then? Or go home?"

I nearly lost patience, but carried out a chatty guided tour with equanimity. We walked back to the car in silence. Grey water from puddles in the yard splashed onto her jeans and white trainers.

She got into the passenger seat of the car, and looked up at me as she fastened her seat-belt, her head cocked to one side and gave me a knowing, sly look from the black-lined eyes. She shifted her gum to the other cheek.

"On your own at weekends, are you?" she said. "Single woman and all that. Mind you, I suppose you can get up to what you want, can't you? Give Arnie my regards. Sorry we missed him. He's usually around, isn't he?"

They drove off. The bouncer still hadn't said a word.

I made my way slowly back to the office, sat down and stared at the paperwork. It was all in order and I was pleased with myself; my first brokerage, even with my dislike of the buyer, but what was left of my good humour faded away as I washed the mugs and thought about her parting words. Something nagged at me; could Hugh's vague ideas have substance, after all? But then, the delightful Miss Downs wasn't Shelly Blackwell; the connection escaped me. Maybe she was a soap-opera, or *Cheshire Wives* fanatic. She looked the type, and then I castigated myself for unfair generalisations.

CHAPTER 12

David phoned me with dates and an invitation to crew for him in May, the first big race of the season, from Pwllheli to Dun Laoghaire in Ireland. His sister Heidi and her current boyfriend, Al, would be on board. They were experienced and I was flattered to bits that I had been asked to join them. I was still a racing novice, but not a sailing dunce anymore.

I put red stars on the calendar for the Bank Holiday weekend and I would ask Arnie to stand in for me. I wanted my own gear this time; jacket, trousers, life-jacket, and safety-harness; plenty in stock to choose from. I'd pay cost and tell Arnie the loss of profit would be a necessary contribution to my training in the job. He wouldn't mind.

For the first time in a while, I felt I was taking part in something I had trained hard for, and could redeem my battered pride after the last disastrous race, when vomit and misery were the prevailing memories. I swallowed hard with excitement, knew I wouldn't be sick anymore, and remembered the sheer exhilaration of fast sailing with David. He'd warned that his hospitality was not quite the same on a race, but I didn't care. I could handle a winch, reef a sail, helm the boat, and keep it on course, even in brisk winds and lumpy seas. I couldn't wait. It was weeks away, but the enthusiasm it engendered in me affected the way I thought about everything else. The new building for the Boat Shed was back on course. Turn-coat, I said to myself, quietly.

Steve said he'd start clearing the remaining vegetation from the rock-face after Easter, and bolt any potential loose rocks. He commiserated with my news about the shed, and I gathered some quotes for a timber-framed building to replace it. Ironically, the disappointment I thought I'd feel about the refusal for residence, dissipated, as new drawings of the log-cabin-style shed I'd originally thought of, took shape on the coffee table.

I wanted a space for storage. Canoeists would need paddles, rowers would need oars, and if I bought a couple of classic, sailing dinghies, sails as well. I had my eye on an old Enterprise. I wanted the same layout as before, a smart, modern cloakroom and shower, still leaving enough room for access to the snack-bar and smoke-house at the back.

Steve had dug out the old, oak counter and the cast-iron stove from the wreckage. The stove was scratched and full of mud, but just needed a coat of heat-proof paint. It had been the heart of the old shed, and would be again.

That was the primary plan. What I really wanted, and kept to myself, was to have the covenant on the property overturned so I had the choice to develop it differently. But I didn't share that with anyone just yet. I'd ask David, when I thought the time was right, and he wouldn't be sniffy about it. If it wasn't possible, so be it, but a classic, small-boat building business would hardly keep me, even in bread and butter.

Then Easter loomed, and the start of the school holidays. It was still cold, the weather unsettled with April showers, snow on the distant mountain-tops and brief periods of welcome sun. The first influx of coaches arrived, and disgorged happy shoppers; children with winter-white faces lined the harbour wall and fumbled with crab-lines in cold hands, and the first sand-castles appeared on the beach, hastily built in-between showers.

The problem of Mr Robinson re-emerged. His berth had been booked for the season and paid for, and we had ignored his demands for payment towards the engine repairs. It was all bluster. He informed Denise he would be arriving from Pwllheli on the high-tide, the Saturday of the craning-in.

"That's fine, Mr Robinson," I heard her say, "but it would be helpful if you could pick up a mooring out on the trots for an hour, until the crane has finished. We may have to shuffle the other boats around on the pontoon. Your berth will be clear by midday, I can assure you, and the pontoon will still be well afloat. You'll have plenty of time."

I heard his voice from the other side of the desk.

"… and I'm not picking up those filthy buoys in the river, either. I've got visitors with me. I'll come straight in, so make sure it's clear. You bloody women don't know what's what."

She'd held the phone away from her head.

"I think you need to speak to Mr Blackwell," she said. "He'll be supervising that day. I'm sure you can come to some agreement about what's best. His number…"

"How are we going to manage him?" she said, as she put the phone down. "He's impossible."

"Could Arnie ban him, refuse to have him here?" I asked. "We can't tolerate abuse like that. Have we got a sign anywhere, about abusive behaviour, or something in the contracts, like they have in clubs and GP surgeries?"

"Never needed it before," she said. "He only brought his boat here last year and I hardly saw him. Phone Arnie, to warn him."

"Me?"

"You're the manager. Happy Easter."

Enthusiasm waned and anxiety crept back into my life, quietly and insidiously, with a subtle change in the way I perceived the day-to-day work-list, which was no different, but the lists grew ever longer. The week before the lift-in, the yard was filled with busy owners who washed green algae off white hulls, polished their boats with the eco-friendly cleaning materials I'd stocked, and expressed surprise at their effectiveness. I was busy all day, talked business over potential sales, checked with Denise I was doing the right thing and organised Don's precious time for his work schedule.

We were in demand every minute, and no-one noticed or cared about our welfare; phones rang, coffee and lunch breaks were interrupted, customers complained and requested instant attention, and had to be placated. I felt as though I'd been picked up from the extraordinary and wonderful solitude I'd experienced on my own out at sea, then beamed up and dumped in the middle of Piccadilly Circus.

My dreams at night were punctuated with arguments and distorted, ugly faces; Tracy Downs, with her sly eyes and tight face, and nasty Mr Robinson, with bald head and piggy eyes. The old nightmare came back to haunt me, and Doug Peterson's eye-sockets with the crawling crabs were enough to wake me from restless sleep well before dawn. I chewed my finger nails, sat up in bed and made lists before the sun rose, snacked on toast and chocolate bars during the day and seriously considered another visit to the GP for some pills.

A lovely, long, email from Helen in Sydney, saved me. I hadn't expected it. I thought she'd shut the door behind this corner of Wales after her Nain died. I felt a surge of something inexplicable, when reminded there was another world out there.

'Love the job. *Silent Witness* eat your heart out. Absolutely fascinating. Don't much like the floaters and murders, but the business of investigating how diseases kill people and the work with the research labs makes it all worth-while. AND, I have a new partner. She's in publishing, so books and body parts over a bottle of Hunter Valley Shiraz after a day's surfing… Come and visit. You'll love it. I want to hear your news. You? Sailing and racing? Really?'

Another surprise, as I answered the phone to an unknown, local number.

"Cassie? It's Veronica. From *Pegasus*. Come for coffee, tea, drinks on the boat? To celebrate Spring and a booking for my first, paid client. Do come."

I escaped from work for the afternoon, and so I could have a drink, took the bus to Pwllheli so I could have drink. I was excited for Veronica at the start of a new venture, although she had exuded such an aura of self-confidence and capability during my training, I had no doubts about her ability to make a success of it. She was also someone you felt you could ask for help, someone who could stare your problem in the face and use life and wisdom to advise.

I was also curious to know about the connection between her and her ex-husband and Doug Peterson. I had a feeling Doug had been more than just an engineer contracted to service *Pegasus*. He'd stolen the expensive powerboat with the intention of picking up the cocaine, killed a man in the process and nearly destroyed it by fire. Would they have known about his other life? Not Veronica, I hoped not. She must be tough to still want the boat after the sordid events on board.

After a large gin and easy chat about life in general, I told her my background and about the inheritance and latest work plans; I didn't spare the ups and downs. She knew some of it. After this, I felt I could ask about Doug Peterson.

"Did you know Doug Peterson well?" I asked, as we sat in the cockpit and soaked up the warmth from the afternoon sun. "I mean, it must have been a terrible shock when you heard it was your boat on fire."

She nodded, then disappeared inside the cabin and came back with topped-up glasses and a dish of olives.

"I'll tell you about that man," she said. "Now that you've told me your story. He was a friend of ours, from way back, and we're talking twenty years or so. That's when we bought our first caravan in Abersoch, like so many other people. We all had a bit of money to get started, small powerboats and sailing boats and a big social life on the site, as well as being members of the club here. Then more money, bigger boats, berths in the marina and so on. We met Doug Peterson in the club. He was way ahead of us in size of boats and had a big fifty-footer in the marina, which he stayed on at weekends; a foreign thing that was built in the Philippines. He'd sailed it back from Bermuda."

"Sounds like good times," I said.

"They were. The boat was big enough to hold parties; people spread out all over the deck on cushions, there was loud music and always cold beer and champagne; well, fizzy plonk. I remember the fore-cabin, all done out in red velvet-type upholstery; very plush. The social life at the club and on boats like his, became a main part of the weekends, after racing. We worked all week and then let our hair down at weekends; a bit of excitement racing, then parties and drinking.

'Then, of course, the inevitable flirting, swapping, creaking relationships, even break-down of marriages; too incestuous, too close, invited back to boats like this, or big yachts, for late night drinks, cooped up in small spaces with too much booze late at night."

I didn't see that as much of a problem, I thought, lots of friends on a boat, but was she ever going to get back to Doug Peterson? She settled back in the chair and tipped her face up to the sun, legs outstretched and eyes closed.

"Well, there's always one, isn't there, to stir up a hornet's nest?" she said. I waited.

"There was a particular woman, twenties, pretty, well, she thought she was, blonde hair, long legs which she flashed around in short skirts, and she had a figure to die for; a real man-eater. Married, but she flirted outrageously with all the other married men, whether their wives were there or not. Nobody took her seriously; she was friends with the wives, as well."

"And you?" I asked.

"Not me, no. Couldn't stand her. She was a two-faced bitch and she called me a snob. Words were said one night, in the club. Common as muck, darling, and that awful Brummy accent. We didn't socialise."

I bit my lip.

She took my glass without asking. I was riveted by then, could have written the script, like a sea-going soap-opera. But not the next part.

"Then," she said. "She struck up a relationship with Doug. Not openly, but people do see things and gossip. She came up during the week, presumably when her husband was at work, and stayed at the holiday home, but she'd been seen sneaking down the pontoons in the marina at night."

I knew before she told me. "What did her husband do?"

"Some sort of recycling business in the Midlands. Oh, and they owned a garage for expensive cars. She always drove something different; flashy, big, foreign things, you know? She arrived in a Lamborghini once, but usually drove a Mercedes. Borrowed from the business, probably."

I would have fallen off the chair, if it hadn't been such a snug fit. David and his 'girlfriend'? Not possible, Cassie. What a ridiculous thought. And Arnie with a posh car garage? Why had I never known that?

I swallowed. "Then, what happened? I mean, if it was true, did her husband find out?"

"I don't know. The summer came and went, people disappeared for the winter and the next time we saw her, she had twin boys in a pushchair and a proud husband. They didn't come to the marina after that for a long while. Then they changed their holiday home to be near Black Rock Sands."

"It was Arnie Blackwell, my boss, wasn't it? His wife Shelly and the twins in the drugs bust? Okay, so I worked that out, but can I ask, was there a connection between Doug Peterson and your husband, other than old friends and powerboats? Something to do with your divorce, you said?"

She swivelled the white, leather chair round and faced me.

"That bitch took my husband away from me. They'd been having an affair for a couple of years; the same MO as she did before. She was here again on her own before she was pregnant with the youngest one; Ben, isn't it? She never wanted him, you know. That's what people said. The twins would have been about twenty and at work and Jason was at school. She never wanted him either, you know. He was about thirteen, then. He obviously had to look after himself while his dad was at work and mum was up here, screwing my husband. Poor lad was left at the mercy of his foul brothers. She just abandoned him."

"Did Arnie know?"

"Not for a while. It was just before your time up here."

"Then…?"

"Then I sued my husband for adultery; took him to the cleaners, darling, and David helped me. Another drink?"

I shook my head, brain fuzzy with the gin and stunned to silence.

"But Arnie took her back, even after that? Doug Peterson and then your husband?"

"Don't ask me why. Mother of his children, I suppose. Maybe he's besotted with her. Who knows?"

"I never knew any of that." I said, "but then, I can't think of anyone who would tell me without upsetting relationships. He's my boss, after all. I'm best kept in the dark, obviously. At least I can make my own judgements and I don't really like gossip. It hurts more than it heals, mostly. But it does make me wonder where his head is."

And where my head was, as I tried to fathom out coincidences with flashy cars and stupidly, unlikely scenarios. David, traditional, formal, and pernickety, and Shelly, tarty arch-bitch? Get real, Cassie.

Veronica walked along the pontoon with me and up the ramp, stopped at regular intervals to say a cheerful hello to other boat owners, and introduced me; a warm, sociable lady, comfortable in her own skin, and with presence, but she had been through tough times. I liked her very much, and still reeling from the afternoon's revelations, I gave her a hug. She stood back and put her hands on my shoulders and held my gaze.

"If you ever need to talk, or run a problem past me, just phone," she said "You've got too many dark shadows under your eyes for someone so young."

She turned to go, and then said, "There was one thing I didn't mention. Did you ever get close enough to wonder why all Arnie and Shelly's children looked so different?"

I could hear Helen's voice as clear as though it was yesterday. The pair of us had stood behind the counter in the snack-bar after Tomas drowned and we'd served burgers to the Blackwell family for the first time. That was a long time ago, but I hadn't forgotten.

"Funny thing," Helen had said. "Those twins have got blue eyes, but their younger brothers, that boy Jason and baby Ben, have brown eyes."

Blue or brown, one could inherit either, but Doug Peterson had blue eyes, steely-blue eyes when he was alive. Was that what Veronica meant?

The bus dropped me in the High Street and I walked back to the yard, head buzzing with questions.

"Where the hell have you been?"

Arnie strode up the yard, arms swinging like a gorilla and biceps bared below short sleeves. He wasn't due until Thursday night, before Good Friday and the craning-in on Saturday. It was only Tuesday, late afternoon and Denise had gone home for the day.

"Hi Arnie," I said, all charm. "Meeting my powerboat tutor. I wasn't expecting you."

I was still in a benign mood from the gin and lulled by the bus-ride back, despite trying to digest the news about the man who stood in front of me, arms akimbo and near enough a scowl on his face. Too chilled to respond in kind, I was scarcely able to look him in the eye. Difficult, when someone has revealed some startling secrets about the wife of the man you are face-to-face with. You see them in a different light, they don't know what you know, and you can't let them know.

"Mr Robinson's been to check that the pontoon will be clear for him on Saturday. Good thing I was here, with you gadding off, God knows where. I thought you'd dealt with it. He said you were useless, and that's not all."

"I told him you'd deal with it. Denise told him he'd have to stand off for an hour, if he came in at the top of the tide. You'll be busy lifting the other boats in, Arnie, and using his space on the pontoon to do so. He'll be in the way. That's all. She was very polite."

This was the other side of Arnie, I thought, and the white streak in his black moustache twitched when he moved his mouth, like an angry magpie with its tail feathers pulled.

"I told you to look after my clients," he said, and jabbed his finger at me.

I was suddenly very angry. The alcohol wore off and the stupidity of the man and the knowledge about his marital disasters fuelled my temper. The worries and tiredness of the last few weeks spilled over.

"Don't you dare point your finger at me, Arnie Backwell. If you think Denise and I are going to tolerate abuse from misogynistic boat-owners with manners like pigs, you can find someone else to run your yard. We're doing a brilliant job, sold one of your precious expensive boats and all the other owners are pleased with the service. The yard is spick and span, the shop well-stocked, the accounts in order and all the engineering work is up to date."

I didn't give him time to reply. It felt good to let off steam.

"So, your Mr Robinson can take a hike if he badmouths me, or Denise, and I'll slap a banning order on him, as stated in the contract and he can take his boat elsewhere. I can do that, I've checked. So, if you can't back me up when you know I'm in the right, I don't want to work for you anymore. And what's more, you won't find anyone else at short notice to rescue the business for the summer. So, fuck off, Arnie and think about it."

I turned on my heel and stormed into the showroom, up the stairs and slammed the door to the flat. Then I howled for an hour.

At eight o'clock, and still upset to consider dinner, cheese-on-toast seemed to be the only option, but the toast stuck in my throat and I threw it in the bin. I considered I'd probably signed the death warrant on my job. How could I face him again?

But by nine, I had nearly talked myself into a state of righteous indignation, the moral high-ground not far away, when there was a tentative knock at the door. He filled the door-frame, huge but stooped, the Zapata moustache peeping out from behind the roses.

"Sorry," he said, from behind the blooms.

He must have cleaned out the flower-stand in Tesco, and he'd brought wine as well, and a meal-deal for two.

"I met Angela. She was on the late shift, stacking shelves. I told her what you said."

"What did she say?"

"She bollocked me. She talked sense, bab. Said you were right to be angry. Said misogyny was never acceptable. I'd never used the word before, just heard it. Never really thought about it, but I have now. She's a good lady."

"Told you she was," I said, closed my eyes and took a deep breath in relief, and put the oven on.

He stayed over in the spare room again, and it was only when he'd emailed Mr Robinson in the morning to corroborate my instructions, and walked out into the yard, that the word 'conjecture' danced back into my head again. Flowers and wine, late visitor. Well, good luck, if anyone was watching. I was fine about it. We talked about the yard; that was all.

I was still unable to understand why his wife had returned to the family home after he'd thrown her out, and he seemed quite happy to have her back, even asked her, maybe. Or had she enticed herself back into his good books? After being unfaithful, twice? He must have known. Or was he blind? Did he ever suspect he was not the biological father of those boys? Was he, or wasn't he?

If it was true, and he'd never known, what would his reaction be to her, if he found out after all those years of subterfuge? Those boys cost him a fortune, so he'd said, and he'd indulged them and his wife for the sake of peace, but they let him down with their criminal activities, bullied their brother, compromised their father's reputation, and wrecked his mental state for a while. If he was their biological father, he'd have to take some blame for it; if not… well, that was a dangerous conjecture. I wouldn't want to be around when he found out. I would say nothing.

The morning had dawned fine for the Saturday lift-in, the sun, a huge yellow globe above the Rhinogs, a promise of summer round the corner with the sky tinted peach and rose. By lunchtime, Don and the crew had craned in the last of the powerboats and the mobile crane from the yard next door had arrived in the nick of time to crane in *Annie* and Paul's little yacht, ready for its new owner. Tracy Downs, with bouncer and friends, filled the cockpit of the Sea Ray and were already laughing and screeching their way through bottles of champagne.

"Thank God the tide's falling. Hope they're not thinking of a trip out," Arnie said, as the
engine roared into life. One of the men had climbed out onto the pontoon and bent down to the mooring ropes. Arnie shot down the ramp, an impressive turn of speed for such a big man. I leaned over the rail and could hear his voice.

"Everything alright after the lift, Miss Downs?"

"This guy wants you, Trace," someone in the cockpit shouted.

She emerged from the cabin.

"Just going for a spin, Arnie," she said. "Want to come? Glass of bubbly?"

General laughter.

I leaned over further, itching to hear how he would handle this one.

"Look, Miss Downs, Tracy, that's not such a good idea just now."

"Why not? It's my new toy. Not going to sit here if I've paid all that money just to look at it, am I?"

The bouncer tapped her on the arm and she bent over him, straightened up and looked at Arnie.

"Why not?" she asked again.

Arnie pointed to the current gathering pace out in the channel.

"It's a spring-tide and it's going out fast. You've missed the flood. It'll kick up a chop on the bar and you might get stuck on a sand-bank on the way back in. It dries very quickly. Best to go tomorrow on the rising tide and give yourself plenty of time and water under the keel." He pulled at his pony tail and scratched his head. "Could be a long night, all of you out there in the dark, high and dry on a sand-bank."

The bouncer nodded his head. Some sense to make up for the lack of hers, I thought. She went back inside and switched the engine off, came out into the cockpit and pouted. I could see her expression clearly, even from up there.

"Have you got life-jackets for all your friends?" he asked politely. "We have plenty in stock."

"How much are those?"

"Sixty pounds or so. Each."

"You must be bloody joking," she said.

The bouncer looked at Arnie and nodded.

"That was interesting," I said, as he came back up the ramp. "He seems to wear the trousers, after all."

"Fucking idiots," he said. "God help us."

But we hadn't finished yet.

"Better radio Mr Robinson," I said, "and let him know he can come over to his berth, now."

He'd brought the boat over from Pwllheli an hour before high water, and I'd watched through binoculars as one of the passengers picked up the link-line between two buoys and looped it over a cleat. He was moored, sort of, but really only loosely tethered, like an obedient horse, and they'd settled down in the cockpit to drink. I could hear the shouts of laughter over the water. I fetched my marine radio from the showroom and walked back outside.

Arnie stood at the edge of the harbour wall. "Something's going on over there."

Two of the passengers stood up and waved frantically. The shouts were drowned by the noise from Tracy Downs and her guests.

"Will you shut up for a minute," Arnie shouted down to the pontoon, his voice as loud as he was huge.

They did, and the words came clear across the water. "My husband's collapsed. I think he's had a heart attack. We need help. Can somebody come over, please?"

I tried the radio, but there was no answer. We ran down to the pontoon. The yard's inflatable dinghy with its outboard engine was always ready to go, and Arnie belted us across the channel to the boat. I climbed on board.

Mr Robinson, his ruddy face now a dirty grey colour, was slumped on the floor, his eyes open. He was conscious and breathing, but in obvious pain. I wished I'd been able to take a photo of the look on his face when he saw me; it wasn't one of relief.

"I've given him his pills. He's got angina but I've never seen him this bad. I'm his wife," the woman beside him said, near to tears. "Do something," she pleaded.

They'd all been drinking and the other guests sat around in the cockpit, shocked from half-pissed laughter into stunned silence.

Squeamish, I didn't do blood, never mind heart attacks. I looked up at the console and the engine-controls and blessed Veronica. I'd be better at this than Arnie, I reckoned. He'd only driven jet-skis.

"I can do this," I said. "Call an ambulance and be on the pontoon to take the ropes." He didn't argue, and sped back over the channel to the pontoon. "Now," I asked politely, "who's the least pissed out of all of you and knows what to do?"

One of the men stood up. "I'm the one who picked up the link-line," he said. "I'm Carl."

"Right. When I tell you to, lift the line off the cleat, throw it well away from the boat, then sit down. When we arrive, throw this one rope to the big man on the pontoon, and don't miss. We'll sort out more ropes afterwards. Okay?"

I put fenders out on the port side, tied one mooring rope mid-ships and bent down to speak to Mr Robinson.

"I'm going to take your boat over to the pontoon, sir. We've called an ambulance. Sit tight and don't worry."

Sir? Look after my clients, Arnie had said. Well, I was, even if this one was a rude pig.

He stared at me, hand on his chest, pain, and disbelief on his face. He said nothing.

I switched the engine on and checked the throttle, forwards, neutral and reverse. I'd only ever made that mistake once.

"Now," I shouted to Carl.

I turned the wheel gently to port and the ebb caught the hull on the starboard bow and helped to turn her into the stream, facing the sea.

"Where are you going?" One of the women stood up, her face tight, and waved her arms about. "We need to go over there," and pointed over to the pontoon.

I'd brought *Annie* into the harbour wall enough times to know the effect of the tide on the hull.

"We're going up to that green buoy, round it and then motor down on the other side of the moorings. There'll be more control bringing her in against the flow of the tide. It acts like a brake," I explained. "Please sit down. It'll be fine."

Compared to manoeuvring *Pegasus* with its fly-bridge, the boat was smaller and beautifully responsive and if it hadn't been for the sick man at my feet, I would have enjoyed it. The hull kissed the pontoon, 'like a maiden's breath,' as Mark was fond of saying, Arnie caught the rope and I switched off the engine.

There was a round of applause and cheers from Tracy Down's guests, drowned out by the wail of sirens, and the welcome sight of blue, flashing lights. If I'd been a man, nobody would have applauded me, carrying out a job that any self-respecting manager of a boatyard should be able to do, but I decided to accept it graciously. I thought I'd done quite well, considering my hands still shook with the stress of it all.

"Not smoking salmon today?" the paramedic asked, with a grin on his face, as he climbed on board. He was the same one who'd held my hand and pumped me full of oxygen on the way to hospital. Small world, round here.

We stood back and waited while the paramedics conducted tests, deemed him fit to be moved, then eased a slightly recovered, white-faced Mr Robinson from the boat and, with Arnie's help, pushed him up the ramp in a chair. His wife and guests followed, sober and chastened, with reassurances that I would moor the boat properly. Arnie walked back to help me.

"Well done, bab," he said, enveloped me in a bear-hug and squeezed gently. Over his shoulder, which I barely reached, I saw Tracy Downs lean over the side of her boat, with her arms up and the phone held high, pointed at us. Taking a photo of the crisis, I thought. Bet she'd snapped the poor man as well. It would be just like her to plaster it over Facebook.

But Hugh's words, 'Give no cause for conjecture', sang in my ears, and I understood then. Arnie, and me, and the hug. Bitch. But I still didn't get it.

CHAPTER 13

The yard settled to a peaceful afternoon, with warm spring sunshine, the tension from the event with Mr Robinson and the lift-in, finally over. Denise brought the business phone, a bottle of wine and some beers outside, and we sat on the harbour wall to celebrate, albeit with thoughts and concerns for Mr Robinson. I rang the hospital. He would be admitted for a few days, but was comfortable. Usual spiel. I sent my best wishes, on behalf of Madoc Marine.

"I thought you couldn't stand the man," Denise said. "I mean, he was so bloody rude."

"That's not the point," I said, at my self-righteous best. "I wouldn't wish a heart attack on anybody."

She sniffed. "He didn't have a heart attack."

"But he might have done," I said. "Perhaps he'll be pleasant in future. Gratitude and all that."

"In your dreams," she said.

I poured more wine and Arnie and I settled to discussing the merits of the boats below us.

"Can you stand in for me at Whitsun?" I asked Arnie, after a few beers. "Just for three days? I've been invited to crew on a race to

Ireland. It's all part of the training for the Day-Skipper Certificate. You could bring Ben and stay in the flat."

He opened another beer and nodded. "It'll be half-term. His mother won't be at home, anyway. She's off somewhere on holiday with a friend for the week. I was wondering how I was going to manage him. The babysitter can't do days. I can't have him running around the scrapyard now, can I? It's a dangerous place. He's better off up here."

So much for sharing and caring. How could she do that? Selfish bitch, and not much net-working there, I thought, opened my mouth, and immediately wished I hadn't.

"Why can't his mum have a holiday when he's back in school?"

He didn't reply. I'd touched a sore spot, and it was none of my business, but I needed to know if I could go on the race or not.

"If the Bank Holiday's a problem…"

"No. I'd have to stay here at night for the security. I'll tie him to the railings, or something, during the day."

"Perhaps Angela could help? She works shifts and she's fond of Ben. Shall I ask her?"

He grunted, drained the bottle and got up.

"I'm going back home now," he said. "You and Denise can manage the rest of the Easter break between you. I've got another business to run. Keep doing what you're doing, you'll be fine, and thanks for this morning. You handled that boat like a pro. Perhaps he'll mind his manners in the future. Good PR for the yard, too. It'll be in the papers and I bet you've put it on Facebook already?" he asked Denise.

"Of course," she said.

He left. It had been a busy week and I thought he looked tired and disgruntled, maybe an anti-climax to the busy day. It had ended well; the craned-in boats were on their moorings, or tied up to the pontoons, and the owners happy. Even the event of the day had been handled successfully. His enthusiasm for the development of the yard seemed to have drained away, and his comments about his wife left me uneasy. Were the wheels coming off, I wondered? Were Hugh's warnings about a potential breakdown of the marriage to be taken seriously? Then I remembered the hug he gave me, and the phone in Tracy's hand pointed at us, and 'conjecture,' stormed back into my brain. I couldn't make sense of it, couldn't connect one thing with another, but knew there was something afoot I should think about.

I wandered down the yard to lock the bottom gates to Madoc Marine for the night, and check the Boat Shed gates were still secure. Then I opened them and walked into my yard. It was eerily quiet, the ground now cleared ready for the new-build, its only occupant, Hugh's little yacht in its cradle. Paul's boat and *Annie* were moored to the harbour wall safely, with their keels just touching the mud and as the tide fell, I checked the mooring ropes for tension. The new shed would be erected during May. The cliff-face behind had been secured with bolts and ivy and brambles were already beginning to encroach on the netting.

I sat down on my favourite bollard. The river ebbed clear and deep-green below me and the sweet evening song of a blackbird broke the silence. Over on Ballast Island, a heron paddled in the shallows and hunted the tide-line. A wave of nostalgia hit me, a longing for the simplicity of this undemanding piece of land, devoid of noisy engines and fussy boat owners, arrogant clients, business profit and loss and the sodding family dynamics that over-shadowed it all.

Then, for the third time, I felt that undefinable sense of a presence, another soul in my space. I'd left the gate open and the gravel that had always crunched underfoot had been mashed into the mud. I turned to see a tall man with a close-cropped beard, a tanned face, light brown hair with sun-bleached streaks swept back off his face, a shambling gait and bronzed arms set off by the sleeves of a white T-shirt. Closer, and I knew those elegant hands and long fingers, and not a patch of eczema in sight.

"Jason?"

He swept me up and hugged me breathless. Where was the gangling teenager? It had only been a year. We'd swapped a few messages, but that was all. He'd left the mess up here that had followed him nearly to disaster, and I respected that. He had his own life down south, and had said he was never going to return.

But here he was, as though the clock had been turned back to the quiet evenings we'd shared at the end of a day's work. All the worry he'd caused me faded away to nothing. He looked down on me, the little brother I never had.

"You've shrunk," he said, and we whooped and shouted and held hands and danced around in a circle. Then we stood and stared at the void where the Boat Shed had been.

"It'll be back," I said. "Same, only different."

His orange camper-van fitted into a vacant spot in the yard and I ordered Chinese to be delivered. After a conducted tour of Madoc Marine and the showroom, I opened wine. We'd never really socialised before; the relationship had been one of reluctant carer to an errant child, even though Jason had been nineteen. I now entertained a grown man, stranger in some ways, and my closest companion in others.

With filled glasses, we sat on the harbour wall above the pontoons and watched as darkness fell over the estuary; the cry of the black-headed gulls as they swooped past to roost, and the sudden silence when the blackbirds turned in finally for the night. Stars speckled the sky in the east. There was no sign of Tracy Downs, the bouncer, and guests, and I presumed they were indulging in the night-life of the town.

The boats on the water were occupied by their owners who could now stay on board legitimately for the night. Their presence on the pontoon below the showroom and over the channel on the trots, induced a feeling of intrusion I couldn't explain; laughter floated across the harbour, and the purr of outboard engines cut through the silence as the inhabitants visited each other by sea, shared meals and chat. My winter solitude was in the past, the night belonged to others now, and the evening chill drove us indoors.

"Your dad only left this afternoon. I'm sorry you missed him," I said, as I set a tray for the meal.

"I'm not. Not much to say, is there? He knows I'm getting on okay."

"What about your mum?" I asked, with a feeling I was, yet again, on dangerous ground.

"What about her?"

The meal arrived, and we shared news over noodle-filled mouthfuls.

"I didn't know what I wanted after dad sent me down south," he said. "I was still shocked and knackered after all that business with Emily and the drugs stuff. I found a bed-sit near the boatyard and made friends at work. The wooden boat-building was great for a bit, learning about the methods and how to use tools and that. And I was going through an environmentally-friendly stage; yachts, driven by the wind, and using natural materials. Like your yard was, I suppose. Then I looked at the glues that we were using, and the power-tools, and it all seemed a bit hypocritical. But that wasn't it."

"So, what made you change your mind?"

"I went to the pub one night and met a guy from a powerboat design and construction yard down the road; son of the owner. We sort of hit it off, and after a few beers, we had a friendly argument about power versus sail."

I could guess what was coming next.

"So, he took me out for a test drive in one of his dad's prototypes."

"Sold, were you?" I could imagine the speed.

He nodded, eyes shining with the memory. "The yard gave me a work-experience slot. Dad helped me out with a bit of money as I wasn't earning much. Had to work in a chip-shop at night to keep me going. 'Anyway, they asked me to stay on and do an apprenticeship in boat-building. I know it's not eco-friendly, but, bloody hell, Cass, doing sixty knots up the Solent is something else. I miss the smell of planed wood, though. It's a bit soulless working with fibreglass and I wasn't sure I made the right choice to start, but, like, when you see the finished hulls finally complete, and all the fittings on, it's like a butterfly emerging from a chrysalis. Know what I mean? Like those ones in your yard, but bigger and so bloody fast. Then, when I get to go on the test drives…"

I understood, completely. He wiped his mouth with the back of his hand like an enthusiastic teenager again, full of ideas about design and hull speed, poured more wine, chilled out and finally got around to his family. I hoped he would.

"Ben said he'd stayed up here with dad in the holiday," he said. "He's got his own phone, so we have a chat now and again. He told me Angela looked after him once. I remember her; Tomas's mum."

"She's great. Even puts your dad in his place," and I told him about the telling-off she'd given him about attitudes to women, and the roses, and how much Ben liked her.

I told him about David, the sailing and powerboat tuition, and the rude but poorly Mr Robinson and the new Boat Shed plans, and then the wine kicked in and I told him about Daniel. Then I told him about my state of confusion over the direction in which my life was going; the whole bloody lot, and then I couldn't stop.

"And to top it all, there's this underlying feeling, like I had with the drugs-trafficking before I knew about it. Somebody doesn't want me here. It's like a shadow following me round, taking care what I do and who I do it with. I don't get it and I don't like it and that's why I thought of selling the Boat Shed and running away from it all. And then I got so busy, I sort of forgot what I promised I'd do, and changed my mind. Oh, I don't know."

I'd rabbited on long enough. He didn't seem to mind, listened intently and with a degree of empathy, I hoped. But I hadn't finished.

"… and then there's this bloody woman…"

I described Tracy Downs and how unpleasant she'd been, even how she looked, with her tight face and over-blacked hair and always chewing gum. I don't know what came over me but it was a release of tension just to be able to talk about her, vindictive though it was. I convinced myself it wasn't really me talking. Too much wine, and the release of stress from the day and the fact that Jason and I had shared so much, I knew I could tell him anything, but on adult terms now.

"She'd even made snide comments about me and your dad being an item. Several times. Now, how ridiculous is that. He's old enough to be my father, never mind yours. And she took a photo of us this morning when he gave me a 'thank-you' hug on the pontoon. But Hugh said…" I stopped, realising I was into the realms of Hugh's theories and I was talking to Jason, whose parents' relationship I was blithely about to discuss. Embarrassed and cross with myself, I cleared away the meal cartons, mortified I'd forgotten who he was for a moment. When I went back into the room, he seemed unperturbed and was on his phone, then he switched it off.

"That woman? What's her name?"

"Tracy. Tracy Downs. Why? And your dad didn't know her, but he said he thought he'd seen her somewhere before, but couldn't think where."

He put the phone down on the arm of the settee.

"This is hard to believe, Cass, but I know about my mum and her relationships and how dad took her back. I also reckon she doesn't want us in her life when Jem and Zac are released. She's moved back in with dad, but I reckon she's up to something."

"That's horrible. But what's Tracy Downs got to do with anything? You shouldn't be talking about your mum like this."

"Yes, I should, if what she's doing affects us all. That Tracy Downs, she's one of mum's friends. I recognised your description. She runs a nail parlour in Dudley. I don't remember her ever coming to the house, so dad wouldn't know her but he must have seen her around somewhere. 'When I was younger, mum used to drag me along when she had her nails done. When you described her, I remembered her. Well, she would buy a boat up here, wouldn't she, probably at mum's suggestion? After all, dad owns the yard. What did you say? Taking pictures of you and dad? I bet she's taken more than one."

"What are you saying?"

"I bet mum's gathering evidence for a divorce. She'll try and get this place for her and the twins and she'll try and screw dad out of it if she can."

"But that's what Hugh thought," I said, horrified I could have been so naïve. Arnie had stayed at the flat, quite a lot of nights, when I totted it up, brought wine and roses, and all the time, I bet the bouncer was up the road taking photos. I hadn't taken the idea of Hugh's 'conjecture,' seriously and dismissed it, because I chose to. How stupid was that?

We sat in silence. He didn't seem upset or surprised and he read my thoughts.

"We were never going to be happy families," he said. "I've got so used to it that nothing surprises me. Now you know why I'm staying as far away as possible. Dad will have to work this one out by himself."

"A court would never believe that photographic stuff. He's the boss. Why wouldn't he stay here?" I asked.

"Clever lawyers," he said, and I thought of Veronica.

"Should I say something to Tracy? I mean, just to get her off my back?"

The thought of a confrontation with another one of Arnie's clients was too much. It was only suspicion, but if he believed his wife had set us up, God knows how he would react; like pouring petrol on water, I reckoned. And I would be responsible.

"Go sailing," Jason said. "Carry on doing what you've planned. It'll sort itself out, one way or another, and the right way. Let it lie for the moment, Cass."

"You think that's best?"

"Yes. That's what I think."

He slept in his camper-van that night, and in the morning, two hours before high-tide, I left a note on the showroom door; 'out for an hour to check on boats' with the radio channel and my phone number, in case anyone wanted me urgently. Tracy Downs had already left the pontoon for a trip out with the tide, as Arnie had suggested. She still hadn't bought any life- jackets, that I knew of. A few other boats that we'd lifted in, had vacated their moorings in the channel.

I made butties and put coffee in a flask, and we took the yard's inflatable with the big Mercury on the back, and zoomed over to the beach at the end of Penrhyn Point with Portmeirion tucked around the other side. It would be open now for the season, to show off its stunning Italianate architecture to the public and would be heaving with visitors. Our beach was deserted, the fake lighthouse a flash of white against the backdrop of orange berberis and yellow gorse that flourished on the cliffs and fringed the paths.

I drove the boat up into the warm shallows and we paddled in the sea and sat on the beach until the tide turned. Within minutes of the start of the ebb, the water would run out like a drain and leave us high and dry. Jason pushed us into deep water, I started the engine, and he jumped in. If I'd looked down at us from above, I thought, I would have seen how comfortable we both were; on the sand, in the sea, on and out of boats, with an easy familiarity with the environment, and remembered that when we first met, neither of us had been much further into water than a warm bath or a chlorinated swimming-pool. Proper water-babies, now.

At the confluence of the river channels, I turned the boat towards the sea.

"We'll go as far as the Fairway Buoy," I said, "just to check all's well with our boats. It's the first time out for some of them. Don't want them stranded," even if I disliked them, I thought. Good for PR.

Tracy Downs, with bouncer and guests, had managed as far as the No1 buoy before they'd cracked open the bubbly.

"Everything okay, Miss Downs?" I asked politely, as we drew alongside, but not too close. I cut the engine.

"Yeah, why wouldn't it be?" she said, and took a long, hard look at Jason. A shadow of uncertainty crossed her face.

"My boyfriend," I said, gesturing towards Jason. He raised a hand, and looked hard at her too. "I'm just making sure all Mr Blackwell's clients are okay. Engine fine? We'll leave you to it, then. The tide's turned by the way. I wouldn't stay too long before you make your way in. Could be a long night out here if you run out of water."

The guests laughed; hesitantly.

I restarted the engine. Then I couldn't resist it.

"Not taking photos today?" and shot off down the channel back to the yard. That'll give her something to think about, I said to myself.

"Was that a good idea?" Jason asked, as we made our way up the ramp. "And 'boyfriend?'"

He hugged me and left, on his way to Dudley to see his mum and dad, so he said. Somehow, I felt he wouldn't. He waved out of the window and the orange paintwork and unmistakable burble of the VW camper disappeared up the road.

There was no sense of loss, only happiness that we could be so comfortable together, and that he was well, and enjoying life. Also, a sense of relief that I'd been able to share so much in so little time, an unburdening I needed, and even though he was part of it, the objectivity to his unpleasant family situation was a comfort. Go sailing, he'd said. Let it lie. I would; just for now.

I stood in the gateway to the yard for a few minutes and let the sun beat down on my back. Heat radiated off the rock-face above me and a single whistle from one of the Ffestiniog engines as it pulled carriages full of happy people across the Cob, filtered over the harbour. Flies and bees hummed in the young nettles at the base of the cliff. How lovely. And it was only April.

The footings for the new shed had settled and baked hard in the sun and I waited patiently for the news of delivery. *Gardencraft* assured me all would be on time. The flat-bed trailer arrived in the second week of May, the sections were unloaded, and work to erect my new Boat Shed began. The yard bustled with activity. Hugh arrived and tutted about the dust on *Capella's* paintwork, I fed the guys tea and coffee, and made brownies to Helen's Nain's recipe. I also started up the smoke-house and turned-out a new batch of salmon and some smoked trout, the fish locally sourced near Criccieth.

Life entered a new phase again, with productive work and a pleasant, chatty, easy-going atmosphere in both yards, and the ugly scenes from the early spring faded away with the glorious, sunny days. There was no sign of Tracy Downs or the rude Mr Robinson, still alive and kicking after his heart scare, other owners told me, and Arnie left us to it; "mad busy down here, bab," he said, on the phone. I sold two new boats, prepared Paul's little yacht, still lying comfortably against the wall next to *Annie*, for the new owners, and phoned him in Dublin when it was ready.

It was the first time I'd had a chat with him since he told me he'd sold it and was intending to buy a new boat. It was good to hear his Irish lilt, even if he had been a dickhead last year. We bantered over his missing finger, exchanged talk of work and the yards and the new Boat Shed. I'd sent him pics of the old one after the rock-fall. Then I told him about my sail-training with David and the race at the end of May.

"I can't wait," I said, "and the night-hours will go towards my Day-Skipper Certificate. Where is your new boat, by the way?"

I couldn't help my enthusiasm and felt guilty I'd talked about myself so much. The phone went quiet for a second.

"Cassie?"

"What?"

"Do you fancy crewing for me, back to Ireland? My new boat is in Holyhead, see, and it's hard to get someone who's had some experience. I mean, if you're doing Pwllheli to Dun Laoghaire with a race crew, Holyhead to Howth would be easy. What about it? I'll pay the ferry back. You can add it to your hours, for the Day-Skipper qualification. End of June. What do you think?"

I didn't think. I said, "Yes. What class of boat?"

"She's a Sadler," he said.

"Okay, good. Bit bigger than your old one, which her new owners are ready to collect, by the way. I'll send you the invoice for the winter season and the crane-in."

At least he'd be unlikely to go aground crossing the Irish Sea, I thought unkindly. Also, by then, I'd have that much more experience. A definite 'yes'.

Fizzing with excitement and the prospect of two Irish Sea crossings, I watched as the Boat Shed took shape. I took pictures daily and sent them to my mother and Trish, and Daniel, back in the UK after another trip Home to Trinidad.

"Looks great. Holyhead on business next week. Will call you. Fancy a night away?"

The cedarwood cladding, expensive but worth it and the beginnings of the long front porch raised above the ground, were exactly as I'd planned; a veranda for easy chairs and chat. I'd asked for big double doors on the gable-end near the slipway so boats could be moved in and out easily and the shed began to morph into a western-style log cabin, my drawings knocked into shape by expert hands.

The front door I intended to paint red, the same as the original, though that had been faded and peeling. I didn't suppose my great-uncle had painted it in twenty years. I'd added more windows for light in the entrance area, but kept the storage part blank, for security. An insulated chimney-pipe poked out through the felted roof. The gulls flew by, perched on the bollards in the yard and looked speculatively at the roof awaiting its protective ridge-tiles.

The days fell into a routine, busy but peaceful and apart from weekends, most owners were saving up their holiday allowance for Whitsun at the end of the month. I sifted through the clothing stock in the showroom and chose a red Helly Hanson sailing jacket, navy salopettes, life-jacket and harness, and put it through the till at cost. More essential gear for training, and I'd okayed it with Arnie.

"I'm enjoying this life," I said to Denise, at the end of one afternoon, mouth full of left-over brownies and feet up on the desk. "It's peaceful and manageable."

"Wait for Whitsun Bank Holiday," Denise warned. "It'll all ramp up again."

"I won't be here to worry about it," I said. "Arnie's problem. I'm going to sea."

I considered Daniel's suggestion of a night in a hotel. Much as I would have enjoyed it, I couldn't leave the yards unattended.

"Stay here, for the night," I said on the phone. "Denise goes home at five. I'll cook a meal."

I cleaned the flat from top to bottom, changed the sheets on the bed, bought best Welsh sirloin steaks from the butcher in the High Street, chose perfectly-formed new, local potatoes from the green-grocer opposite, and wheedled Angela's salad dressing recipe out of her from across the till in Tesco. She divulged it, reluctantly, but only on threat of death if I shared it with anyone.

The starter was easy; my best oak and apple, wood-smoked salmon, Welsh cheeses for dessert and two bottles of expensive Burgundy. Slightly uneasy about spending a night with him in the apartment and not understanding why, I fussed around, moved furniture about and vacuumed underneath, and left Denise alone downstairs in the office.

"For God's sake, what are doing up there?" she shouted up the stairs at four o'clock. "I'm going early for a hair appointment. Day off tomorrow, remember? I'm covering Saturday for you. Take over, Cassie, will you? I've been here since eight, anyway."

Friday morning, I would be away by eleven, ready for lunch and a briefing on David's boat, then off on the tide. My stomach lurched with excitement, and I had Daniel's company tonight, to boot.

I bounced downstairs to the showroom. Daniel had said he'd be there about six o'clock. I'd said, no earlier, please, and lied, or I might not be there, but I didn't want him to bump into Denise. To explain I'd been sleeping with her previous boss would be too much to explain. I hadn't forgotten how totally smitten she was when he first came to the yard; 'he's gorgeous she'd said.

I had it all planned out. If there were no owners in the yard, I would shut the gates at five and still have an hour for the final touches, like a shower and a change out of work-clothes into something more suitable. Not silver fish tonight, though, or the little, black dress; just me in a pair of clean jeans and a T-shirt. This was my domain after all.

I opened the bottom door into the showroom. The main doors whispered open and Daniel stood in the entrance as Denise walked out of the office door. I stood in the middle. Her hand flew to her mouth. She stopped dead.

"Oh, Mr Freeman," she said, flustered and looked at me. "So nice to see you again. Have you come to see how the yard's doing?" and she held out her hand. "You remember Cassie, of course?"

"Of course," he said, and offered his hand, the tissue-wrapped bottle of wine in the other.

"You'll have to excuse me," she said. "Cassie will look after you, I'm sure. She's the manager, you know," and favoured me with me an unfathomable look.

"Yes, I know," he said and smiled at me.

"Excuse me for a moment," I said to Daniel. I followed her out.

"You bloody dark horse, you." Trish's words again. "How the hell did you do that?"

"Explain on Friday. Bye," and shut the driver's door for her.

In the morning, I opened the bedroom window wide and let the birdsong flood in on salty air. We sat up in bed with strong tea and I conducted a virtual guided tour round the mountains in the distance, blue and hazy, with the pointed summit of Cnicht unmistakable. High pressure dominated the whole of the country and light northerly winds were firmly in charge.

"Can you stay?" I asked, tucked up against his shoulder.

"Not now. I have business in Holyhead for the next two days and then up to Scotland."

"Can I ask about Holyhead? I thought you'd abandoned the project you were discussing."

"Early days yet. Do we have to talk?" he asked, and we forgot about breakfast until later. At nine o'clock, I unlocked the main gates and bolted them back while he turned the Porsche around, got out and perched on the bonnet with his arms folded across his chest.

I remembered the first time I'd seen him in casual clothes, and this morning, the slim-cut jeans and fitted white T-shirt he wore, defined his chest muscles and contrasted with the tan that spoke of a life in warmer places. God, you're beautiful, I thought. He stood up and watched me walk towards him, a studied, serious look on his face. He ran his hand over the designer stubble, then reached out and wrapped his arms round me. He held me tight for longer than I ever remembered, then kissed me, lightly, and stood back with his hands on my shoulders.

"Hey." A voice broke the moment. "Is that shop open yet?"

Tracy Downs marched through the gate. "I couldn't get in before. The car's up the road. I need those life-jacket things."

"Don't you have the code, Miss Downs?"

"Yeah, well, I forgot it, didn't I?"

She looked Daniel up and down, stared at the car and looked at me. For a moment, she stopped chewing.

"My boyfriend, Miss Downs. He's just leaving. Do excuse me for a moment while I say goodbye."

Daniel nodded politely, got into the driver's seat and I put my head through the open window.

"Who's she?" he asked.

"A nasty bitch," I said. "Give her something to talk about." She couldn't hear me.

The Porsche, sparkly-blue in the morning sun, purred out of the yard, and he blew me a kiss as he turned through the gate and onto the road. Her face was a picture of disbelief and confusion and I knew she was desperate to ask about him. Two different boyfriends in two days? She'd have a field day with that; like, did one boyfriend know about the other? Then what about the fictitious affair with Arnie? I had to stifle the laughter that bubbled up in my throat and escorted her into the shop at the back of the showroom. None of the nonsense with the pics she'd taken seemed serious any more. Two can play at that game, I thought, and relieved her of three hundred pounds for four life-jackets.

"Mike told me to get them. He's paying. Expensive, this boating stuff. He said he wouldn't go all that way to Pwllheli without them. Might drown out there," quite chatty for a change. Wonder why? "We're going over to the marina for the weekend and I'm taking friends. And we're going to the Sailing Club on Saturday."

"Very nice. Do you know someone to sign you in?"

I had to explain. She didn't like it.

"Perhaps take plenty of food and drink for a party on your boat, then," I suggested. "Or you could join the Club? I'm sure they'd be delighted."

"How much would that cost?"

I tapped into the website and turned the screen towards her.

"Fucking hell," she said, grabbed her purchases and left.

I didn't sleep much Thursday night, my head full of the charts of St George's Channel and the Irish Sea, and my calculations for the race based on wind forecasts. Although David would share his own plan at briefing, he said that I should use the experience as though I was the skipper; it could contribute to the requirements for the Day-Skipper Certificate, when I would have to navigate through a three-day practical, whenever I could find the time.

That was nothing to the barrage from Denise on Friday morning, when I bundled my sailing-bag downstairs to the showroom, life-jacket slung over my shoulder and a bacon butty in one hand.

"I haven't got time to explain," I said. "I need to go now."

"No, you don't. You haven't got to be there until twelve, you said, and you're not sneaking off for the weekend without telling me how, when and where you managed to snaffle that creature. I mean, he's just gorgeous and charming, was the owner of all this and God knows what else, and just look at the state of you, most of the time in your old overalls and grubby hands. As for your nails… Sit down and tell all. Now. You've got ten minutes."

So, I told her. Some of it.

"Wow," she said. "I mean, is it serious? You'd be made for life."

"For God's sake, Denise, why are you always trying to pair me off? First David, now Daniel. They're just friends. I'm not in love with either of them."

"Yeah, but this one stayed over."

"Well, he's good in bed," I said, and picked up my bag. "We had a lovely time. Going now. Bye," and I'd shot through the door before she could draw breath.

CHAPTER 14

Sunset, and with barely a breath of wind, the fleet ghosted through Bardsey Sound into the Irish Sea. A copper sky blazed over the landmass of Ireland, a barely-visible grey smudge on the horizon. The distant land seemed to nibble away at the setting sun, and the blood-red orb diminished in bites, until it finally disappeared in a panorama of indigo and midnight-blue. Then darkness fell like a blanket, and the white hulls and masthead lights of the racing yachts were just visible, but slowly disappeared into the dark as the boats separated and skippers varied their courses. The weather-stations had warned of increasing wind strengths later in the night, and the multi-coloured cruising-chutes and spinnakers were packed away in their bags down below.

High pressure had settled over Scandinavia and a run of easterlies with cloudless skies was forecast for the next few days. Porthmadog would bask under these conditions; the town, nestled in its protective armpit of Snowdonia and the Lleyn Peninsula, would trap the heat, and was often rated the hottest place in the British Isles. The warmth would sink into the pavements on the High Street, bake the sand on Black Rock Sands and warm the clear pools left by the tide; a children's paradise for buckets and spades and model boats, the wrappings of winter clothes discarded for bare skin and Factor 50.

But out at sea it was a different matter. By two o'clock in the morning, it was freezing. David and Al, Heidi's partner, had settled in for some sleep after the first watch out of Bardsey and at midnight, Heidi and I took over. Dressed in my new and expensive gear, with thermal hat and gloves, and at a steady five knots on a reach, Heidi and I took turns at the wheel as the wind increased, and the self-steering complained. The course, 290 degrees should, theoretically and according to David, stay constant, accounting for six hours of flood countered by six hours of ebb, at least until we neared the Irish coast.

"You shouldn't need to touch the wheel," he'd said. "Unless, of course, the wind picks up or changes direction." Which it had.

I'd only spent time with David's sister once; she held the bucket while I threw up on my inaugural race to Ireland, and reassured me that my sickness would pass, which it didn't and the seas would become less nasty, which they didn't. This time, with David and Al asleep off-watch, and without the curse of sea-sickness as well as my increased confidence and knowledge from the training, we'd sat for a while and let the self-steering do the work. She chatted about her job as a geologist, full of enthusiasm and funny stories.

"I move around between the Irish and North Seas, wherever they send me. We're drilling constantly for new oil and gas supplies. The oilrigs in the North Sea are something else, though, especially when it blows and you can feel the vibrations from the waves bashing around the base. The wave-heights scare the pants off me sometimes, but at least it's outside and I'm tucked up inside on my computer with central heating and excellent food."

A wave splashed over the pram-hood, wet my face and white water surged down the side-deck, and dribbled into the cockpit.

"This is getting a bit silly," I said. "My arms ache."

"Not silly enough for the skipper. I'll take over in five minutes. Keep going. You're doing great. We'll do thirty minutes each, okay?"

I nodded, slightly anxious now. It had never been this rough during my sailing weekends. The waves were short and steep and the bows crashed through them, flinging sprays of water high above the surface. My gloves were wet and slippery on the wheel and I had to work hard to keep the boat on course, veering off to avoid the worst wave-crests and then back on course. Heidi seemed unperturbed, which boosted my confidence. Perhaps it was supposed to be like this.

"Funny thing is," she went on, as though we were sitting comfortably in a café drinking cappuccinos, "every time I sail over here, I think of oil and gas under the sea-bed and what it was like at the end of the Ice Age," and she waved her arm at the sea, "that's what makes it interesting; all this covered by fresh-water lakes and forests and animals. I mean, you could walk across to Ireland, like the giants…"

"Should we put a reef in?" My stomach tightened.

Sylvie lurched off course as a large wave hit the bow and the speed dropped off.

"Better check with the skipper first," she said. "He'd be more pissed off if we did the wrong thing and slowed us down, than he would be waking him up. You know he's a speed freak, don't you?"

David's head appeared, bleary eyes squinted and the black curls tousled. He looked up, studied the sails, and shook his head.

"Carry on," he said, and closed the hatch behind him.

"He's very trusting," I said.

"He speaks very highly of your ability," she said.

Oh yeah, I thought. Only sometimes. And only when helming his boat. And doing what I was told. As for the rest of it, I was too busy keeping the Irish Sea out of my eyes to remember and fret over his numerous disapprovals about my personal and business life. Heidi took a long look at my face, unclipped her safety-line and clipped it back on behind the wheel.

"I'll take over now," she said. "You've had enough. We're quite safe, really. Sit and enjoy. There's only an hour of the watch to go, then we can hide down below. At least it's not raining," and she touched my arm, gave me a big smile and took the wheel.

The wind and wave-heights remained steady and I'd sat with my back against the bulkhead, faced aft and watched the waves as they boiled up, lifted the hull, and swept underneath and away, leaving a broad wake, momentarily smooth, until the next wave.

Without the responsibility of helming, lulled, then mesmerised, into a hypnotic state of unreality, the world outside ceased to exist, and I disappeared into a heightened state of sensory awareness confined to the immediate; black sea, curling crests foamed white, shush of the sea as it broke and creamed alongside, the whine in the rigging when we surfed down the back of a wave, the constant, physical onslaught of the wind, cold hands, salt water on my tongue, and wet cheeks.

The hatch opened and the aroma of fresh coffee filtered into the cockpit. David shook my arm. "Coffee in a flask and ham butties in foil. They're wedged in the sink. Have a good sleep."

My expensive gear dripped in the wet-locker, and I lay down fully-clothed, pulled the sleeping bag over me and barely remembered to pull up the zip. I dreamed of nothing; a dead sleep, a total blackness of subconscious mind; asleep and only separated from the wildest, most inhospitable environment imaginable, by a thin shell of fibre-glass, the outside fraught with dangers, devoid of safety-nets and totally in the care and trust of one human being.

At seven-thirty, Heidi and I rolled from our bunks early, the motion less violent, and daylight a welcome sight through the side-windows. I cooked masses of bacon in the oven, buttered baps, and David came down below to update the course.

"We're heading north to avoid the overfalls this side of the Codling, then over to the north Kish at slack water at the latest. Don't want to get swept onto the bank when the ebb starts. Keep the course until eleven then call me. All hands after that, until Dun Laoghaire."

The wind stayed fair in the east, the sun shone and the Kish and Burford Banks were left behind in the realm of fictitious horror possibilities, as we swanned into Dun Laoghaire Marina. David poured the mandatory whisky to celebrate our arrival and we waited for the rest of the fleet to appear. Twenty yachts in total had set off, all different classes, and Heidi talked me through handicaps. We waited patiently for the results in the ambient surroundings of the Royal Irish Yacht Club and downed several pints of Guinness during the inevitable and exacting debrief from David.

"Not bad," he said, to sum up.

Heidi punched him in the arm, but then siblings can do that to each other and get away with it. Al sniffed and rolled his sleeve up to show off the bruises where he fell against the coaming whilst furling the genoa, and I sat back and enjoyed all of it. Showered and changed, with pre-supper drinks and a meal at the club, we were entertained to live Irish music, drank far too much, and danced until midnight.

We won. Of course, we did. Not many skippers would have pushed so hard, I was told by a fellow sailor who congratulated us later.

"We don't do pink and fluffy on *Sylvie*," I said, then wished I hadn't, knowing full well that I'd been scared at times. But nobody else heard me, and the guy was drunk, anyway. Heidi and I left ahead of David and Al, who were deep in conversation with another crew. We swayed along the pontoon arm-in-arm, sang Irish songs, and giggled like a couple of teenagers. She stopped, turned, and put both hands on my shoulders.

"What?"

"Oh, nothing," she said. "It'll keep."

With barely enough sleep to kill the hangover, we prepared to leave after an early breakfast, and with the morning ebb, follow a reciprocal course, pick up slack tide in Bardsey Sound in the early hours of Monday morning, and arrive in Pwllheli on the flood, to go our separate ways and back to work on Tuesday. I thought I could sit back and relax for this return journey, until David called me down below.

"All yours," he said, as he vacated the chart table. "I'll check your calculations when you've finished."

"You're joking," I said.

"You want your Day-Skipper Certificate, don't you? The forecast is good, the wind hardly worth mentioning, so use your judgement to get us back in time."

Heidi and I stood on the pontoon after lunch, ready to untie the mooring ropes. During the afternoon a resident yacht had appeared next to us on the opposite pontoon. It was slightly longer than our Sigma, with stainless-steel davits glittering on the stern, and a dinghy strung up precariously between them. I didn't envy David the job of reversing out of the narrow berth around it and out into the main channel. Heidi followed my gaze and shook her head.

"Rather him than me," she said as he started the engine, then jumped off the boat onto the pontoon.

"Take us out, please, Cassie. It's no more difficult than Pwllheli."

And no, he wasn't joking. He stood on the foredeck, while my hands sweated on the wheel, thanked the heavens there was no wind and inched the boat straight out, the davits so close I could have touched them. The stern swung around beautifully in reverse, and I shifted the gears and motored out of the marina. David favoured me with a quick nod, disappeared below and went to sleep.

"The stress was too much for him," Heidi said and I couldn't disagree. I dried my damp hands on my T-shirt, and motored out into open sea. Heidi and Al put the sails up without a hitch and I headed for the Kish, puffed up like the proverbial bullfrog with achievement. Al sat on the foredeck and absorbed himself in his phone, but Heidi stayed in the cockpit. She seemed relaxed, but I saw her eyes flick to the compass and the instruments more than once. She watched me like a hawk.

The ebb pushed us along at five knots for a few hours, and the wind stayed light and veered southerly; then it became barely a whisper. The sails flogged.

"What should I do?" I asked Heidi, uncertain whether to tack and catch more wind, or sit there like an idiot, miss the tide at Bardsey and risk the wrath of skipper and crew. My initial pride in the negotiation of the marina took a serious tumble. Not for the first time did I appreciate the contrast between all being well, and the immediate effects when plans went awry.

"You're in charge. It's your call, the skipper said."

The speed dropped to three knots.

"We'll motor," I said, and looked for her approval. She nodded, clipped her safety-line on and joined Al on deck to lower the main while I switched the engine on. I hadn't asked. He said to use my judgement and I sat back and let the autohelm do the work. I knew that Heidi, an experienced sailor, would have corrected me. I also knew that if we missed the tide at Bardsey, I would not be popular, and I hoped the diesel tank was full.

Innocuous wavelets flattened to a grey, undulating swell, the glassy surface punctuated by groups of little auks and bunches of floating seaweed. It was too far from land for gulls and gannets, but the auks bobbed up and down like toy ducks, sea-miles from nowhere, and totally at home. I altered course to steer clear of two fishing boats pair-trawling, and gave a coaster a clear berth as it tramped up to Scotland and beyond.

Al made tea and passed the biscuit tin up through the hatch.

"Skipper's still asleep," he said. "Must have been all that Guinness."

The engine ticked over comfortably and pushed the boat at six knots, despite the slow-down effect of the flood tide. There was time to chat.

"Do you miss London?" Heidi asked, out of the blue, after swapping student stories.

I wanted to say no. I wanted to say how much I envied her childhood in the country with the sea just down the road. I wanted to say I'd seen her childhood home on Google Earth and how stunned I was by the size of the property, but I couldn't admit that, I thought. Then I didn't need to.

"Have you been to our place?" she asked. "Well, mum and dad's place."

I shook my head. Why would I?

"You know my dad, though? He did all your legal stuff, David said. Funny old stick. Mum still irons his handkerchiefs, you know. He insists on a clean one every day."

I know, I know. I know more than you think. But I couldn't say.

"Hell of a big house," she said, "and all that land, but it's mostly rented out to farmers, but David's well entrenched in properties and management. He always knows who to ask when mum and dad need help. Developing quite an empire, my small bro."

"Really? I thought he was just a solicitor. I know he does divorces."

David and properties? He never said. But then, I never asked. Private joke, and I smiled to myself.

"You met the lovely Veronica, then? David's her hero forever. He made sure she got what she deserved; cleaned her husband out. Silly man, having an affair on his own doorstep, especially with that tart. Veronica's quite a character. Of course, you did some powerboat training with her, David said. And she's started her own business Wonder if she'll present the race trophies in the autumn. At the laying-up ball, you know."

I didn't know, and, 'that tart?' Good description of Shelly, I thought, and wondered what Heidi would think of Arnie, his wife, and the 'conjecture' still spinning in my brain.

"Why would Veronica present trophies?" I asked.

"Commodores usually do," she said. I wasn't surprised.

David appeared, iPad in hand.

"All right for some, idling around while the rest of us work," he said. "I see you got this far without a disaster."

We laughed then stopped. The engine had coughed once, and then nothing. The silence was palpable.

"Prop? Fuel? Check the engine, will you, Al?" and leaned over the side.

A carpet of matted weed floated to port, the fine tendrils spun to a brownish-red mossy felt and intertwined with orange and blue strands of twine. A heavy-duty fishing rope, coiled in the middle of the mass, had spread tentacles, woven itself through and out to the side, and one long length had disappeared beneath the hull. From the stern, it was clear to see how it might have wound itself round the prop, too heavy to lift with the boathook.

"I'll go," I said. "I've done this before," stripped off shorts and T-shirt and dropped into the sea. David handed me a knife.

"Be quick," he said. "We can't afford to lose any time."

The engine coughed back into life; one of the fuel filters had blocked, and Al had worked furiously to change it.

"How could two things go wrong at the same time?" I asked, knowing the answer.

"Comes of gossiping and a modicum of bad luck," said Heidi, "and we were having such a nice time."

Back on course, we were summoned for a briefing. David was unusually serious.

"We'll have to miss slack tide in the Sound," he said. "It wouldn't matter that much if the wind stayed light, but I've checked the forecast and it's going to blow hard in the early hours. We'll have to go through while the ebb's running and the wind's reasonable, or we can't risk going through at all. I'm not putting us through strong wind against tide in the middle of the night, or anytime, come to that. You've all read the warnings in the pilot. It'll be rough, though."

"How rough?" I asked. Couldn't be much rougher than the night passage on the way out, I thought. He side-stepped the question.
The anti-cyclone over Scandinavia had intensified, the isobars closer together over the UK and the wind, Force 5 to 6 easterly, was due to pick up before our original plan for passage through Bardsey.

"It's that, or go south of Bardsey and I don't fancy being anywhere near Bastram Shoal and Caswenan Rock in the dark with a big sea running. Not only that, we'd have Devil's Ridge and Muddy Hollow to negotiate. What do you think, crew? The Sound, and batten down the hatches? It'll only be rough for a short while."

Out of my depth for any contribution to decision-making, apprehension bordered on anxiety, but I did as I was asked, prepared sandwiches and flasks, and Al and Heidi readied the boat; anything that could move or fall was stowed away; mugs and pans stuffed into cupboards, bottles sandwiched between cushions, kettle tied down with a bungee cord, cooker gimbals bolted home, weather-gear and harnesses ready, hatches locked, sea-cocks checked.

"This is like preparing for war," I said, down below out of David's hearing. "I feel sick already, and it's not sea-sickness."

"She's a good boat," Al said. "She's designed for speed and a bit of abuse. It's always the humans that fail. You'll be alright. Just sit tight

and do what David tells you."
He gave my arm a reassuring squeeze, which did nothing to help at all.

My easy-going sailing mates were transformed; one minute happy to chat and gossip, drink and dance and laugh; the next, they morphed into an experienced, focused team, prepared for a tough job, and their quiet preparation instilled in me some confidence, and a considerable dose of humility. It would take years of this tough sailing to produce that level of efficient preparedness. I sat out of the way in the cockpit, watched them and kept quiet, while Al and Heidi set the genoa into a handkerchief and reefed the main. We were ready.

Pitch dark, and at two in the morning, the wind began to increase, straight out of the east, as they said it would, and David angled *Sylvie* a fraction off the wind. It caught the sails, and she picked up speed as the ebb tide, still running strong off The Tripods, met the wind head-on and threw the boat around like a toy.

Water broke over the bow, surged along the side-decks into the cockpit and sluiced round our feet as the drains struggled to cope; waves rose in peaks from all directions, picked us up and dropped us off the crests in a welter of white foam. David shouted once to hold on tight, and the boat seemed to drop, disappear into a hole, the bows buried completely. Clipped on, my hands gripped onto the coaming, frozen in terror, I thought the boat would founder, and we would all drown. Nobody moved, the engine surged but kept going, and I watched David as he jinked the helm, on and off the wind, to power us through.

Then it was over; the sea rough, but bearable, and we were out of it, headed for Trwyn Cilan to miss the north end of the Devil's Ridge.

"Well, that was fun," Heidi said. "Anyone for a sandwich?" Rigid, speechless, muscles tensed to the point of snapping, I lifted my knees up onto the cockpit seat and crouched against the bulkhead, unable to move, shaken, shocked, traumatised by the violence, and unable to pull myself together. A strange, unaccountable bubble of hysterical laughter formed in my throat but there it stayed. Al thrust a sandwich into my hand and a beaker of hot tea into the other, bent down and peered into my face. I was still unable to form words to thank him.

"Drink," he said, and waited while I drank it. "Now eat."

Like a robot, I lifted the sandwich to my mouth. Spaced out, on another planet, distanced from reality, I chewed and swallowed, as a sharp voice cut through the whine of the wind in the rigging.

"Take the helm, Cassie, if you please, while Heidi and I clear up below. Straight through the Roads and try not to pile us up on the Tudwals. You've done it before. We'll be able to sail free after Trwyn Cilan. Al will trim the sails for you."

A hint of pearly dawn in the east with the Tudwal Islands and Llanbedrog behind us, I helmed the boat to the Pwllheli Fairway Buoy as though nothing had happened, but I smarted at the skipper's peremptory instructions, when what I wanted was comfort, sympathy, and a reassuring hug from someone. But I knew, deep down, that's what he had to do to rescue me. There were no prisoners on this race; there or back.

Heidi and Al furled the sails, and David took the wheel from me with curt thanks, berthed the boat back into its customary place in the marina, disappeared below and came back into the cockpit with four tumblers and a bottle of Glenfiddich.

"A toast," he said, green eyes bright with enthusiasm. The black curls, tousled with wind and water, fell untidily over his forehead, as unlike a working solicitor as I could imagine. "That was hellish scary, and you were all bloody marvellous."

At least he admitted that it was scary, but he didn't say he was scared. Different entirely. Unlike myself, still a rookie sailor with delusions of grandeur in becoming more than just a competent crew and boatyard caretaker, I now knew the feeling of true fear for the first time in my life; uncompromising, immobilising terror with no control over its effects, and only saved by those more experienced than I imagined I would ever be.

There was no redemption gained by my reasonably competent boat-handling and easy sail back from Bardsey. I'd done it before, as the skipper said, and whether it was self-doubt that I would ever be able to make those decisions under those circumstances, or fold up in a heap and cry, I would never know, unless tested.

After breakfast, Heidi and I used one of the marina trolleys to wheel our gear along the pontoon and up to the car-park.

"Are you okay?" she asked. "You're very quiet."

I couldn't answer. She stopped and dropped the trolley wheels onto the pontoon.

"Look," she said. "I know how you're feeling; deflated, embarrassed, exhausted…"

I stared at her.

"…'cos we've all been there, bashed around in huge, confused seas for the first time, well and truly terrified. You were frightened because it was outside anything you've ever experienced before and shocked by the physical violence of being thrown around. We were all apprehensive, verging on scared, probably, but we've sailed with David many times in foul seas. He knew what he was doing, and if he'd thought he couldn't get away with it, we'd be heading back to Ireland now, rather than weather hours of gales hanging around out at sea. Al and I knew that, but you didn't. It was as bad as gets, Cassie, but it was only a short, sharp bit of nastiness. Next time, if you ever go cruising again and you hit bad weather for a long time, you'll be better able to measure your reactions against it."

Lecture over, we pulled the trolley up the ramp to the gate.

"Actually," she said, when we'd drawn breath, "it doesn't get much worse and Bardsey Sound is notorious, so you did well to pull yourself together and sail *Sylvie* back. It's now, when the adrenaline drops, you feel like a bit of road-kill."

The vision of a flattened squirrel, horrible though it was, made me smile. Just. But I'd listened, and was grateful. I wouldn't forget what she said.

We unpacked our gear into respective cars, walked to the front of the marina reception, and watched David and Al as they left the boat and followed us up. Heidi stood by my side with her arms folded, legs apart, freckled face and no-nonsense short hair, solid, and reliable as the rocks she studied. I watched her, as she watched her brother wait for the security gate to swing open, then she turned towards me.

"You know he's in love with you, don't you?"

CHAPTER 15

I'd never been in love with anybody and I hardly ever considered it was not the same as simply loving someone. I'd loved my dad, and Milly, even Helen's Nain, to a degree, and decided that the level of love was related to the misery of loss that ensued without them. I had a serious affection for Jason, and Denise, and Will Roberts, and Hugh, and all the other friends who were a part of my working life. As for Daniel, what I felt was not much more than an enjoyment of the passionate melding of bodies, and a lot of fun. Would I miss him if I never saw him again?

I'd pulled into the layby at the top of the hill on the way out of Criccieth, parked and looked back towards the castle and the town. The sea, as blue as the sky, glittered and sparkled; the early-morning land-breeze ruffled the surface and caught the sunlight, the swell rolled in gently, without fuss or foam, to kiss the shingle beach below me.

It promised yet another hot day, and a group of holiday figures had already gathered on the jetty below the castle. Cars began to fill the parking spaces on the promenade, resident dog-walkers gave way to families with buckets and spades and a lone kayaker skimmed out into the bay with a leisurely dip and swing of the paddle.

I needed to take stock, to consider Heidi's words about David, before

I returned to face work and boat-owners, and I needed sleep above all else before I could consider the implications rationally. Fat chance of that back at the yard, I thought, with Bank Holiday demands, and Arnie in charge.

With eyes closed and my head back on the headrest, the first thought that entered my head was one of disbelief and to dismiss it as rubbish and nothing else but the playfulness of a loving sister. However, none of that rang true with what little I'd come to know about her. She wouldn't make something like that up. Then the chatter began. On what basis could she possibly say that?

He'd been curt and brusque in his instructions, which he hadn't been on the training weekends; even sarcastic once, made me work when I was exhausted, traumatised, and needed a dose of TLC. He was angry, I'd thought, with my fragility, my shocked submission to extreme fear; disappointed, disgusted even.

Had he said something to her, a close confidence between the best kind of siblings, who could share secrets without judgement? I had no experience of siblings, and was still learning to be more circumspect with whom I shared anything; except Jason. He was as near to a confidante as anyone could be.

Then one thought led to another. If it was true, if David Hughes, solicitor, and now, as I'd discovered, property developer and a whiz-kid with divorces, a personality with a bizarre mixture of conventional family values and attitudes, a passion for a dangerous sport, but over-cautious with others, charming but not sexy, still single, then he had a strange way of showing his affection. Was our skipper-crew relationship, all part of the test? Was it a test? And, my brain in overdrive, why was he still single? And then, I remembered, the glitzy girlfriend with the flash car I'd been told about, and his short replies after my polite enquiry as to her welfare post-Covid.

So, who was this strange man? I'd never really sat down and thought about him, apart from his penchant for irritating me in the past with his overcautious opinions, and now grateful, if not a little bemused by his recent offers to develop my sailing skills. The next question, if it was true, how would I feel about it? Then I opened my eyes.

Perhaps it was the sight of Criccieth Castle, castles generally associated with keeping people out, and in, and all the unpleasantness associated with incarceration, that unsettled me further; the image of a dark cave, a stifling blackness of oppression and entrapment as opposed to the wide-open sea below me, a silky sheen of blue stretching far into the distance, one vast stretch of water connecting with another, for thousands and thousands of miles.

A picture flickered in my brain, from one of the Hans Christian Anderson stories my dad read to me as a child; the picture of tiny Thumbelina, crouched against a dark wall of earth and how the mole captured her, took her far below ground to his maze of tunnels, and kept her there to prepare for the marriage he'd planned with her, to be underground forever, and never to see the open sky again. I remember recoiling with horror at her fate, until the swallow she'd rescued flew her to freedom. But for this story, I would have to rescue myself.

To have someone in love with you, someone like David Hughes, intelligent, well-read, attractive, capable, and to have nothing in your emotional arsenal with which to reciprocate, was beyond my tired mind to analyse. All I knew, as I switched the engine on and turned into the road, was that it brewed a strong feeling of choking claustrophobia. I would have to pretend I never heard it, carry on our relationship as before, hope he took the hint and let him teach me as much as I could learn. Then I could escape and sail away, be my own swallow, with white sails instead of wings.

"Fanciful rubbish," I said to myself. "You're bonkers from lack of sleep," switched the engine and the radio on, and was blasted into reality by the blessed, heavy guitar riffs of an old *Foo Fighters* song, drove off and turned off after Pentre Felin, to take the single-track road leading to Black Rock Sands and Morfa Bychan.

I passed the church where poor little drowned Tomas, my great-uncle and his children, my great-nieces and nephew were buried, stopped to gaze at the sweep of the estuary below me and away to the east, the sand-banks high and dry and the channel a winding snake out to the bar with the Rhinogs grey and hazy in the distance.

Seven years ago, it had meant nothing to me. Now, I knew every inch of its shifting dangers and my gaze followed the buoyage out as far as the Fairway, and beyond, and beyond that, and something tugged at me, like a dog straining on the leash. I drove on through Morfa Bychan, turned off towards the harbour, couldn't face Madoc Marine for the moment, carried on straight past the gates and turned into the Boat Shed yard.

It was finished. The guys from *Gardencraft* must have worked over the weekend. My new Boat Shed stood, in all its cedar-planked glory, the covered veranda at the front begged for chairs and a bottle of wine, the new windows glinted in the sun and someone had tied a pink ribbon and balloon through the door handle. I laughed and then cried a bit, wiped my eyes on my sleeve, and opened the door to several envelopes on the floor; a card from Steve Lewis to say 'Welcome Home, from Steve and Jackson', another from Will Roberts and Mark, and the invoice from *Gardencraft*. I didn't mind. No surprises there.

On my old, but newly-installed counter to my left, polished and burnished to a rich brown, stood a bottle of champagne and a glass jug with pink roses, and behind, the old stove with a new coat of black paint, was laid ready with sticks. A new electric kettle stood on the window-sill by a jar of coffee, some dried milk, a tin of assorted biscuits and some new mugs. Who was it that put all these things for me to find?

My tired mind in a whirl of things to buy, to replace, to restore the ambience of the old shed, and fill its dark interior with the gear I'd ordered, wiped away the desperate desire I'd had, only an hour since, to run away. I wanted to light the fire, sit in the armchairs with new plaid rugs, and share chat and coffee with Mr Roberts and Mark, and Hugh outside with the comforting whine of his planer on *Capella's* hull. Who was it said you can never go back; to think you can recreate something that's been lost? I knew that, but chose not to believe it. For a short period of time, after the fluctuating love and hate, the Boat Shed was the only place I'd called 'home;' a hub of friendship and the beginning of a meaningful enterprise.

But that home was demolished, dead and buried, people changed and moved on, grew older, died even. Could I recreate it, the same, only different? I shut the door, stood on the veranda and the gulls cried and wheeled over the harbour. I looked over the channel at the blossom-coated trees on Ballast Island, and up at the rock face behind me, secure with its new nets and bolts, and thought I'd try, at least. What else was there to do?

Then I was back in the yard, and wished I wasn't.

"Good race?" Denise asked. Ben sat at my desk; a jigsaw-puzzle of an emerging safari park covered the surface; lions and tigers and giraffes, and a polar bear on the edge of a pool.

"Instructional. I need some sleep. Just for a couple of hours. I'll be alright then. Hi, Ben. Had a good time? Are you taking over from me?" I ruffled his hair. "Where's your dad?"

"Gone home," he said. "Will you help me, Cassie? I can't find this piece of lion."

"Yeah, in a minute. What do you mean, gone home?"

Denise ushered me out of the office door.

"He had a letter he brought with him on Saturday when they arrived. He kept taking it out of his pocket and reading it when he thought I wasn't looking. Then he was busy on Saturday, being nice to owners and organising berths and stuff. I didn't work Sunday, but when I came in this morning, he was steaming. He kept whatever was bothering him hidden from Ben, and was lovely with him as usual, but he rang Angela to see if she could keep an eye on him today, until you got back. She changed her shift and she's got today off. She's upstairs now, just clearing up and preparing a meal for you tonight. She said she could look after Ben all week during the day when you're working, and do late evening shifts at Tesco."

"All week? That's amazingly good of her. So, he's left Ben here with us? Why, for God's sake, is something so important he needed to leave him here? And won't he be homesick at night?"

"Ask him," she said. "Angela's been great with them both. I think Arnie's told her something."

I found the lion's leg and helped with the mane, fetched him an ice-cream from the freezer I'd installed in the shop, and asked him.

"It must have been something important at work, if your dad had to go home. How do you feel about being here without him?"

"Okay. I like it here. I won't cry at night. I'm not a baby. And there's pancakes for breakfast. You can put them in the microwave, Angela said, and she's taking me on the train tomorrow. Dad gave us money for the tickets. It's a steam-engine, with smoke an' that."

Angela came down from the flat. She looked at me, cocked her head and I followed her upstairs.

"Something awful has happened with Arnie. Ben doesn't know, but he thought his dad was in a funny mood, so he's been ever so well-behaved."

"Well, what? Is it business?"

She hesitated. "It's not good, Cassie."

I was so tired I couldn't think straight, but somehow, I knew the answer. It wasn't a matter of his guard-dogs eating someone, or a decomposed body discovered in the crushing machine. I looked out of the window towards the channel, and abreast of the harbour buoy, I saw Tracy Downs, bitch, on the fly-bridge of her boat with the bouncer on the helm. The boat slowed down, manoeuvred neatly into the pontoon, and stopped.

"His wife, Shelly. She's divorcing him," Angela said. "She's not coming back, from her holiday, not at the end of the week, or ever, telling of violence from him. Evidence going back over a few months, he said, and the biggest set-up he'd ever heard of for adultery. It's not fair, Cassie. I like him very much and he's a great dad. How can she do that?"

"Adultery? Who?" as if I didn't know the answer.

She hesitated. "You, Cassie, of all people. It's ridiculous. He was furious. He's gone back home to see his solicitor tomorrow and didn't want Ben around. Then he texted me to say he was changing his solicitor for one recommended further away, as it was too close to home down there, and he and Shelly had shared the same one. He said they all talk to each other and he didn't think he'd get a fair hearing. You know what she's like. Probably slept with them all at some time or other. She's got a terrible reputation. It's just horrible."

What was there to say? I expected it, Hugh had predicted it, and it was all rubbish. Angela knew it, too. But I couldn't explain just then. If ever.

"I'm going to bed for a few hours," I said. "I can't think straight. Thanks for looking after Ben. Catch you later."

"I've made a meal for you tonight," she said. "You don't mind?"

"Then stay for tea and we'll talk then, when Ben's in bed. And thanks. I owe you."

"No, you don't. Go and sleep. I'm taking Ben to the beach for the afternoon. Go," and she pushed me through the bedroom door, where I slept, despite it all; a sleep of total exhaustion and woke at five o'clock.

"Five o'clock," I shrieked to the empty room. "Denise'll kill me."

But she'd gone, locked up the showroom and Ben sat at the table with Angela, a boiled egg, and soldiers in front of him, as Angela checked his manners. She didn't need to, but I could see she was perfectly at home with this small child beginning to fill a gap in her life.

Then I thought about Arnie, and Angela sharing his space that weekend, and hoped Tracy Downs hadn't transferred her photographic allegiances at Shelly' requests. But then it wasn't Angela she'd been told to photograph. It was me, and Arnie, my boat yard and my lovely new Boat Shed, and a surge of anger propelled me towards the window. Yes, she was still there, moored up from her trip to Pwllheli, but hopefully going home tomorrow, Bank Holiday over, job and damage done.

After Ben had been bathed, we argued over the bedtime story. I won, and he fell asleep before the ending, while Angela washed-up. We sat on the settee and finished a bottle of wine. Our shared history of Tomas's death was the one thing we had in common, apart from my hope that she would run the snack-bar for me, but I felt she needed to know, and I knew I could trust her. She was also liked by Ben and Arnie. That was enough.

"So, you need to be careful," I said. "In case that bitch wants to include you in Arnie's fictional affairs."

She sat quietly, eyes down and sipped her wine.

"Oh," I said, shocked, but happy, and it was so obvious now. "You and Arnie?"

She shook her head. "Not yet, no, but we could be, if his divorce is settled. He's going to fight the allegations and demands with all guns blazing, and divorce her anyway, and we talked about how to go about it. He was so angry, he needed someone to talk sense. She never came back just for him and Ben, and he chose to ignore it. Silly man. It seems right, us being together and I think Ben likes me. I mean, I've known the family for years, even those horrible, older boys, and I'd always felt sorry for Jason when he was younger and spoiled him when his mother wasn't around."

"That would be wonderful, really, but how do we get on with our lives?" I asked her, "with all this going on?"

No hesitation, and she said, "Carry on as normal. You get the Boat Shed and the snack-bar up and running, hire out your rowing boats to keep the solicitor happy, and manage Madoc Marine. Let Arnie's new solicitor do his job, whoever he is. He's very good, I believe. You'd be surprised what I hear at work.

'One of the guys has a fishing boat in Pwllheli and he was telling us about a woman who has started her own business, bit like you, but doing powerboat training, and her boat was the one Doug Peterson did his drugs run with. You remember *Pegasus*? She and her husband owned it and then she sued her husband for adultery, and this solicitor made sure she got the lion's share of the property, including the boat. They were all rooting for her at the club and he's left the area and gone off somewhere with his tail between his legs."

My skin started to prickle. "Who's the solicitor? Did you know?"

"Well, yes, of course. Can't keep secrets round here. You know that. He's the same one looked after you and the lobster. From the firm in Port."

I felt as though someone had propelled me into the cast of a soap-opera. David could not have possibly known who his one-night stand was; the blonde one with the long legs and the bling car. A false name? A fictional background? Maybe they didn't talk at all and it was just sex. Why would he know, and should he know, especially now? He couldn't possibly represent Arnie if he'd had a fling with his wife, even just a one-nighter. Or could he? I opened another bottle of wine after Angela left, took a glass out into the yard, and sat on the harbour wall. All was quiet in Tracy Down's boat and I was tempted to throw the glass down onto the cabin roof, but remembered I was now responsible for a sleeping child, and pancakes for breakfast.

It was nine o'clock and too late to phone someone I barely knew, but the question gnawed away at me. I didn't think she'd mind.

"Veronica. It's Cassie Jones. I hope…"

"How lovely," she said. "I'm dying to know all about the race. I hear you won. Well done. What can I do for you, dear girl?"

I apologised before I'd even started.

"I can't explain just now," I said, "and I know this is really personal, but could you tell me, is it likely that David would have bumped into Shelly Blackwell in the club, maybe before or after she met your husband and…"

"…had an affair with him?" She laughed. "How diplomatic of you, dear, don't worry, it's all history. I'd love to know why you ask, but no, probably not. Quite a different set of people. She loved the parties and events and David hardly ever socialised in the club in Pwllheli; solicitors are a bit like GPs, I think. They'd rather not bump into their clients off-duty. He always kept to the boat after a race and entertained the crew on board, if at all. I seem to remember he mostly went straight home and only went into the club for race meetings. She'd hardly be there, would she? Will that do? Why, may I ask?"

I skirted round that one, and thanked her very much. "Just curious," I said.

After breakfast, where Ben gave me strict instructions about the pancakes and I insisted he ate a Weetabix as well, I sent him downstairs to wait with Denise for Angela to arrive. She called upstairs ten minutes later, to ask where he was. That cold, sinking feeling crept into my stomach, and I grabbed my phone, rushed down the stairs, called and called, checked the shop and the cloakroom, now in a flat panic and shot outside. Not this, please, not a missing child, not with Angela around, of all people. She was already at the top of the ramp, and I leaned over the rail. Down below, on the pontoon, Ben sat in the cockpit of Tracy Downs' boat, his sun-hat on and a chocolate bar in one hand. She sat opposite him, her feet up on the seat.

I ran towards the ramp, and Angela took one look at my face and put a restraining hand on my arm.

"He's okay," she said. "Don't let him see you're angry. Time to go to the train, Ben," she called, and he climbed out of the cockpit onto the pontoon. "Say thank you to the nice lady for the chocolate."

We waited. He clambered up the ramp towards us, chocolate smeared round his mouth, apprehension on his face; he'd disobeyed the strict instructions from his dad, from me, from everyone, about being outside the showroom on his own, but I knew he'd been coerced.

"Ask him what happened," I said to Angela before he reached us. "Do it so he'll tell the truth. Was he inside the showroom, but bribed to go with her, or did he break the rules and was wandering around out here on his own? Tell him he's not any trouble and we won't tell his dad, either way. Text me straight away."

I reassured him with a smile, wished them well for a lovely day on the train and walked down the ramp to Tracy Downs. The phone buzzed; 'inside, but promised chocolate'.

I stood on the pontoon, seething with anger. Any nearer, and I would have hit her.

"Don't you ever, ever do that again," I said, barely able to keep my voice under control. "Don't even look at that child while he's in my care. That lady up there lost her child, not feet from where we're standing; missing, drowned. He was only nine, and you cajoled Arnie's little boy, and you knew who he was, with no life-jacket, onto your boat? He doesn't even know you. Why, for God's sake? Are you trying to invent some more shit against his dad for leaving him with me and saying I can't look after him?"

"Don't get your hair off," she said, not even on the defensive. "He was wandering around on his own in the yard. I was looking after him," she said, and shifted her gum to the other cheek. God, I hated that bitch "No harm done."

I lost it then, heard my voice high, shrill, ranting over the still morning.

"You're lying. You bribed him out. What sort of lesson did that teach Ben, that he could just wander off with a stranger on the promise of a chocolate bar? You stupid, stupid woman. And while we're at it…"

"Everything alright, Miss Jones?"

Will Roberts leaned over the railings above us. I nodded briefly, turned back to her, and lowered my voice to quietly vicious. I wasn't going to pass up this chance, now I'd worked it out.

"…and while we're at it, don't you dare take any more photographs of me or Mr Blackwell. How much has Shelly paid you? You don't really think those pics you took will stand up as evidence of an affair? His wife won't stand a chance in the divorce settlement if it goes to court. I know what she wants and she won't get it through a trumped-up case of adultery that never happened. It's laughable, Miss Downs, and she's made a complete fool out of you."

She stood there, chewed her gum, uncertain, not so quick to answer back. I didn't give her a chance to ask how I knew.

"And if you ever cross me again, I'll have you removed from this yard for harassment and make sure that Pwllheli Sailing Club know your character before the committee considers your membership. I happen to be friends with the Commodore. Got it?"

She got that alright, made a face, but I knew she was not that easily intimidated. I only guessed she'd applied for membership, cost irrelevant.

Will Roberts met me at the top of the ramp, his comfortable burly figure in a white short-sleeved shirt, clean and ironed.

"Don't ask," I said. He didn't.

We sat outside the Boat Shed on the new veranda in two plastic chairs from the snack bar. I'd made coffee with the new electric kettle and took the mugs outside, the simple task of hospitality helped to settle my thumping anger. We sat, like old times, and chatted about the hot weather, and the race and my training. He'd sold his sheep to Emily's dad, and spent time at their farm when he wasn't on duty, nurturing the new fruit trees they'd planted during the winter.

"I'm going to retire at the end of the summer," he said. "Mark will apply for the job, but there's no guarantee he'll get it. He knows that. And I'll sell the farm and move closer to Port, I expect. All change, then, Miss Jones. And you? What will you do when Mr Blackwell takes over?"

I didn't mind him asking. I just couldn't say, 'cos I'd no idea.

He left, and the energy in his stride as he walked back to the pickup, reassured me that he was coping with his grief and moving on. I was glad; he'd been a major critic of my silly adventures, but he supported and rescued me in such a quiet, unassuming way, I'd hardly noticed, and never took umbrage at his caustic remarks. I shut the Boat Shed door and walked back through the yard to the showroom.

David's Audi was parked outside. He sat in the office, chatting to Denise. Carry on as normal, I said to myself, nothing is different, except the awful possibility he'd had a mad night or two with Arnie's wife, but had no idea who she really was. His choice of bed-mates made me wonder about him even more.

"You left your harness on the boat," he said, "and I was just passing. You'll need it for your next trip to Ireland. When are you going? He's the chap who went aground on the bar and lost a finger, isn't he?"

He knew that perfectly well, I thought. I just nodded. I wasn't going to be side-tracked from my burning question about Shelly. It was too awful to imagine. And should I tell him I knew? He'd have to drop the case, be made to look stupid, it would be unprofessional, if not criminal, if he didn't know the truth. I had to find out.

We walked to the door. I'd worked out how to engineer the question.

"I hadn't thanked you properly for taking me on the race," I said. "I learned a lot; mostly about myself."

He laughed. There was no need to explain.

"Would you do it again?" he asked. "I know it was a bit tough coming back."

"Possibly," I said, "when I've forgotten the terror. Will you race a lot this summer?"

"A few races round the cans, out in the bay, but the big trips are hard to fit in with work."

Here we go, breathless, my stomach in a knot, I said, "I can imagine. Better than last year, though. Everything stopped, didn't it? I lost touch with so many people. Will you be able to see your girlfriend again after last year, with all those Covid restrictions? I couldn't remember her name."

"Oh, Amelia, you mean?" he said, still easy and chatty. "She went back to New York as soon as she'd finished business dealings here. We met at Harvard when I was on a short sabbatical and she bribed me out with one of the classic American cars her family deal in. Ironic that she had to come to the UK to buy the ones they wanted."

"Harvard?" I said, barely able to swallow. "You never told me."

"You never asked," he said with a grin, and slid into the driver's seat. I hadn't time to berate myself for sheer stupidity, or faint with relief, and thought he'd drive off, but he hadn't finished what he'd started, question after question about Paul's new boat; age, condition, previous owner, Paul's experience at sea… I stopped him.

"Look," I said. "I appreciate your concern, but I promise you, if I'm not happy with it, I won't go. You've taught me enough for me to be able to judge, I think."

"Think?" he said. "Is that enough? Shall I give you a list of things to look for?"

"Like what?" I asked, annoyed now.

"Like sea-cocks that work, and a gas alarm, and hatches that lock properly, engine service and in-date flares, radio, and GPS, all the electronics. And checking the forecast. Do you want me to come with you? To look at the boat, I mean."

"No," I said, horrified at the thought. "I can work all that out. It's only a short trip. We'll do it in daylight, easily, but thanks, anyway," and tried to shoo him off as politely as possible, with work excuses.

He leaned out of the car window. "I'm sure you already know that I'm representing Mr Blackwell in his divorce case. Just to let you know. It's close to home for you. He is your boss, after all."

"Nothing to do with me," I said. "I keep well away from births, deaths, and marriages, and especially divorces, if I can. Thanks for the harness and advice. Bye," and he drove off, a puzzled look on his face.

I locked up, bounded up the stairs to Ben and Angela, as though a ton weight had been lifted form my shoulders. His girlfriend, Amelia, and Shelly Blackwell, both with classic American cars? No such thing as coincidences, they said. Rubbish, I argued.

Life didn't seem so bad that night. I put Ben to bed after Angela left, found the story of Thumbelina on my Kindle, watched him drift off to sleep and knew I'd miss him terribly after his dad took him home. I didn't envy Arnie the difficult task of explaining that his mother wasn't coming back – again, offered mental apologies to David for tarring him with a very dirty brush, poured a large drink and cheered myself up further with the prospect of another sailing trip; a well-found, comfortable yacht, an easy trip, and no Bardsey this time, with only slight trepidations about the skipper.

Arnie drove into the yard on Friday tea-time and joined me in the office. Denise had left early, and I was glad. I hoped he would talk to me openly. I'd never seen a man change so much in such a short time. In one week, the white streaks in his moustache and hair, still tied back in a ponytail, threatened to take over from the black. The contrast was startling. His cheeks were sunken and his foot tapped continuously on the floor as he sat at my desk with Ben's nearly-finished jigsaw in front of him. He pushed the loose pieces around in the open lid of the box.

"Here's how it is, bab. I've just come from the solicitor, that one who looked after your lobster. Right on the ball, he is, recommended by a friend, and seems to think there isn't an adultery case to answer on my part, which there isn't, but she's got a solicitor at home who's going for the jugular with the estate. Even if the adultery crap doesn't stand up, the divorce is going ahead. She's gone too far this time, and yeah, I've been a bloody great fool, I know that, so don't remind me. She'll try for custody of Ben, though God knows why; out of sheer spite, I reckon. But I'll tell you what, I'll fight that, if it's the last thing I do."

"What are the chances of you losing this place to her?"

He shrugged. "It's not just this place. There's the main, big scrap-yard, two smaller recycling centres, the Classic Car business, the house at home, the static up here, cars and vans…" He ran his hand over his face. "Stuff, Cass, a lot of stuff and she wants the best of it, this place, especially. Don't even ask about pensions."

Divorces were only what I'd read, or heard about, from people like Veronica. They sounded painful, messy, long-drawn-out, and they reinforced my thoughts about marriage in the first place.

I led Arnie upstairs to a happy, brown-faced Ben, fed and cuddled up to Angela in front of the television. He ran to his dad, who lifted him high in the air, put him down, then a warm, but restrained greeting for Angela. It had to be. But I saw their eyes meet; they were so right together. No risks, not now, but I knew they'd be alright when the dirt stopped flying.

"How are you going to manage Ben without his mother being there?" I asked, as he strapped him into the booster seat.

"I've cut my hours in the yard to suit school hours," he said. "Had to increase my right-hand man's time, but it's good money for him. I can work from home in the evenings. When this divorce is over, we'll see what to do next." He looked around the yard and up at the showroom. "But I'm not giving this business up, Cassie, or Ben. Whatever it takes."

I looked at his barrel-chest and enormous forearms, the strain and anxiety on his face and the controlled anger, and thought that I would never want to cross this man. I would not want to be in Shelly's shoes, or those of Tracy Downs, if he found out she'd been spying on him at her request. Then secretly wished he would find out and drown them both in the fucking harbour.

CHAPTER 16

That weekend, and the end of the Bank Holiday, the daytime temperatures hit thirty-five degrees in sheltered spots. Porthmadog was featured on the national news as the hottest place in the UK; lawn-mowers in Morfa Bychan lay idle in sheds as the sun baked the grass crisp and brown and the gulls stopped screeching. By the barrier-blocked road to Black Rock Sands, the council digger had cleared sand from the access road and piled it up on the sand-dunes either side of the entrance.

High-tide at ten-thirty in the morning, and the water was so still, it barely lapped on the tide-line. Where it met the hot sand, and for first few feet of the shallows, it was embroidered with a ribbon of soft, brown weed, but the sea beyond that and away towards the south, stretched out in a pale-blue sheet.

I scooped out a deep hole in the sand-dune, took my trainers off and paddled in the lukewarm water, the sand soft under my feet, then sat in the hollow I'd created. I watched the tiny wavelets crest and topple in lines of evenly-spaced bubbles, like the glass bubbles in Helen's Nain's old-fashioned jelly-mould, the one I'd brought back from the empty house and had yet to practise with.

Visitors began to arrive. They pulled buggies loaded with small children and all the paraphernalia necessary for a day on the beach. Family groups set up their camps surrounded by windbreaks, barricaded themselves in with castles topped with turrets and decorated with flags; happy fathers dug out moats for the smaller tots to amuse themselves, as they tried to fill them with buckets of water, only to watch it mysteriously disappear into the sand; rather like social services, and charities, I thought irrelevantly; a bottomless pit that never seemed filled, no matter how hard you tried. That's what Helen had said, and I thought about her in Sydney at the beginning of her winter and wondered if she still surfed in the cold weather; well, relative cold.

Figures stood, silhouetted against the glare of the sea and sun, up to their knees in crystal clear water; torsos of all shapes and sizes. An overweight lady with her trousers rolled up and her arms akimbo watched eagle-eyed over her brood. Older children in inflatable ducks and swans floated in the safe shallows and a man, covered in tattoos, attached a dog by its harness to his paddleboard for a free ride.

Hats and sun-cream. The tide, now on the turn, ebbed as fast as it had flooded in over the baking sand and left it hard and wet. The social life of the beach, at that moment, seemed a reflection of home lives; for some, the proximity to others afforded comfort as they crammed their cars together and shared their lives with others' barbecue smells and barking dogs; others chased the tide, and parked in open, isolated spaces of wet beach.

I stood up. The sand burned the soles of my feet, the sun beat down on my head, and I had to put my trainers back on to reach shallow water, walked a bit, then when I saw the beach ahead filled with cars, changed my mind about the walk and turned round to go back along the footpath. Mark drove past in his patrol car and I flagged him down.

"Alright for the idle rich," he said.

“I’ve worked all week,” I said, only slightly indignant, “while you’ve been swanning around in that truck of yours trying to look busy.”

“Very funny,” he said. “Have you seen how many people there are? There’ll be some rescues before the end of the day, I bet. Can you believe this heat? It’s only eleven o’clock. See you around.”

The snack-bar was up and running just at weekends to start with. A notice outside Madoc Yacht Club warning visitors about NO PARKING on Boat Shed premises, did not deter the walkers on their way to and from Borth-y-gest, and it became so popular, that Angela decided to finish work at Tesco and opened up full-time. She served gourmet fish dishes served on slate platters with posh paper-napkins decorated with oystercatchers, and grilled succulent lamb-burgers, courtesy of Mr Gilbert’s sheep. The hot weather drew in the tourists from far and wide, and Emily arrived down from the farm on Saturdays to wait on.

“Bored with town,” she said, “and as for the boys my age, they’re so silly. Can’t wait for college,” and I left them to it, a capable, practical couple of women with a creative flair and a promising business.

Mine however, seemed to be in its death throes. I abandoned the idea of hiring out rowing boats after quotes for insurance and the idea of running a website for classic boat chandlery had as much appeal as a cold haddock. I couldn’t have cared less about fids and baggywrinkles. I just smoked the salmon for Angela.

I pottered about Madoc Marine, asked Don to teach me to use the crane, passed a test or two for insurance purposes and managed the smaller boats with the daily business of lift-ins and lift-outs. I organised the berthing and anti-fouled a couple of boats. There was no sign of Arnie, and Tracy Downs or the rude Mr Robinson, which was a relief. But I was fed-up and I knew the fragility of my future here was beginning to affect me.

"For goodness' sake," Denise said, one evening, shutting the office up and following me upstairs to the flat. She'd never done that before, and she closed the door behind her, meaningfully.

"Why don't you ask that solicitor of yours if you can overturn the covenant on the Boat Shed, so you can use the yard differently? There's only Hugh's yacht to show it's got anything to do with classic wooden boats. People do it all the time. I mean, Cass, this is ridiculous. Unless you sell it and go and make a new life somewhere else, like go back to journalism, I can't see what else you can do. We can't have you hanging around with a miserable face. It's not good for business, apart from the fact that I care about what's bothering you. Is it money that's worrying you?"

I'd paid the bills for the sale of Tai-Pilots, the new Boat Shed, Steve's for the work on the rock-face and I'd happily bought all the new stock and special quality extras for the snack-bar, to Angela's delight, and was quietly astounded. Not because I'd run out of money, but because there was a lot left; enough to play with, enough for a deposit on a house or flat, but not enough to buy a home outright, and with no future employment prospects there was no chance of a mortgage. Then there was my change of mind-set after Heidi's revelation about David, the feeling of oppression and being hemmed in, and that strange moment when I'd stopped in Criccieth on the way back from the race and looked out to sea, and the horizon, and the impact it had on me.

I started to share all this with Denise, faltered, and stopped. She sat back in the white leather swivel-chair Doug Peterson had kindly left behind and put her feet up on the stool.

"You need to talk, girl," she said, phoned her partner, said she'd take a taxi home and I put a pizza in the oven, opened a bottle of wine and was so grateful to her, I gave her a hug.

"So, I'm not going to starve," I said. "I just don't know what to do next. This divorce is bothering me, and I've still got this feeling the woman's not finished with me yet. I've nowhere to live, a lapsed career, and I haven't written more than a shopping list for a couple of years now. My journalist qualifications are probably worthless now, anyway."

"You've got your degree, though? Just start over."

"Where? In a city. No ta."

"What did Jason say? I know you're close?"

I thought back. It was only a few weeks ago. He'd know about his parents' divorce by now, but I hadn't liked to phone. Platitudes would be totally inappropriate, remembering his reluctance to go home to see either of them.

"He told me to go to sea, so I did. On the race with David."

She looked at me thoughtfully.

"Something's changed since then, hasn't it? You're different, your attitude's different, all that enthusiasm you had for the Boat Shed: it's all drained away. So, what happened? Come on, Cass, talk it out. My ears only. Right?"

So, I told her about David. Everything. "Good God," she said.

There were no answers, but I'd felt better, got on with work, cheered up at the promise of a sail, with no strings attached, and drove to meet Paul in Holyhead on that Friday night after work. Arnie had said he would arrive on Saturday morning with Ben and cover for me until Monday when Paul had booked the ferry back from Dublin for me. I wasn't sorry I'd miss him. I didn't want all the acrimonious details of the divorce to spoil my weekend.

Paul and I met in the bar of Holyhead Sailing Club. He hugged me and bought me a pint of Guinness, fresh off the ferry, I was assured.

"How's the finger?" I asked.

"Long-gone food for the crabs," he said with a grin, and held up his maimed hand. The stump had healed up nicely. He seemed unfazed by the reminder of his accident when he'd grounded his little yacht on the sand-bar and sliced his finger off in the anchor chain.

"Very tidy," I said, wrinkled my nose and stuck it in the glass. I'd never been good with blood or injuries; scratches were about my limit. He looked as young and scruffy as ever, fit and full of enthusiasm about his Whitsun sailing holiday in Scotland with his dad, and said this trip was just like going down the road. He'd done it loads of times.

"How many times?" I asked, but he'd gone back to the bar for a refill. The window at the back overlooked the harbour with the boats that had previously been berthed in the marina, now on swinging moorings out in the bay. I'd seen the footage of the disaster and Hugh, still recovering from the shock as he'd been there when the storm hit, had told me about it. The space over towards the breakwater where the marina had been was now empty, except for one pontoon for loading and unloading was still connected to the walkway.

"That's her," he said, and pointed to a yacht tied up to the pontoon. "I've booked a table and we'll eat here in the club, then go on board for the night, off at about nine in the morning to catch the tide. They'll allow us one night on the pontoon. Okay?"

"I'd like to look round her first," I said, "just so I know where everything is. I presume she's ready for sea?"

"Oh yeah, the owner's assured me she's up to scratch. Engine serviced and all that."

"No broker?"

"No, private sale. He's an old friend of my dad."

"Service history? Rigging? Sails in good condition?" I asked.

"It's fine," he said, "Dad said his mate was reliable, and Wanderer is an okay boat. Stop fussing. Let's go and eat."

I wasn't going to be told to stop fussing by anyone, but kept quiet, with

David's words in my ears. I had time to do what I wanted.

It was nearly dark when we left the club. Paul drank a lot, chatted and entertained members with his sea stories, but I decided to stay sober, even to the point where if I was uneasy about his capabilities the following morning, I could just drive home and leave him to it. But I was desperate to go, wanted the sea hours and above all else, the chance to prove to myself I could crew this boat competently. There was no crack race-crew to advise and help me on this trip.

At six, I crawled out of my sleeping-bag in the fore-cabin and threw on a track-suit. Paul was still asleep. He snored and reeked of beer, dead to the world, so I turned the gas on, boiled the kettle, made tea, and took it up on deck. He still hadn't moved. A fine mist hung over the bay and obscured the top of Holyhead Mountain but the cloud had already begun to thin.

The shipping forecast promised light southerly winds, increasing after lunch, but no more than a Force 4. With one check on my list ticked off, I stood at the bow and looked aft. She was a pretty boat, only twenty-six feet in length and perfect for Paul to manage. She'd take him safely over to Scotland and around the islands, with plenty of room for a mate or girlfriend. The standing rigging was taut and there was no evidence of wear around the chain-plates.

He emerged on deck an hour later, bleary eyed and decidedly worse for wear, thanks to the pints he'd drunk; he wasn't a tall man, had a slight frame and still looked like an overgrown schoolboy. There was time to change my mind. We breakfasted on toast and then I asked for a guided tour around the chart table and the instruments. Although the panel was nowhere near as complicated or comprehensive as David's, the radio worked and I called for a radio check with the coastguard. Paul didn't mind, he seemed glad to leave me alone to study the course he'd scribbled down and transferred to the plotter.

"Where are the charts?" I asked.

"Oh, I gave all those to the previous owner. They were taking up too much room. I've got my phone as well as all the nav electronics."

But David said, David said, David would never… he whispered to me, as though he was in the cabin. I checked my watch. Eight o'clock. One hour, in which to decide.

"Food?" I asked. "Water? Diesel? Engine checks? I mean, do you need to start it up and let it run for a while?"

"For Christ's sake, what is this?" He glared at me through blood-shot eyes. "The bloody Spanish Inquisition?"

"No, but I'm still learning, Paul. I need to know all this, anyway. It's no criticism of your preparation. Sorry if it sounds like that," I lied and had already decided I didn't want to spend ten hours in his company in the middle of the Irish Sea. I hoped I could find something to justify my decision, apart from sheer intuition and a gutful of unease.

Hungover and grumpy, but slightly mollified, he disappeared up the steps and back into the cockpit. He started the engine, and I could hear him talking on his phone. What else should I check while he was on deck? Sea-cocks, David said… Sea cocks for the galley, wash-basin and toilet, sea-cock for the engine cooling-water; any holes in the boat, like the transducer, to check depth.

I scouted around in my memory banks and realised I knew more than I thought. I'd helped Hugh a couple of times on *Capella*, while he screwed and glued new anodes, and I'd watched Don replace skin-fittings in powerboats. It wasn't rocket-science to understand about holes drilled into boats, the sea-cocks being the safety valves for letting only necessary water in and out. If badly maintained to the point of failure, a boat could be scuttled in minutes.

The torch on the chart table, shone bright in the dim cabin and I unclipped the cover to the engine compartment. Copper-blue corrosion surrounded the fitting, and it looked as though it hadn't been turned on, or off, for years. Then I checked the sea toilet. A steady drip of sea water from the seal behind the bulkhead dripped and ran into the bilge. Back in the cabin, I lifted a floor-board with a ring through it and looked underneath.

Filthy water, six inches deep, stained with a film of diesel and oil, sloshed around in the deepest part as the wake from a passing boat rocked our hull. The sides and bottom of the bilge were coated with matted hair which had blocked the drainage holes between the frames; a red-setter, I could have guessed, had it been a dog. The pump didn't work, despite a cheerful red light on the switchboard.

I put the floorboard back, quietly, but he thumped around on deck and wouldn't hear me above the engine. The boat rocked again as he bashed up and down the deck, preparing the mooring ropes to be loosed when we set off. No chance, I thought, and crept into the fore-cabin, squashed the sleeping-bag and clothes into my sailing bag, carried them through the cabin and up the steps. He was at the helm, the mooring ropes loose on the deck. But now, we were ten feet away from the pontoon, motoring out into the bay.

"What the fuck do you think you're doing?"

I stood on the top step, not believing what had happened.

"You bastard," I said. "You knew I was going to leave, didn't you?"

He laughed. "Thought I'd surprise you. You should see your face, Cassie. Get real, it'll be fine. You just got cold feet. I thought you were a hardened sailor now. Go and put the kettle on and don't be a wuss."

I put the bag down on the cockpit seat, stood in front of him at the tiller and put my hands on his.

"You turn this boat round right now, Paul, or I'll call the coastguard and the police. There's six inches of water in the bilges and the toilet seal's leaking. I couldn't even see the bilge pump for shit floating around, and it doesn't work anyway. You'll never make Ireland. You'll sink, breakdown or drown, and you're not taking me with you. Got it?"

The colour left his face. I thought he was going to be sick, but he pushed the throttle into neutral.

"You're not joking?"

"Does it look like it? Has this boat been in the yard for ages? When was it launched? Did you even check it was seaworthy? It's a disgrace. How dare you even think about a passage and as for asking me to come with you… You lied, Paul, or you've been lied to. Your dad's friend, was it? Some friend," but he'd already pushed the tiller over and headed back, his face as white as a sheet. He crunched the bow into the pontoon and I leapt off with the mooring ropes.

"I don't know what you'll do now," I said, "but it's your problem, not mine. An apology won't cut it, by the way. You could have got us both drowned. I'd take up golf, if I was you. You're safer on land. And I shall let the Harbour Authority know the boat's not safe to be taken to sea. That way, you won't be tempted," and I left. I was angry, and it was cruel, but I didn't care. I hoped he wouldn't play the same trick on anyone else, through sheer ignorance, even if not intentional.

I set off on the road to home. Home? I didn't want to go back early, to face Arnie and his problems, and not even Ben's sweet little face could tempt me. I'd rather sleep in the car for two days. I rang Daniel.

"When are you coming back this way?" and tried to keep the pleading out of my voice.

"Now, actually," he said. "Just passing Preston on my way to Holyhead for a week. Change of plan, but I thought you'd be in Ireland."

There is a God in heaven, I thought, and booked us into a posh hotel in Trearddur Bay, treated myself to a swim in the sea and paddled in the glorious little coves until he arrived.

CHAPTER 17

Arnie had left on Sunday, and I reached the yard late on Monday morning. I'd had an unusual text from Hugh; 'can you meet me at the Boat Shed at twelve o'clock, please, Miss Cassie, before I return to Scotland with Alistair?'

"Tell you later," I said to Denise and chucked my sailing bag on the floor in the office. "I didn't go, I'm still alive and I've had a lovely weekend with Daniel. I must meet Hugh."

That'll be the end of *Capella*, Hugh's classic wooden Vertue in my yard, I thought. He's come to tell me it's sold, or he's going to sell it, the last of my old boats gone. I'd been expecting it for a while. His new relationship didn't include the restoration of old boats; he didn't need that any more, I could tell.

He had arrived early, and stood on *Capella's* deck with the hatch open, and some bags piled on the coach roof. I'm right, I thought. He's sold her. He climbed down carrying a small brief-case, and two plastic bags. I unlocked the shed and put the kettle on. We sat on the veranda, mugs of coffee and the biscuit tin on the table, as though he'd never left. The last time I saw him he'd given me warnings about Shelly Blackwell, and he'd been right. I'd texted to let him know as much as I could.

"The divorce will go ahead," I said, "but Arnie said she'll do anything to get her hands on Madoc Marine and leave him the scrap business. God knows what a court will decide, and it will go to court, Arnie says. Shelly hates me, though. I don't think she's going to let it go, Hugh. She wants Madoc Marine, but she doesn't want me here. I keep looking over my shoulder for bad things to happen."

He shuffled his feet and drank his coffee.

"That aside, Miss Cassie, I need to talk to you about the boat."

I waited. He leaned down and opened the brief-case, took out a sheaf of papers in plastic wallets and put them on the table.

"This is for you. Hear me out, please. I have cancer. A brain tumour. I have a few more years of good health, but eventually it will kill me, and life may be difficult for a while as I lose my faculties."

He lifted his hand as I opened my mouth. To say what?

"Alistair and I are going to be married, just a civil service, you understand, and I shall be returning to Scotland with him to live. We are blessed we met each other and at least will have a few happy years together."

I couldn't speak. I swallowed, nodded and a gull wheeled and screeched overhead. It settled on the mooring bollard and cocked its head as though listening. Watching it gave me a second to catch my breath.

"So, we need to talk about *Capella*," he said, and smiled. "Half a life's work for the wrong reasons, in hindsight; a way to keep my mind occupied in my dark days, instead of having to face my mental health problems and ask for help. The plotting, planning and working on the restoration, has been carried out to a degree of perfection, I'd like to think. I'd never intended to sail her, Miss Cassie, but this place and the work in Boston Lodge gave me an anchor for many years, and I've been privileged to have the pleasure of your care and company in the last year or so."

"Stop it, Hugh, I'm going to choke. Please stop."

"So," he said, ignoring me and carried on. "These are the ship's papers. They're all in order, with the transfer to your ownership up-to-date."

"But Hugh, I can't afford to buy a boat, any boat. I haven't even got a home. She must be worth a lot now. I mean, how much would you want for her? I'll sell her for you, if you like. I can do brokerage now."

"You misunderstand me, as you have done so before, I seem to remember. This is a gift, Miss Cassie. *Capella* is yours, to do with as you please. Use her, sell her. She's yours, to say thank you. And before I forget, if you would like to join us, the Railway are putting on a special train for us on Wednesday; just friends, you know, a short trip across the Cob to the Lodge to celebrate our marriage. A small party, you understand."

Reeling from the news, I clutched the papers to my chest as he stood up to leave.

"Don't forget to close the hatch. They've forecast showers for tonight."

I climbed up *Capella's* ladder, stood in the cockpit and stared at twenty-five feet of wooden planking, fashioned into a purposeful hull with lovely lines and a reputation for successful ocean voyages, sitting headroom inside, the woodwork finished and varnished to the point of perfection, fiddles and lockers, tailor-made to fit the tiny galley, and every inch imbued with Hugh's soul. Was this a wonderful gift or another ball and chain? But he said I could do whatever I wanted with it.

Unable to compute what this meant for me, I sat for a while, upset about his desperate news, but knew that however long he lived, at least he'd been happy for a short time, happy and strong, and amazingly philosophical about it. His partner must be a special man, I decided, and looked forward to meeting him. But what the hell was I going to do with this boat? The phone saved me.

"Are you coming back today, this year, or what?" Denise asked, decidedly snappy.

"Now, I'm coming now. Sorry. I'll be there in five," and shut the hatch.

But it felt like five years; a short, nasty, five-minute encounter, that felt as though it had put years on my life, stunned me with its ferocity, and exhausted any resilience I thought I'd built up.

Shelly Blackwell, tight white jeans and T-shirt, heeled sandals, her long hair tied back in a pony-tail and her face made-up like a mannequin, walked down Madoc Marine's yard towards me. I hadn't seen her since I was seventeen, nearly six years ago, and she wore clothes too young and too tight for her forty-year-old figure, with a distinctive roll of fat above her waistband; 'mutton dressed as lamb' my mother used to say, and in this case, much as I disliked her critical comments, she was so bloody right.

We drew closer. The skin around her jawline had been tightened, and the blonde hair, scraped off her forehead and tied in a stringy pony tail at the back of her neck, gave her face a mask-like appearance without a shred of character. Except spite, perhaps.

We stopped, six-feet from each other, sandwiched in between boats, and she looked me up and down, then said, "I've come to look at my property."

"Really? Mrs Blackwell, I presume? It's been a long time. Rather premature, don't you think? I thought that had yet to be settled. If you'll excuse me," and I tried to move past her, but she stood her ground. She's come to stake her claim, I thought.

"Not for long. My solicitor says there's every chance I'll get it, and when I do, you'll be the first to go. Who the hell do you think you are? A jumped-up little shit of a nobody, living in that apartment and getting what money you can out of Arnie. Thought you'd make a play for him, did you? Well, I saw the photos, love, and they weren't that innocent."

"Mrs Blackwell," I said, as politely as I could. "You're quite wrong. We've nothing to discuss. It's none of my business."

"Let me tell you something, Miss Jones," she said, and narrowed her eyes. "I'll never forgive you for what you did to my boys. I'll make your life a misery until I fire you, just see if I don't." She turned on her ridiculous heels, and walked off to the end of the yard.

I fled into the showroom, and upstairs, out of breath with my heart pounding. Denise followed me up.

"I saw her walk in, but she'd parked up the road. I hadn't got any right to say she couldn't come in the yard, anyway. She collared you, didn't she? What did she say Cass?"

It took coffee and toast before I calmed down. First Hugh's news, his illness and the boat, and now this. I needed space to think, but I needed to work. I didn't tell her about *Capella*.

"Let me finish the invoices while you deal with customers," she said, "then I'll cover for you this afternoon. Go scrub a boat or something, and then go for a walk. It's no good trying to solve all these problems when you're in a state. Mountains out of molehills, and all that. She won't come back now."

But she did come back. She never left the yard. She watched me from the harbour wall as I worked on the pontoon; she leaned against a powerboat and watched me move trailers around; she sat on one of the chairs by the crane, and watched me while I cleaned the hull of a prospective purchase. There was nothing I could do, or say, to get rid of her. Then it was lunchtime, and I escaped.

It was quiet in Borth-y-Gest after the frenzy of the Bank Holiday, and I sat down on a bench near the bus-shelter. The sun beat down with renewed vigour, reservoirs were low, lawns parched, huge tracts of mountain side covered in tinder-dry heather and ferns above Llangollen had smouldered, then blazed into fires, and in south Wales, even houses had been threatened. Pleas were issued by local authorities for careful use of water.

In a fit of desperation, slightly disorientated with tiredness from the weekend and the morning's events, I forgot the time difference and rang Helen in Sydney. I reckoned she was a safe bet, dealing all day with corpses who couldn't answer back, and would listen objectively, without the emotional baggage of an active medic in an A&E unit, which she could easily have been.

Now away from the heart-breaking job of bailing out sick and starving children, I'd noticed a change in the tone of our emails and occasional Facetime slot; she had more time to listen, ask questions, show an interest in my exploits, good, bad and indifferent, and I needed a neutral ear and sharp brain, distanced from all the sordid mess I was up to my neck in. That included the amazing gift, or poisoned chalice, of the Vertue. Still up and watching a film with her partner, she paused it without comment, and listened carefully.

"Well, I know what I would do," she said, "particularly with that nasty piece of work threatening you. You can't stay there, Cassie. It'd be bad enough if she wins the case, but the effect on you until then could be devastating. These divorces can take years. You'd be wrecked, if you didn't kill her first and end up in prison."

"Very funny, but that's no help. Where would I go? I haven't got a home, I've only a certain amount of money, I don't want to sell the yard, I've decided, and it's pointless owning a wooden yacht if I'm not going to sail her."

"Why not?" she asked.

"Why not what? Sail her, you mean? I know Hugh spent years restoring her to perfection, but she's been on land all that time. I hate to think how much water she'd take up if she was launched. I just couldn't be bothered with all that angst, watching her like a hawk with the bilge pump on overload. And then there's that varnishing. And I've been on a small boat only last week. It wasn't much fun. Not like David's. You don't seriously think I'd sail around here in twenty-five feet of old planking with a deep keel, do you?"

"The old slate-trade skippers seemed to manage it," she said. "Not to mention the fact that the slate trade out of Port was based on hundreds of ships made from wood." I could hear her partner chortling in the background. "You just have to watch your sandbanks. Oh, and teredo worm, if you sail to the tropics." More laughter.

"Are you still there?" she asked, after a pause. Was she making fun of me? Not like her at all.

I didn't know what else to say. I was disappointed. She didn't really have any useful advice after all. Then she did.

"Anyway, seriously, Cass, just listen. From what you have told me, you're really hooked on sailing, aren't you, despite the rough stuff in Bardsey Sound? And you've got skills now, and qualifications and sea hours. Well, this is what I would do."

It wasn't so much a lecture, as a rational suggestion for a complete, life-make-over. I stood up, walked through the car-park and up to the pill-box, and said hello to Helen's Nain, resting quietly in the memorial garden.

"What should I do?" I asked.

Be yourself, cariad, I imagined she'd say. Just that, whatever 'myself' was, and sat down on a bench in front of the church, for a while, then carried on along the cliff-top path, my head down, one foot after the other, one thought after another, and ideas raced into my brain and kept pace with my feet.

The chirrup of the resident robin, always there on the cliff-top path, stopped me. Fearless of passers-by, with a backdrop of thick yellow gorse to retreat into, he perched on the fence. He was only a foot away, cocked his head, considered me with a black, beady eye, as much as to say 'get a grip, Cassie Jones, stop pissing around with your life ticking away in months of threats and unpleasantness; think of Hugh, with only a few years left; stop singing to everyone else's tune, sod the business ideas, and the offer of love that'll swallow you up.'

I left him to twitter and marched on, as though on a mission, through the soft sand and down the steps to the beach, up through the narrow path carved into the sand-dune the other side of the bay hemmed in with blackthorn bushes and the pink stars of ragged-robin peeping out from the marram grass.

At the top I veered off the path to a tiny terrace just above the sheer rock that fell away to Samson's Bay, and sat with my back against a rock with my bare legs on the grass. The estuary stretched out below me, shimmered and glittered in the heat, the tide fully in and not a sign of a sandbank, just the buoys to point the safe passage out to sea.

Now, here, in this special place, on my own, with the sea stretching in front of me to the horizon and beyond, I could stop, and try to piece it all together; an objective focus on what I had been, to what I had become; a self-centred appraisal that sat uncomfortably on my shoulders, but had to be addressed. I started to look at my life from other people's point of view, like my mother's, which was easy; 'I care about you, but I've got my life and you've got yours, Cassie. Don't bother me, just get on with it.' Fine.

Everyone else, I thought, would see me as flaky, indecisive, playing at forging a life for myself with the golden spoons I now owned, and mixed up in a soap-opera with its smutty domestics, conveniently forgetting that I was partly responsible, if all for the right reasons.

Then, of, course, I could have said 'no' to Arnie's offer to put me in charge of Madoc Marine. I questioned why I didn't reject it. Vanity? Self -esteem? To prove that two women could manage just as well as the Doug Petersons of this world? Or the thought of a smart, modern apartment to live in as opposed to a grubby caravan?

I got myself into this unhappy situation, so it was up to me to get out of it. I couldn't dismiss the underlying message and impatient tone in Helen's voice. She'd found herself in a career situation that threatened to damage her health, and was brave enough to admit it. Now there she was on the other side of the world, with a new partner and a job she enjoyed. The laughter said it all. I couldn't remember the last time I laughed.

Dismissal of her advice, then self-doubt, then practicalities, followed by more self-doubt, then a frisson of excitement, and I sat a while longer as the afternoon became still and oppressive. A milky haze reduced the heat of the sun, lower in the sky now in the late afternoon as wisps of cloud appeared from the south and streaked the sky with mare's tails. After weeks of heat, the weather was finally about to change. I set off back to Borth-y-Gest, just a fraction nearer to resolution than I had been on the way up, walked faster to beat any rain, but I needn't have worried. The breakdown of the heat was to be a slow process.

A thunderstorm was forming somewhere up in the troposphere, and the sky had glazed over almost completely. Where the sun poked through, it cast a copper light on the grey clouds and pooled sunbeams on the sea. It wasn't pretty, not in a 'red sky at night, shepherd's delight' way, it had more of a jaundiced look, a copper-yellow, malevolent tinge that spread across the horizon.

At 'A'-level, I'd learned about 'pathetic fallacy', rife in Wordworth's poetry and his wanderings amongst the daffodils, and in Bronte's '*Wuthering Heights*,' with Heathcliff and the accompanying storms.

But that was just terminology. Besides, I already felt a glimmer of optimism and could hardly imagine anything unpleasant would happen for the rest of the day. For me, the only immediate drama unfolding was the thought of being caught out in a downpour.

I stopped briefly outside *Tai Pilots*, the scaffolding still up and the newly-grouted chimney-pot had been stripped of the ferns that had embedded their roots in the ancient mortar. The windows and front door had been replaced with smart new double-glazing, the stone steps leading up to it had been weeded, and the patches and holes cemented over. I looked at the house long and hard, examined my heart for regret, found none, and moved on down the path and across the car-park.

The sight of David's Audi, parked on the road outside Helen's Nain's old house, stopped me in my tracks, surprised at first, but it had now become a holiday let, and David would perhaps know the visitors. Then I noticed that decorating was still in progress; ladders and paint pots stacked by the garden gate and curtains removed from the bay windows. It was beginning to look cared for again, the colour of the masonry a delicate violet and the white surrounds to the windows marked out to perfection. She would have loved it.

Puzzled, I stood for a moment, my heart this time not quite so unaffected by the change of ownership. Then the door opened and David walked out and behind him, from the state of his overalls, the decorator. We stared at each other across the road.

"I'd love you to explain," I said, when he'd walked over, "even though it's none of my business."

We sat on the wall and dangled our feet above the fringe of sand below us, the muddy bay revealing more of itself, minute by minute as the tide ebbed.

"I bought it. Well, my company. Obviously," he said.

"Oh, I see." That explains it, I thought. So much for homes for the locals. “Heidi told me you bought and sold property. I didn’t know. Well, why would I? As well as the sail training? And dealing with sticky divorces? Not to mention feeding lobsters, on occasion.”

He laughed. “Just that one lobster, I can assure you. I didn’t like it much, either.”

“How on earth do you find the time?” I asked.

“If it’s important, you’ll always find the time,” he said.

“That sounds a bit sanctimonious. And is this house important?”

“Yes. Very. More than *Tai Pilots*.”

“You bought that as well? But that was mine, David. Why didn’t you tell me? Why keep it in a company name, so I wouldn’t know?”

“Well, because we’d had that conversation about you renovating it to live in. You weren’t exactly open to suggestions, but I could see its potential. It was too good to miss. I just thought it would be difficult if I did what you wouldn’t, if you know what I mean.”

I think I did.

“What about Helen’s Nain’s house? Is that going to be a holiday let as well?”

He didn’t reply, kicked his heels against the wall, then turned to me and said, “you loved being there, didn’t you?”

This time, it was me who didn’t reply.

“I bought it with you in mind, Cassie. I bought it because I was going to ask you to reconsider our conversation when I talked about partners. We’d make a good team, and it’s a house you’d be happy in.”

I still didn’t get it.

“I love you, Cassie Jones. Will you marry me and live there?”

Heidi was right after all. I didn’t fall off the wall, but it wasn’t the place to hold such a conversation. We walked, back up to the cliff-top, sat on the bench as the sun died behind the village and the last rays coated the sandbanks pink and apricot. I swallowed the platitudes, the words of polite rejection, of unworthiness, honoured, too shocked to make decision, all the phrases I could conjure up to make him feel better. I just said no.

"I don't love you back, David. Without that, all the property and money and charm in the world would be irrelevant."

"Is there someone else?"

"No, nobody else. Just me, trying to find out what makes me happy and I think I know what I'm going to do. I'm not ready for marriage and babies and living here for the rest of my life, although I know if I married you, I'd never want for anything. But I'd be like a mad dog on a leash. You'd hate me. So, thank you. I am deeply honoured, and hope you'll find someone, one day, who can do you justice. You just haven't met them yet."

He took my hand and kissed it, patted it and put it back in my lap, rather paternalistically, I thought, like a father acknowledging a child's opinions.

"Would you have wanted to live there, though?" I asked. "I mean, you'll inherit…" I stopped. That was crass. He just laughed.

"One day, but not for a long while, I hope. Then it stays the family home. I'd never sell it. That's why I'm working to make sure Heidi and I aren't left with a white elephant. The property and land must pay for itself. I think you, of all people, would understand that."

I nodded.

"I thought you'd say no, and I'm sorry," he said, and smiled. "You're the only person I've ever met who I'd ask. Heidi warned me. But it was worth a try. Can we be friends, still?"

"Oh, definitely," I said. "Tell you what, though, I really need some advice. Can I buy you a pint?"

All night, thunder rumbled around the mountains; first over the

Rhinogs, then Cnicht and the Moelwyns, closer and closer, then receded to an occasional grumble, as though looking for something well-hidden and, when frustrated, disappeared to search elsewhere. Lightning flickered out at sea, a faded light-show that never quite materialised to the expected jagged shapes or streaks of something more serious.

By dawn, the heat stored in the mountains had enveloped the town in a stifling blanket of warm air. Windows flung open made no difference, the sun struggled to make an appearance through a grey early morning and Denise was irritable from lack of sleep. I'd tossed and turned in a tangle of sheets, damp, but not unhappy, and had enjoyed a pleasant evening with David in *The Ship*.

We'd supped beer and I soaked up facts and figures and treasured every scrap of advice and personal experience he could give me, after I'd shared my decisions with him. He was enthusiastic and supportive, the relationship now on a practical footing again; easy, comfortable, and strangely I guessed, an unspoken relief to both of us.

He'd accepted my rejection with perfect, but bizarre equanimity. Perhaps his declaration of love had been based on elements grounded in his family background; the need for continuity of the family name. I was young and fit, and my Welsh heritage fitted the bill. Also, I thought unkindly, perhaps a half-million pounds-worth of dowry might help. Strange, lovely man, and terribly useful.

"That'll give the locals something to talk about," he said, jokily out of character, as we left, but my stomach knotted, as through the glass panel in the door to the other bar, I saw Tracy Downs and Shelly Blackwell together, drinking and laughing. There was no sign of the bouncer.

There was no sign of the storm either. Mysteriously, it disappeared, after a few heavy, desultory drops of rain, followed by a muggy, misty Tuesday and Wednesday, when I worked on *Capella* over in the Boat

Shed yard, out of sight of Denise, but on call in case she needed me, but mostly to avoid Shelly Blackwell and her mate, of which there was thankfully no sign. I remembered she still owned a static, or maybe they just went home. Wherever they were, the decisions I'd made had pushed her threats into the realms of simple nuisance; I didn't need to be afraid any-more.

On Thursday, after yet another sticky night, the sun broke through with a welcome blue sky, in time for Hugh's marriage celebrations. The heat returned and the air in the harbour was stifling. After coffee and Danish pastries Denise had brought in, I walked down the yard and exchanged pleasantries with a couple of owners.

"It's a job to do anything this morning," one elderly, boat-owner said. "My legs feel like lead in this heat. I was going for a trip round the tide, but now I don't feel like going out at all. Doesn't look very inviting, does it?"

An oily swell rolled down the harbour, the water coloured a steely grey. Even the birds were quiet; the early morning blackbird song and the incessant screech of gulls had faded to nothing. It was mid-week, and most visitors had gone home, boat-owners were back at work and children were in school.

The yard had taken on a ghost-like quality, with the bright, white boats and colourful jet-skis lined up; lifeless, soulless machines, waiting patiently for the weekend, when hulls would be washed down and engines cranked into life as the crane worked overtime to catch the tide. I'd ignored the inheritance conditions and jet-skis were launched from the Boat Shed's slipway now; nobody'd complained, and I wanted the money. Only my solicitor would know and I could always apologise. I changed into tidy clothes for Hugh's wedding party.

The platform buzzed with staff from the offices and Boston Lodge. *Welsh Pony*, paint-work and brass gleaming as usual, and with one carriage attached, waited with steam rising into the still air. The engine-driver leaned out of the cab and chatted to a guard, the engine decorated with buntings and the handles of the carriages had ribbons attached; at the rear of the carriage, was a large 'Just Married' sign.

The happy couple were surrounded by friend and well-wishers, and the feeling of affection was palpable, a bitter-sweet occasion with Hugh's diagnosis. The Ffestiniog Railway had seen him through bad times with care and understanding, the common bond they all shared, the love of the Railway and its history, the amazing engines, and all the paraphernalia that went with it, had bred a friendship out of unhappiness. Crammed into the carriage, we left the station to loud cheers from visitors and sight-seers, always present, and shouted and waved to those taking photographs as we chugged across the Cob to Boston Lodge with much whistleblowing and fluttering of streamers.

The party went on all afternoon. Alistair was a man who anyone would seek out when in a pickle; he was tall and gracious, had wonderful eye-contact, natural attentiveness, and kept an eye on Hugh all afternoon. I dared not think about the awful times that would be ahead for them and, slightly pissed from drinking too much Prosecco, hugged them both and left before I disgraced myself with tears. I didn't tell Hugh what I intended to do with his boat, and he didn't ask.

CHAPTER 18

Arnie phoned me that night. I could hear the rage in his voice. He couldn't come over at the weekend, he said, but it didn't matter. The yard was quiet and there was little to do, apart from launch jet-skis. I'd looked at the weather charts and didn't think anyone would be playing around in the bay this weekend. The storm that had fizzled out was now set to return on Saturday, with thunder and lightning, and heavy rain. That's okay, I reassured myself, with the new Boat Shed four feet above the ground on its concrete plinth and worth every penny for peace of mind.

"Do you know what the bitch has done?" he said. "She's only trumped-up accusations of violence as the reason why she left the house and won't come back. I never laid a finger on her ever, I swear, Cass, even though I wanted to sometimes, and I don't have to explain why I never did."

No, he didn't have to explain. One look at his huge muscles and the power behind them, said it all.

"I've got things to sort out. I'm taking Ben to stay with his nan for the weekend. Will you manage?"

"Of course. Arnie, I know you're angry, but you won't…? I mean, you wouldn't take things into your own hands, would you? You've got to leave it with the solicitors."

"Yeah, right. I hear you. Speak to you soon."

I didn't believe him. The old uneasiness crept back; that gnawing sensation in the pit of my stomach, and an edginess that forbade relaxation. I'd opened all the windows in the apartment, but the air outside was as hot and humid as inside. Pitch dark now but, towards the west, lightning flickered and a faint rumble of thunder broke the silence. Another storm in a teacup, like the last one, I reckoned, and a part of me embraced the heat and the changeless days and the certainty that the sun would shine forever.

Comforted by the list of possibilities I'd found that would allow me to extricate myself from the unpleasantness of it all, I checked my listing on eBay. Three seriously interested people were watching *Capella*, with offers well above the reserve price, but I was determined to be realistic and not greedy. Then I indulged myself in the websites David had recommended, trawled through forums, and sent a lot of emails. Was it too late for this year, I wondered? Did I have enough experience? I would have to wait until *Capella* sold and the money was in the bank. At least I knew what I was doing with the brokerage, and for the first time in a while, I blessed, rather than cursed, my time with Madoc Marine. I wished Daniel was here and I could lose myself in a night with his beautiful body. I'd have to tell him my plans, but not yet.

I was up at dawn and out in the yard when Denise arrived. We walked over to the harbour wall and leaned on the railings. Tracy Downs had moved her boat further down the pontoon. It was tied up fore and aft, but the nest of tangled ropes had been hastily wrapped around the cleats and the loose ends trailed across the planks.

"I'd go down and sort those out," I said, "if I didn't think she'd sue me for imaginary damage. Lazy cow. Somebody's going to trip over those."

"Best not," Denise said. "She's on board, and guess what? So is Shelly Blackwell. Thank God Arnie's not up this weekend. She must have known, or she wouldn't be here, would she? Their cars are out on the road. They must have arrived late last night. I can have a polite word with her later, if you like. Anyway, she won't be going anywhere in this. Look at it," and she nodded over to Ballast Island and beyond, over the estuary with its sandbanks high and dry, and up to the skyline of the Rhinogs, where the sun had appeared through a red-streaked sky.

"Finally," she said. "Shepherd's warning and all that. Oh, for the smell of rain on dry ground," and laughed. "Croissants?"

By mid-morning, small dapples of grey clouds showed dark against the paler sky, cloying heat blanketed the yard, and even the blackbirds gave up, their cheerful songs to be replaced by muted voices and the occasional buzz of a drill. I wandered around the yards, checked bin-lids, tightened loose covers on new boats, and chatted to people who were happy to be away from work after a busy week, no matter what the weather.

Despite the forecast for thunderstorms, the tuition course for the jet-skis was to go ahead, possibly without the practical side on the water, and cars arrived by the minute and lined the narrow road outside. I'd kept the space in front of the showroom open, and the tuition group had already gathered with Andy, the lead instructor, in the early stages of a safety briefing.

I saw him glance up at the sky a few times, but he had his fall-back plan for inclement weather. He planned to amalgamate the theoretical sessions and move into the showroom, with one jet-ski already in place for demonstration; the others were moored to the pontoon.

Satisfied that all was well, I leaned over the railings and looked down onto Tracy Downs' boat. There was no sign of the occupants and the ropes still lay in a knotted mess. Then the sliding door to the cabin opened. I pushed back from the railing out of sight, just in time to see her sit down in the cockpit, a cartoon of orange juice in one hand and a bottle of bubbly in the other.

"Bring the glasses, will you, Shell?" I heard her ask.

I fled back into the showroom and spent an hour staring at the screen, reading through forums around my future escape, being careful not to let Denise see.

A boat-owner poked his head in. "What time's high-tide, Cass?"

"12.40," I said.

"Cheers. Someone having a party down there? Music's a bit loud. Can't you hear it from here?"

"Bit early for parties," I said, surprised, and closed the screen.

"Must be a hen party, then, with all that cackling. Christ, what a racket."

Denise looked up. Our eyes met, we stood up at the same time, and followed him out of the showroom door.

The stage was set, the curtains open, the cast in place; a tableau of white boats, the busy figures frozen in their appointed places, an arm raised with intent, a mouth opened in silent reply, a finger pointed, a head turned, and way out at sea, the sound effects, as a faint rumble of thunder broke the silence.

Into this arena, at the top of the ramp, Shelly Blackwell stumbled, regained balance, and walked a few feet with the concentrated gait of someone, not just gently inebriated, but undoubtedly drunk. Car keys dangled in her hand and she veered unsteadily over to the railings.

"Plenty in the car, Trace," she called down, "How many bottles?" and turned round.

"At least she's wearing trainers," Denise said. "God, she's barely on her feet, even with those on. Should we do something?"

"What, like arrest the owner's wife for being drunk in his yard? I don't think so. Leave it. She'll go back to the boat and probably drink until she falls asleep. Coffee?"

"Suppose she falls in?"

Best not to answer that, I thought. We studied her, the jet-ski trainees turned their heads and the boat-owners stopped work as she weaved her way past us, focused entirely on putting one foot in front of the other, towards the gate. Then she stopped and lifted her head. Arnie stood in the gateway, feet apart and arms by his side, fists bunched, head lowered like a bull about to charge.

The figures on the stage shifted, shuffled, glanced at each other, the atmosphere as electric as the storm brewing out at sea.

"Found you," he said. "Bitch," loud and clear, the air heavy and suffocating. The words seemed to be held in its clutches; it resonated off the hot rocks on the cliffs behind him and rolled around the yard. Denise clutched my arm.

"Do something, Cassie, for God's sake. Everyone's watching."

I couldn't. What could I do? It was a reckoning, and it needed to happen, but I couldn't have guessed it would be in public and so terrible. It was unstoppable and we had no choice but to listen, an unwilling audience gripped in awful fascination as the voices rose, the participants oblivious to anything or anyone, except themselves.

"Ben told me."

"Yeah? What?" She was upright, sobered a touch, sassy now.

"I'll tell you, bitch. I dropped him off to stay with his nan for the first time. Know what he said?"

She shrugged her shoulders and made a face.

"He said, 'Nanny won't leave me alone tonight, like mummy did, will she?'" He mimicked a child's voice, but nobody laughed.

"Don't know what you mean, Arnie. Let me past," and she took a step forward. He blocked her way solid as a rock, arms folded now.

"You left him on his own one night in the winter, after you'd come back home. Baby- sitting, you were supposed to be."

"I never. I don't remember. If I left the house at night, it was only for ten minutes, maybe to put the bins out. Don't you dare fucking tell me how to look after my kids. He's lying."

"Ben never lies."

His voice was menacingly quiet now, but the yard so still, every word could be heard. The play unfolded, the language choice, and the audience listened intently, if not uncomfortably.

"He'd just learned to tell the time at school. Not that you were interested. He could read the clock, Shelly. You came home at three. You'd left him on his own in the house. Is that the way you treat our kids? Pick and choose which ones you care about and which ones are irrelevant? And you want custody? No fucking chance. Our kids, Shelly," and he tapped his chest. The six-pack strained tight beneath the black T-shirt. "Even Jem and Zac, and right shits they've turned out to be, no thanks to you."

She ran her hand through the blonde hair, and wisps escaped from the pony-tail, hung untidily round her face, her head went up, her eyes wild. Then she laughed, a manic,

drunken laugh.

"Jem and Zac. Our kids?" She tapped her own chest. "My kids, Arnie. My fucking kids. Not yours. Never were yours."

If the silence was palpable before, now it was profound. The yard seemed to hold its breath; the boats, the people, even the birds. From where I stood, I could see his eyes narrowed in puzzlement. He took a step towards her and I saw him mouth, "Who?"

Stupid woman, with a silly, misjudged, coy look on her face. She fiddled with her hair.

"Doug Peterson," she said and smiled.

"Oh, no," Denise said, and tightened her grip on my arm.

Arnie lifted his arm, swung it back, and hit her, a flat-handed smack, full on the side of her head. The force knocked her off her feet, and she fell against the nearest boat and slid down the hull onto the gravel with her hand to her cheek.

"You bastard. You'll pay for that," and she scrambled up and ran, unsteadily, back to the ramp and down onto the pontoon. Arnie took a step to follow her, his face a mask of anger, but a strange thing happened. The men gathered around him and blocked his way. One put a hand on his arm.

"You're alright, mate. Let it go. Come on now," and they ushered him into the showroom, into the office and sat him down. He was pale and his hand shook when someone offered him a glass of water. The men towered over him in a protective shield, a hand reached out and touched his shoulder, voices whispered in support. Denise and I stood back, as if at the scene of an all-male ritual. We were excluded. We were women, a woman had humiliated him, the story had been heard and the actions judged. He was not to blame; Arnie was the victim.

The end of Act One, but there was no applause. The cast dispersed to their boats with heads bent together in hushed, disbelieving chat. Only the air was left; hot, humid, and oppressive. I shepherded Arnie upstairs to the apartment and fetched cold lemonade from the fridge. He was worryingly quiet, drank his lemonade and stared out of the window down the yard.

When I was a rookie journalist and sent out to cover horror stories for the paper, I'd once sat on a parent's settee after their child had been killed, and I'd regularly faced recipients of life-changing court decisions. It became clear that the more tragic the circumstances, the less likely people wanted to discuss them, until the time was right.

Shock, disbelief, grief, the sheer enormity of it all, most responses to tragedy quickly squashed my assumptions that normal conversations would ensue. The reality was mostly one of stunned shock, and Arnie sat in a vacuum of emotional disbelief that had yet to materialise into reality. I left him alone, with gentle but firm words to stay put. He'd already played into her hands and that was bad enough. She was lucky he hadn't killed her. He nodded, and when I put the cushions on the settee and told him to lie down, he did so, like a child. I put a pillow under his head and went downstairs.

"I don't know what'll happen now. I mean, will she phone the police and have him arrested?" I asked Denise, as shocked as I was.

"Bet she won't," she said, harnessing her hair back into its band, "and fancy that? Doug Peterson. I should have guessed, but then I wasn't around then. But those twins, they were blue-eyed like Doug, and just as foul. Do you think she ever told him she was pregnant with his kids?"

"Probably not," I said. "She'd have known which side her bread was buttered when she got pregnant, and Arnie had money and a promising future, then, so Veronica told me. She wouldn't rock the boat. How unforgiveable is that? Adultery, screwing both men and covering up the twins' paternity. Conniving cow. She must have worked it all out, timing and that, so he never had any idea."

"It's not going to do his case any good, hitting her like that in full view of all those people. Do you think they'll take their business away? I mean, it was pretty personal stuff, and horrible."

The door opened and Andy stuck his head in.

"I've cancelled the course for the day. The weather's not good for later. The group was a bit taken aback by all that outside. Nasty business. Is he okay?"

"Funny how everyone's rooting for him," I said, "considering he smacked her. Yeah, he's okay, just needs to be on his own. She might have called the police, for all I know,"

"I don't think so, Cass. That's what I came to tell you. She went back to that boat of Tracy Downs. I was down on the pontoon checking on the jet-skis. They were drinking hard, she was crying, then laughing, and I was down the other end of the pontoon when that woman, Tracy, let go of the ropes and they've gone out. Pissed as farts, they were, and the tide's on the ebb. It's running out like a drain and that storm isn't going to stay away for much longer. They might get stuck out there. Bloody dangerous, I'd say, with all that drink and her being hit like that."

They were out of sight by the time we'd run outside. Should I let Will Roberts or Mark know? I just hoped nobody else was out there when they'd passed the speed limit. I knew Tracy would hit the throttle and heaven help anyone in their way. Denise turned the radio onto dual watch, and I called up the boat on the working channel. There was no answer. The lights in the showroom flickered and the thunder grumbled ominously. It was only a thunderstorm and no serious winds were forecast. I was more concerned about the ebb tide, the increasingly shallow channel, the drying sand-banks and two pissed-up women in the aftermath of a domestic drama.

"Let's hope we don't get any water-spouts," Mark said, when I'd phoned the harbour office. "Never seen one and don't want to. Do you reckon they'll come back in soon? There's not much we can do. The water's too low to go out safely in the launch. Have you tried her mobile, like? Just to remind her about the tide?"

Good idea, but there was no answer from Tracy Downs.

"Try Shelly's phone. I've got her number," Denise said. "Hurry up. We're already at half-tide. They'll never get back in now. Should we let the Coastguard know? It's not a Mayday or anything, but maybe the lifeboat should go out?"

"Yes, you do it," I said, then rang Shelly's number.

She answered the phone.

"Shelly…" I started. How did she know it was me?

"Fuck off," she said and rang off. I left a message, two messages. What ese could I do?

'Go to Pwllheli,' I'd suggested. 'Don't try to come back here.'

"Do you think they're counting hippopotamuses?" I asked, lightly, but felt as heavy as the air. A crack of thunder put the storm only five miles away when the first drops of rain hit the window.

I checked on Arnie. He was asleep, my bottle of Glenfiddich half-empty on the coffee table. I didn't blame him and tiptoed to the bedroom to look at the lightning show over Snowdonia. The storm was breaking in all directions; jagged flashes lit up the dark sky over Cnicht and the thunder rolled around the mountains on all sides; an unwelcome stab of serious concern for those two out at the Fairway Buoy hit my stomach. They must be terrified by now. My dislike for them both turned to anxiety. I couldn't see an end to all this, but I knew that Arnie's actions that day, despite the reasons, had jeopardised his future.

We sat in the office, and he crept downstairs stinking of whisky. He brought the bottle with him, plonked it down on the desk, disappeared into the kitchen and returned with glasses. We didn't argue, sat in silence in the dark and listened to the gods play with our mortal fears; the thunder-claps overhead, the lightning flashes that lit up the showroom, the ping of hailstones on the window and the comforting red light of the marine radio, open on dual watch, silent in its watchfulness.

Then the power failed. The red light faded, Denise reached for the portable ship-to-ship, switched it on and used her phone to light up the numbers and tune in. The radio blared out the insistent bleep for the land-based Coastguard, the zero channel for the lifeboat, and Holyhead

Coastguard asking for 'vessels in the vicinity…'

The storm passed in an insignificant downpour, the thunder rolled away to the east and the lightning spent the last of its energy over the Rhinogs, flickered once and then died. The afternoon lightened to a grey mist over the estuary, the tide at its lowest and the sandbanks stretched a dull brown over to Harlech, the channels of the Glaslyn and Dwyryd reduced to a mere trickle.

On the grass outside the church above Borth-y-Gest, we gathered to watch, the folk of the village alerted by word of mouth and the crowd grew steadily in numbers. The helicopter had landed, way out in the middle of the estuary and obscured much of the view, but it was clear to see the hull of Tracy Downs' boat, high and dry and canted over on its side. The helicopter crew, like black ants, stood around, but the figure of one could be seen as he clambered with difficulty onto the tilted flybridge. They seemed in no hurry to lift off. They were on their own, the water so low not even the inshore lifeboat could reach them.

The scene meant nothing if you were unfamiliar with the channel and its buoys, the vagaries of the shifting sandbanks, the soft and hard sand, and the quick-sands in-between. It meant nothing, if all you saw was a sheet of unblemished water stretching in front of you, and you believed it was kind enough to afford the same depth for safe passage from shore to shore, with the freedom to speed away across it with no visible dangers.

But it meant a great deal if only inches of water lay below your keel, terror and disorientation played tricks on you and convinced you that all was well, until your only goal was to arrive at your destination by running from a hostile environment at breakneck speed.

The papers and television said it all, even internationally; a story so bizarre, so tragic, two lives cut short, both mothers and wives, enjoying a boating break on a stunning part of the Welsh coast. The estuary and its access had claimed two lives, the history would tell of many more, and the captains of the slate-trade ships one hundred and fifty years ago, would nod their heads sagely and understand.

The powerboat had lost its way in the channel, the news said, returning to the harbour of Porthmadog in the teeth of a violent storm, but the speed at which it was travelling as it hit a sandbank head-on, could have been equivalent to a fifty mile-an-hour crash on a motorway. Both women were on the fly-bridge when it hit the bank. They were found dead at the scene with catastrophic injuries.

For weeks, the shock of the event eclipsed the aftermath of confused emotions. Nobody would speak 'ill of the dead' but many, I was sure, had thoughts best kept to themselves. It seemed the investigation would never end. Arnie's divorce proceedings became irrelevant and life continued much as it was.

At the weekends, I moved back to sleep in the caravan in the Boat Shed yard. It was fusty with lack of use, but it didn't leak, and I didn't mind. It was not for long, and Arnie and Ben needed the apartment. They arrived every Friday night after school and Angela joined them after work. She'd changed her shifts again to keep the weekends free. Ben was receiving counselling, his dad said, but couldn't tell if he was distressed. Whether he was, or not, Shelly was still his mum, and the circumstances of her death would be difficult for a child to embrace.

His face brightened when he heard Angela's footsteps on the stairs; she brought goodies and hugged him, then kissed Arnie, a little shyly, I thought, perhaps because I was there. We shared a meal before I walked back to the yard and left them in peace. Whether Angela stayed over was none of my business.

Jason and I discussed very little by phone after the accident, apart from polite well-wishing; condolences were not on the agenda, and we both knew it. He had a new girlfriend and I hoped he would talk to her, if he ever needed to. He hated his mum for what she'd become, he'd told me, but like Ben, she was still his mum. It was painful to talk, until I told him my plans, and then there was a great deal to talk about. As for the twins, with a few years of custody left, I was glad I wouldn't be around when they were released and didn't care how much grieving they had to suffer, if any.

At the end of July, the space that had been occupied by *Capella*, was now home to four jet-skis, only temporarily and just for income, and the boat-cradle that Arnie had so lovingly built, was transferred to Madoc Marine's yard.

I made an appointment to see Mr Hughes, David's father, and he explained in detail the process of overturning some of the ridiculously rigid rules for the Boat Shed business my great-uncle had bequeathed me. He raised his eyebrows when I told him my plans.

"Insurance, Miss Jones," he said. "Conditions can be modified, if you're prepared to pay. You're not selling it?"

"No. It's an investment. I'd like to think the rent will give me a small income, and Mr Blackwell has agreed to lease it from me and will manage it. However, I still want to retain the spirit of the inheritance, so I'd like you to you to include new conditions, if you can."

He phoned for refreshments, and we chatted about the summer's events over the china teacups, until we returned to business with the usual formality.

"The conditions to the lease," I said, "must include the use of the yard and Boat Shed yard premises purely for sailing boats, storage for small sailing yachts, use of the slip for dinghies, and the new building could be used as a hub, a meeting place, if you like, for like-minded folks to gather and chat and drink tea. Obviously, yachts will have engines, and there will be outboards around, but no powerboats and no jet-skis are to be stored there or launched from there. Also, I'd like another appointment to make my will, just in case I get trashed in the ocean."

He didn't smile. Did he know that I could so easily have been his daughter-in-law? Mother to his grandchildren, ensuring continuity of the family name? Possibly, I thought, but not a discussion we were likely to have.

He escorted me to the door.

"I wish you well, Miss Jones," he said. "Be assured we will look after your affairs as you have requested. I'll ask a colleague to draw up the will."

He shook my hand, held it for a second, and said, "Delighted to see the diamond nose-stud is in place, Miss Jones. Long may it remain. Do keep in touch."

I touched the stud, and remembered Helen's Nain's words when she advised that I removed it for my first meeting with him; a formal, conventional man. 'Play the game, cariad. It's only for an hour,' she'd said. But it was my game now, and I knew she'd be content with that.

I'd taken photographs of *Capella's* craning-in and sent them to Hugh. She settled neatly against the tyres on the wall, then I sat up with the new owners for the best part of two nights as the tide came in and the water eventually swelled the timbers. The bilge pump worked overtime until the cry, "there's nothing coming out now," was heard.

She was destined for Oban in Scotland, entirely appropriate, and I hoped Hugh would be well enough to travel to see her. Then, I thought, he wouldn't want to. She set off on a bright morning, her perfect varnish caught the sun's rays and the hull carved out a gentle trail on the still water. I stood on the wall and waved goodbye.

The train to London took forever, and for the second time, I knew I was doing the right thing, but I had to tell my mother, Trish my best friend and her mother Felicity. They welcomed me with open arms and sympathies for all the tragic events I'd gone through. The last time I'd shocked them was in my revelation about living in the caravan in the Boat Shed yard, the overtones of 'itinerant' almost too much for my mother to bear. I had a feeling this would be little different and probably, much worse.

The design business had flourished post-Covid, the supply of money had never ceased to flow from the east to furnish the apartments of wealthy business folk, and was evident in the clothes they all wore for dinner. I'd brought the black dress; it was nearly all I had left after my major clear-out to charity shops.

"A special occasion, darling. We haven't seen you for months," my mother said. "Lovely little dress. And the choker? So retro, but it suits you."

The banalities only reinforced my satisfaction from their responses.

I'd brought the very last of the smoked salmon, and the meal, superb as ever, the opulence of the room, the easy chat after their desperate questions concerning the accident, lulled me into a generous frame of mind as I laid out my carefully-edited plans.

"So, I'll fly out in a few weeks and then we'll leave the Canaries in November, to be in Antigua for Christmas."

"Darling, a cruise. How lovely. And Christmas in the Caribbean. That must have been expensive."

I hadn't said it was a cruise, exactly, then I explained about Hugh's gift.

"Alright for some," said Trish. "How do you manage to invite gifts like that?" slightly put out, I could tell. "Nobody gives me stuff. I have to work for everything." There was no answer to that. I let it go.

"So, what next?" asked Felicity. "It sounds as though your boss is taking over Madoc Marine from you. You'll be out of a job, and a home, and it's nearly the end of the summer. Where will you live? Will you try and develop the Boat Shed business, as you said you would, when you come back?"

It was time to tell them,

"I'm not coming back," I said.

Daniel booked the hotel this time and I packed my best posh outfits. I'd vacated the apartment completely and moved my meagre belongings into a cupboard in the shop at the back of the showroom. Arnie didn't mind and Denise said she'd send them on to wherever. There was nothing I needed for the trip, but wherever I settled, I would want the jelly-mould and the oystercatcher teapot and Helen's Nain's recipe for brownies.

The confirmation emails arrived. I liked the tone and just hoped the boat-owners were as charming as their letters. They looked forward to having me on board, said the Moody owners, husband and wife, who had received a testimonial from David. Could I cook as well as sail? Oh yeah, I'll do anything, I said, perhaps rather rashly.

I'd booked my flight to the Canaries ahead of time, well before the race was to start in November, but found a vacancy as a care-taker on an empty powerboat in a marina until their owners arrived for a long, Christmas break.

I broke the news to Arnie first. Angela was his therapy, and he arrived each Friday night after a busy week with a smile, flowers and wine.

"I knew something was up, bab. I'm happy to run the Boat Shed for you. I've got Angela now and anything's possible. I'm going to move in and put Ben in school up here ready for the new term. He's already made friends when he's been out with Angela, crabbing and stuff. He can say a bit in Welsh already. He'll learn quickly."

Then the serious bit. "I've made my will," I said. "In case I drown out there."

"Good idea," he said. "Who knows?"

"I've left the Boat Shed to Jason," and waited for the response. His eyes filled, and no, I hadn't told Jason yet, but I would phone him later. "He'll understand the conditions. We shared a lot, Arnie. He's the brother I never had. He can always pass it on to his own kids."

I told Denise, then Will Roberts and Mark and emailed Hugh who was receiving radiotherapy and hoped for some remission. Mixed reactions from all, no mixed feelings for me. Will Roberts brought me a present; a new, expensive, hard-backed diary.

"Write your travels," he said. "It might come in useful." Prophetic, but I wasn't to know at the time, and promised him I would.

I joined Daniel for an excellent weekend in Llandudno.

"And when you get to Antigua, I can fly or sail up and meet you. We could have Christmas together. Then if you come back to Trinidad with me, I'll put feelers out for the leg through Panama and the Pacific. There's always someone off to Australia on deliveries, or just cruising. There are lots of live-a-boards out there who need crew, Cassie, but you must be careful you pick the right ones. It's a big deal sailing the Pacific, but I've got reliable contacts."

I remembered the hitch-hiking and the pervy salesman, Paul with his blocked bilges and corroded sea-cocks, and knew he was right.

Much later, he said, "You could always change your mind, be my love, and stay in Trinidad. My mum would eat you."

"Oh yeah? With you gallivanting back to the UK every five minutes and leaving me with an apron full of brats? No ta."

We fell off the bed laughing, then opened more champagne.

"See you on the ocean then," and we clinked glasses.

CHAPTER 19

JANUARY 2023

The speaker that evening had flown in from Perth. He'd been invited to address a packed club, and the crowd, having moved from the bar into the lounge, sat on chairs set out to face the front, and waited. The windows open to the river, failed to invite a cool breeze, and when a slight movement of air brushed the hot faces, it brought with it the tang of smoke.

Outside, many miles away, over the marina and the broad stretch of water that led downstream to Sydney Harbour and eventually, to the vastness of the Pacific Ocean, the sky glowed red. The fires were far enough away to defer any serious anxiety, but near enough to instigate vague uneasiness; many of the members had properties on the city outskirts.

A spoon tinkled against a glass, the speaker moved to the space cleared at the front, and the room settled to a respectful silence. All the members who attended that night, were hardened sailors. Many raced in Sydney Harbour, some in the Bass Strait or as far away as New Zealand; a few had sailed short, holiday stretches of the south coast in the UK.

No-one there, only the speaker, a well-known, globetrotting Pom, had circumnavigated the UK, but all knew its reputation. The speaker began, and finished, to a rapturous, if slightly sober applause.

He'd caught the eye of a woman who stood on her own behind the back row, remembered how she listened intently as he talked about navigating the Goodwin Sands with its hundreds of sunken wrecks, about freezing in the grey rollers of the North Sea, nearly foundering in standing waves crossing the Pentland Firth, and how he was awed by the beauty of the Western Isles of Scotland.

He talked of passing Liverpool and the entrance to the Dee Estuary and then bashing through the Irish Sea spattered with wind-farms and taking a roller-coaster ride along the north coast of Anglesey and the overfalls in Holyhead deep. But as his voyage headed for the Lleyn Peninsula, the woman craned her head forward. He'd made a mistake with the tides, he admitted. It took the members by surprise; you could tell by the stillness in the room, to hear such an experienced sailor admit his failures.

"I'm sure there are other evil places in the world that sailors have encountered and survived, but this was my nemesis," he said. "Never, ever, have I been so scared, never have I actually thought I might die, swallowed up, dropped into a huge hole, never to come out, with a wall of water around me so high that it reached the top of the mast."

The woman nodded to herself and lowered her head, as if in thought.

"Who is that?" the speaker asked the barman afterwards, and gestured to a table where the woman now chatted to a couple of members with tanned, weather-beaten faces. They laughed a lot, and hands touched arms in gestures of friendship. "The one with the purple streaks and the nose-stud?"

"That's Cassie Jones," he said. "Lives on her boat in the marina."

"Does she work here?"

The barman polished a glass and held it up to the light.

"Yes, and no. She crews on all the big races and writes features for sailing mags when she's asked. But mostly, mate, she's the Marina Manager."